WATERLOGGED
A NORTHWOODS MYSTERY

What Reviewers Say About Nance Sparks's Work

Secret Sanctuary

"I love the combination of action and romance. ...The crime plot is fast-paced and the story is action-packed and exciting to the end, with some unexpected twists."—*LezReview Books*

"I buzzed through all the action sequences. They felt real and very dangerous, with just enough vulnerability from the main characters to heighten suspense. I was never unsure of who was where and what was going on. The romance made me happy, because both characters have a deep need for love but their lives are highly secretive, giving it a nice tension."—*Lesbian Review*

Cowgirl

"I fell in love with *Cowgirl* by Nance Sparks. This is the author's debut novel, and I'm very impressed with her writing. In fact, I see myself adding a new name to my list of favorite authors. It is the setting that really made the story special to me. The author set this novel on a farm near a tiny town in Michigan, and something about her descriptions of this place really touched me. I kept thinking, 'This sounds and feels like home.' ...I recommend this book to everyone. I will also be looking for more from this author."
—*Rainbow Reflections*

Starting Over

"This novel works because it's built on a relationship that's grounded, authentic and genuine. Sparks crafts the romance in such a way that it feels believably sincere and honest. She capitalizes on the emotional depth of the characters and their relationship. There's a chemistry between these two ladies that's compelling. Readers see their potential, and they root for them. *Starting Over* reminds readers that love endures and heals, even when one thinks it's lost forever."—*Women Using Words*

Visit us at www.boldstrokesbooks.com

By the Author

Cowgirl

An Alaskan Wedding

Secret Sanctuary

Starting Over

Appalachian Awakening

Waterlogged: A Northwoods Mystery

WATERLOGGED

A NORTHWOODS MYSTERY

by

Nance Sparks

2024

WATERLOGGED: A NORTHWOODS MYSTERY

ISBN 13: 978-1-63679-699-4

This Trade Paperback Original Is Published By
Bold Strokes Books, Inc.
P.O. Box 249
Valley Falls, NY 12185

First Edition: December 2024

CREDITS
Editor: Barbara Ann Wright
Production Design: Susan Ramundo
Cover Design By Tammy Seidick
Cover Photo: Nance Sparks

Acknowledgments

I'd like to thank J.B. Owens for the amazing suggestions and feedback. You continue to be an amazing beta reader. Thank you to my editor, Barbara Ann Wright, for your amazing input. And thank you to my wife, for taking a few days to explore the Turtle Flambeau Flowage. Our trip confirmed that it was the perfect setting for this Northwoods mystery. What an amazing place.

Dedication

I dedicate this book to those looking for something like family. Sometimes, a found family gives you all the support you've ever asked for and everything you need. May you be wrapped up in hugs and protected by those who love you like a family would and should.

Dedication

I dedicate this book to ... and ... for
something that family ... Sometimes, a noted family
gives you all the support you ... you ask for
... May you be ... when
hope and perseverance, that you love you ...
in ... braid words and should ...

CHAPTER ONE

G entle waves splashed along the bow of the boat as Jordan slowly navigated around the big island. Tucked way back in the cove, she cut the engine and closed her eyes for a moment, soaking in the stillness of nature and the seclusion offered by her favorite out-of-the-way spot on the lake. The cove offered a quiet reprieve from the chaos of the summer holiday weekend kickoff occurring on the main lake. Large rocks and old tree stumps from long before they'd built the dam hid just below the water's surface, keeping most boaters out of this area.

The sandbar on the back side of the island offered a perfect place to beach. She hopped off the bow and tied her mooring line around a large rock. The ability to stand and stretch her legs was just what her body needed. Her muscles were stiff from sitting in the boat all day. She walked a few laps back and forth. After a bit, she sat on a downed tree at the water's edge, a perfect place to enjoy a late lunch and savor the sound of waves gently lapping against the sandy shore.

Faint whiffs of suntan lotion teased her nose, along with all the earthy, organic happenings above and below the surface of the water that, once combined, could best be described as the scent of a lake on a warm sunny day. My, how she loved her job. Scattered, wispy clouds softened the deep blue sky, and the gentle breeze kept her from overheating in her uniform. Getting paid to enjoy nature's wonders was heaven on earth. The heat from the sunshine felt good, tempting her to lean against a stout branch and rest her eyes for a brief spell.

The solitude of her private oasis was interrupted by the roaring, high-pitched engine of a Jet Ski, with the stereo blasting and children screaming for the driver to go faster, faster, faster.

Jordan sat up and looked toward the action. "Seriously? This guy again?" She'd just talked to him an hour or so ago. She removed her tie line and pushed off the sand. As soon as the engine was running, she hit the throttle while also flipping on her flashing blue lights and siren. She knew this side of the island like the back of her hand and kept wide to avoid hitting something just below the surface. She needed to get the driver's attention and slow him down before someone was seriously injured.

The first really warm weekend on the lake seemed to bring out the recklessness in some people, as if it had been bottled up all winter, eager to burst free on a sunny spring day like the cork in a shaken champagne bottle. The driver of the Jet Ski was all that amplified to ten. He hugged the island at full speed, fanning a tube full of children out where the dangerous obstacles hid beneath the choppy water. He cut hard to the right and darted back out to the main lake, sending the tube off on another velocity laden arc. Luckily, the children hung on.

Jordan hit her air horn twice, hoping to grab his attention before he circled back around to do it again. It was obvious when he finally saw her because his shoulders dropped, and he shook his head. At least he cut the engine and didn't attempt to outrun her with three children in tow.

Maneuvering her boat perpendicular across the bow of the Jet Ski, she shifted into neutral, and kept her emergency lights flashing. She reached down and enabled her body cam, required for all interactions where ticketing occurred. Over the years, she'd made it a habit to turn it on for all interactions, period.

"Aw, jeez, Warden, I thought for sure your shift would've ended by now. Do you work twenty-four hours a day or what?"

"Hello again, Mr. Knowles. Please pull the children in closer." She waited quietly while he pulled on the rope until the tube was next to the Jet Ski. "Is this your daughter?" With an open palm, she motioned to the child sitting in front of him.

He nodded.

"Please have her transfer to the seat behind you."

The little girl, perhaps five, was wide-eyed with the situation and climbed carefully around her father from her perch directly behind the handlebars to the back seat.

"Thank you." She pulled out her citation book. "I assume you know why I stopped you."

"Don't suppose you'd let me off with another warning?"

"You've used up my very last warning along with my patience. License and registration."

"Come on, Warden, have a heart. It's Memorial weekend, and for once, it's actually warm and not pouring rain."

"All the more reason to be cautious. The lake is extremely crowded today."

"Look, Warden Pearce, like I explained earlier, my boat is down, and the kids won't stop hounding me to take them tubing. They drive me utterly insane unless they're out on the water."

"And as I explained earlier, you can't have a young child in front of you while driving a personal watercraft. You don't have a spotter, and you're still not wearing a life jacket."

"But there are tantrums if I leave one of the kids behind."

"Okay, leave two, take turns, figure it out. How long have you been boating on this lake?"

"I've been coming up here since I was a kid. I grew up spending my summers on these waters."

"Then don't pretend like you don't know the boating regulations. The law is clear. You must wear a life jacket when operating a personal watercraft. Nothing and no one can be between the operator and the handlebars, and you must have a spotter or mirrors to know when a tuber goes in the water. I don't care what kind of swimmer you are, you're of little help without a life jacket when trying to rescue someone in distress. In the event of an emergency, there's no way for you to get everyone safely to shore, and back there, behind the island with the rocks and the stumps, you were just asking for an emergency."

"Aw, come on. The kids are all wearing life jackets, and they're on a six-foot inflatable disk. It's no different from playing by shore." He opened a compartment and pulled out his wallet.

"Sir, there's a big difference, and you know it. You're towing your children around at thirty miles per hour on one of the busiest weekends of the year, unnecessarily putting yourself and others in danger." Jordan accepted his license and boat registration. "You've been on this lake long enough to know the dangers behind that island."

"Yeah, but over the years, the ice has broken off all the stumps. Look." He pointed behind the island. "The danger is gone."

"They broke off at the surface, but believe me, they're still back there. How would you have felt if one or more of your children went off the tube and crashed into something just below the surface? Injury is the best-case scenario in that cove. Trust me, I've been on enough recoveries to know, and while not illegal, taking them back there at that speed is irresponsible and flat-out dangerous. You're not getting out of it this time."

She filled out the citation with ease, having long grown accustomed to writing while bobbing on the rough wake from a lake full of boat traffic. The engine had to be engaged to realign her boat and bring her closer to the driver. She'd done this so many times, she accomplished it with muscle memory as much as conscious awareness.

"Sir, how far away is your cabin?" She held out the citation along with his license and registration.

"It's on the other end of the lake. Kilts Point. I promise, we'll head straight home."

"Keep the little one behind you, and next time, wear a life jacket and get a spotter." She put away her citation book and sat behind the steering wheel. She knew right where Kilts Point was. She'd keep an eye out for him the rest of the weekend.

He pushed the tube full of children away and started his Jet Ski. It ran for a moment, then stalled out when he tried to give it gas. He tried starting it again and again once more. "Say, Warden. Don't suppose you have a gallon of gas on the boat?"

"My spare cans are empty. It seems you're not the only one who forgot to check the gas gauge."

"So how about a tow home?"

"I'm sure there's someone you can call. I'm on patrol," she said, knowing she should help but already beyond annoyed with Mr. Knowles.

"See, the thing is, I don't have my phone with me."

"You can use mine." She stared down at him.

"Like I know anyone's numbers. Besides, like I said earlier, my boat is down."

"Fine. Pull the children on the tube back up. They can ride with me." She pulled out a neon orange life jacket and handed it down to Mr. Knowles. "Put this on."

Without a word, he put the life jacket on and fastened the chest strap. Once all four children and the tube were in the boat with her, he secured the rope to the front of his Jet Ski and tossed the other end up to Jordan.

"Are you a police officer?" the little girl asked.

"I'm a DNR conservation warden. My name is Warden Pearce. What's your name?"

"I'm Chrissy. What's a DNR?"

"Department of Natural Resources. We're the police for the parks and lakes and state land."

"So that's why you get to carry a gun?"

"Yes, because I'm a law enforcement officer, I carry a gun," she answered honestly.

"Warden Pearce, can we tow Dad with the lights and sirens on?" the oldest child asked.

Jordan guessed his age to be nine or ten. Having kids in the boat brought back memories of her two younger sisters when she was about the same age. As kids, she'd been their primary caretaker before and after her parents had divorced. When she'd finally escaped that responsibility, she'd dove into a career where she was the one in control of all aspects of her life, responsible for no one but herself. Still, in moments like this, with young children in the boat, it reminded her that she lived a solitary, lonely life.

"Please, no lights and siren," Mr. Knowles said from behind the boat.

"What's your name?"

"Timothy, and that's my little brother, Steven, and that's our cousin, Carl."

"Well, Timothy, if you flip this switch and Steven flips this one and Carl pushes the horn button twice, we'll be running with light and sirens."

"Cool!" The boys took turns performing their assigned tasks.

"What do I get to do?" Chrissy asked over the siren.

Looking back, Jordan checked to see if the towline was a safe distance from the prop. Satisfied, she looked down at Chrissy. "You get to start the boat. Turn that key all the way, then let it go." The engine started on the first try. "All right, everyone, take a seat."

She maintained a slow, no wake speed and hugged the shoreline all the way to Kilts Point. Mr. Knowles was tormented relentlessly by his family and neighbors who witnessed his lake version of a walk of shame. She hoped the jeering would serve as a reminder not to head back out the moment she was out of sight. Once the family was safely on land, she cut the flashing lights, started her boat, and made her way back to open waters. Being a visible presence on the lake helped keep most boaters from doing silly things that led to accidents. It was always a good day when it ended without injuries or fatalities.

Late in the afternoon, at the end of her shift, huge thunderheads developed on the southern horizon. Boat traffic on the lake had already thinned out quite a bit, and the storm that was coming in would send the rest to shore in a hurry.

She was almost to the ramp. A good thing too. Lightning streaked across the sky off in the distance. There'd been no mention of rain in the forecast, but the clouds that were back building gave every indication of a supercell storm. Something must've popped. Jordan tied her boat to the dock at the public ramp and walked across the parking lot to retrieve her truck and trailer. Her phone rang just as she reached her driver's door.

"Hey, Lieutenant Grace, uh, sorry, Chief, what's up?" Jordan climbed into the cab of her truck and let its Bluetooth system take over the call while she backed down the ramp.

"It's okay. I'm still getting used to the new position myself. Listen, Jordan, you submitted a transfer request not too long ago for a property specific post up on the Turtle-Flambeau Flowage. Are you still interested in moving up to the Northwoods?"

Water enforcement on some of the busiest lakes in Wisconsin had been an adrenaline-laden blast early in her career, but she'd grown weary of the congested waters and overcrowded state parks in the southern counties surrounding Madison and stretching west to the Minnesota state line. No doubt it was great to see the resources used, but how she longed for a calmer, quieter area to patrol.

"Ma'am, has an opening come up?" Blood pounded in Jordan's ears, and her heart flip-flopped with excitement at the prospect of finally being assigned to a permanent post. No more bouncing from lake to park to state land. To be stationed in the Northwoods, her favorite area of all time, was more than she could have asked for. Memories of time spent on one of the larger lakes in Wisconsin, the Turtle-Flambeau Flowage, was the main reason she had become a conservation warden. She drew in a deep breath, hoping to calm her racing heart.

"Seems one may have, and your name popped as next in line for a transfer. I think you know Deb Ryder?"

"Sure, I do. Some say she's my doppelgänger, but I don't see it. We've paired up on a few training classes and several exercises. She's good people."

"Do you know her well?"

Jordan considered the question. "We're not best friends or anything, but she recently invited me to come up and go fishing. I know she was super excited to be assigned up there. Did something happen to her? Is she okay?"

"That's the million dollar question. Seems she just submitted her resignation via email, effective immediately, which is quite irregular. After which, she's been unreachable. Given that you know Deb, I'm hoping you could help us figure out if she really did up and walk off the job. Her resignation said that the solitude was too much, and life in the Northwoods wasn't what she thought it would be. Do you think she'd walk away from her post like that?"

"That doesn't sound like her. But like I said, I don't know her all that well. If she wasn't happy, wouldn't she put in for a transfer instead of walking away from her entire career? She always said how much she loved being a warden."

"I'm hoping you can head up soon and help us figure that out. We'll need you to meet with the county sheriff and check out the property. Be our eyes and ears if something doesn't seem quite right. The other warden assigned to that county is on vacation and without cell service for another week. The district supervisor is here in Madison for a conference that starts on Tuesday, but she could cut her trip short and head up to meet with the sheriff tomorrow if you need more time."

"That won't be necessary. I'll pack up tonight and hit the road."

"I was hoping you'd say that. Report to Lieutenant Foley from the Rhinelander office after you've met with the sheriff at the residence. You have my cell. Please keep me in the loop."

"Will do, Chief."

"Hey, Jordan...be careful. Keep a watchful eye."

"Chief?" Jordan's breath caught in her throat. "Is there something more I should know?"

"Nope, but I'd be remiss not to remind you of your training."

It was a known fact that conservation wardens were seven times more likely to experience assault than other law enforcement officers. Jordan had heard the warning before. She'd experienced several close calls over her career, but it seemed as if Chief Grace was sharing more than the standard message. "Understood. I'll report my findings."

"Thanks. I knew I could count on you."

Disconnecting the call, she thought about Deb and hoped she'd simply found another calling. If that was the case, Jordan just might have a chance at her dream assignment. She did a little fist pump as she climbed out of her truck. Before long, the boat was secured to the trailer, and she was on the road well before the storm hit. She needed to pack so she could get up north.

CHAPTER TWO

One minute, Hanna had been teaching a course on harvesting beneficial herbs for tinctures at a co-op in southern Missouri, then the next, she was pushing the limits of her vintage 1973 Winnebago Indian. She wasn't even sure she'd said good-bye to anyone.

Thirteen hours before, she'd picked up a call from Aunt Ruthie. Aunt Dottie had cancer, stage three, and Ruthie needed her help.

Winnie, the wildly original name of Hanna's camper, hadn't been running all that well when she'd left Branson, but somehow, it had survived the journey to the northeastern corner of Wisconsin, clunking, clattering, and coughing out plumes of dark smoke those last twenty miles.

Pulling into the all too familiar driveway, Hanna parked off to the side just in case ol' Winnie refused to ever start again. She gripped the wheel tightly, drew in a deep breath, and let it out slowly, unsure of what the future would hold. Stage three... stage three was bad...not the worst but close. Had Dottie elected treatment, or would she refuse and simply enjoy her remaining days?

That last part was too much to think about.

Through the open driver's window, Hanna heard the rusty spring screech in protest as the screen door on the house opened, then the reminiscent thud as the door was released. It was surprising how a simple sound could conjure up such a rush of fond memories and heartwarming emotions. Her two and a half years with her aunts had been a life-changing experience.

"Ah, there's my favorite niece."

Pulled back to the present, Hanna opened her eyes. Her aunt's voice was unmistakable, with her Irish accent still so pronounced, but the person standing at the top of the steps looked nothing like dear Aunt Dottie. For some reason, Hanna had thought she'd only recently been diagnosed, but she'd clearly misunderstood. One thing was certain: cancer sucked.

Aunt Dottie had dropped at least twenty pounds. Her once snuggly fitting clothes now swayed with the gentle breeze. The knit cap pulled over her ears was likely not only keeping her head warm but also hiding the fact that she'd lost her beautiful ginger locks. Her face looked different too, devoid of both eyebrows and lashes. Hanna hadn't realized how a few fine hairs could create such defining features. Without them, Dottie's striking green eyes had morphed into sunken orbs peering out of dark, cavernous sockets.

Hanna kept up her end of the favorite niece game. "Favorite doesn't count when I'm your only niece."

Aunt Dottie balanced herself with an aluminum walker, and her bony knuckles grew white with the effort. Hanna tried to fight back tears while wrestling with Winnie's driver's door. A strong shoulder shove proved successful, and she jumped to the ground the moment it released.

"Aye, doesn't mean you're not my favorite." Aunt Dottie's response was exactly as it had always been.

"Oh, Aunt Dottie, I've missed you so much." Hanna rushed around the front of the Winnebago, ran up the porch steps, and wrapped her arms around her most treasured person in all the world. She inhaled deeply, wanting all the smells that she associated with her aunt, but they were oddly absent. The unique scents of her fabric softener, shampoo, and conditioner were missing, as was the faint sweet fragrance of her perfume. Now, she smelled like nothing, almost sterile, devoid of anything familiar. It didn't matter as long as Hanna could hold her close.

"Oh, careful, honey, don't squeeze so hard. You might pop my head clean off. I'm not as sturdy as I once was." Dottie's voice was a squeak.

The mental cartoon image of her head popping off forced Hanna to stifle laughter through her tears. She'd always been one to laugh when she cried, often at the most inappropriate times. She loosened her grip. "Shit, so sorry. Cancer sucks balls."

"You can say that again."

"Cancer sucks!" At least Aunt Dottie said it with her this time. "How are you feeling?"

"I'd be lying if I said I haven't been better. Your auntie Ruthie's doing her best to keep up with me, get me to my appointments, and keep the diner open. It's been tough on her too."

"Yeah, she said her hands were full, but I had no idea it was this, that you were already getting treatments. When were you diagnosed?"

"A few months ago."

"I wish I'd known. I could have been here to help so much sooner. Cancer is a lot without a business to run, but Ruthie has the diner…Jesus, Aunt Dottie, I didn't know you were—" She couldn't stop the tears.

"Oh, honey, we decided against telling you right away. There wasn't much to do at first, and you need to be able to live your best life. Besides, seeing you mope around wouldn't do much to boost my spirit. You know that Ruthie and I have always found a way through tough times. We called you home when it was clear we needed help, and here you are, such a ray of sunshine." Dottie reached for her again and held her close for a long moment. When she pulled away, Hanna realized she was also crying.

Hanna gently wiped away her tears. "Do Mom and Dad know?" she asked, not wanting to bring up her parents but knowing she should.

"Yes, of course. I called your mother while Ruth was talking with you. Ruthie still won't speak to her."

"A mess of my making, I'm afraid. We were always like oil and water. She was so jealous of the relationship I have with you two. I'm sorry that I came between you and your sister."

"Nonsense. She had her own role in the mess, and she's supposed to be the adult in the room. She'll snap out of it someday."

"It's been twenty-five years. I'm thinking that ship has sailed." Hanna hoped that someday would come sooner rather than later. Who knew how much time Aunt Dottie had left?

"Never mind your mother. I'm so glad to have you here. Look at me, carrying on like an old ninny. We just called you yesterday, and it seems you've been on the road nonstop to get here. Come inside. I'm sorry we haven't cleaned your room. I'm not even sure there are sheets on your bed. Anymore, just breathing wears me out."

"Don't worry about it. I can take care of my room." A soft breeze rustled the leaves above her head, and Hanna caught a whiff of another one of her favorite scents. She drew in a deep breath through her nose and looked at the sky. "Smells like rain."

"Storm's coming. Supposed to be a gully washer. It's headed this way at a pretty good clip. The good news is, if it comes in fast, it'll be gone just as fast."

"If it's the one I drove through on my way up, it'll clean out the gutters, that's for sure. Let's get you inside." Hanna followed her into the house.

It was torture to watch her hobble and navigate the walker. The living room, once perfectly configured for curling up on the couch and watching a movie, had been transformed into a bleak hospital suite. The cozy furniture was shoved to the side beneath the front window. A mechanical bed with side rails was now the dominant feature. Next to it sat a portable commode and a rolling food tray holding the TV remote and a glass of water. On the other side, Hanna recognized Auntie Ruthie's easy chair. They'd always sat next to each other; at least that hadn't changed.

It hadn't been that long since she'd last been back. A year or two or maybe three. Her aunt had appeared perfectly healthy during that visit. How could so much have changed in such a short time?

"Can I make you a cup of your favorite tea or some tomato soup? Anything at all?" Hanna asked.

"Thank you, honey, but I can't keep much down these days."

The house had to be ninety degrees. Hanna peeled her sweatshirt off. Even then, her tank top and jeans felt like far too many clothes. She'd find some shorts when she closed up the camper.

"Sorry. Ruthie does the same thing when she gets home. She says it's like a sauna in here. I'm just so cold all the time. I think it's from the chemo. Feels like a meat locker to me." Aunt Dottie's arms quivered, and her legs looked as if they were about to buckle.

"Here, let me help you into your chair."

"I prefer the bed. Sitting hurts my back too much. The treatments are doing a number on me." She flopped on the edge of the hospital bed and tried to push her walker off to the side, but all it did was teeter a bit and return to the original spot. Hanna moved it up by the head of the bed, unsure of how else to help. "Don't move it so far away. Jesus, my arms aren't made of rubber." Aunt Dottie weakly wiggled her butt back. "Be a dear and lift my legs up. I swear, Ruthie puts twenty pound weights around my ankles to keep me from doing too much."

Her legs were skin and bones compared to what Hanna was used to. Was it the cancer or the treatments that had her so weak and feeble? Probably a bit of both.

"Come up here and let me wrap my arms around your neck. You can help me scooch up on the bed better."

Hanna carefully helped her get better situated. She seemed so fragile that Hanna was afraid of hurting her.

"Could you hand me that controller thing? And pull my blankets up?"

Aunt Dottie pressed a button that elevated her upper body. She grimaced, lowered it a bit, and readjusted. When it looked like she was as comfortable as she was going to get, Hanna draped the blankets over her and tucked her in, just as her aunt had done for her when she'd stayed home from school with the flu.

"Ah, that's nice."

The portable commode had been used a time or two. Hanna pulled out the pail and walked toward the bathroom.

"Ruthie can do that later."

"Ruthie needs some help, no?"

"You're still a stubborn little shit, aren't you? You don't need to be dealing with my piss bucket." At least her aunt hadn't lost her snarky wit. "This whole situation is for the birds. I tell ya, it's hard to feel sexy when your wife has to help you wipe your ass."

"I bet." Hanna choked on the unexpected comment. She emptied the pail, rinsed it, and washed her hands before returning to the living room. "Where are you getting treatment?"

"We've been driving to Woodruff. I had chemo for three cycles before surgery with a month's break after. No ringing of the bell, not yet, anyway. Now it's back to chemo for who knows how long. I'm too weak to drive myself, so with you home to take care of the diner, Ruthie can take me to treatments. I swear, if the cancer doesn't kill me, the treatments just might." Dottie coughed into a crumpled napkin. "I have an aide that comes a couple of times a week to help me bathe. Ruthie's a good sport. You know how she hates to have strangers in the house."

That was an understatement. Anytime Hanna had brought a friend home, Auntie Ruthie had had a fit and given them the third degree. "Oh, believe me, I know. Can they do anything for the nausea?"

"Ah, they stick a patch on my arm every so often. It keeps me from puking nonstop, but it hasn't helped my appetite one iota."

"I'll look through my books and see if there are any tinctures in my stash that might help."

"Thanks, honey. You're a good egg." Aunt Dottie's blinks were getting longer and longer. Her head drooped and then lifted again when she popped her eyes open, much like a child desperately trying not to take a nap. She shivered.

Hanna reached beneath the blanket and held her hand.

"Hmm...your hand is nice and warm." Aunt Dottie's hand was freezing cold, even beneath the blanket.

"I don't suppose there's room on that bed for one more? It'll be a tight fit, but we could snuggle, just like you used to do with me on the couch when I was freezing from a fever."

"I'd like that."

The bed looked to be narrower than a standard twin, but Aunt Dottie was nothing more than a twig and didn't take up much space. Heatstroke be damned, Hanna lifted the blanket and wiggled into the small open space. She turned onto her side to not take up too much room. Her aunt curled up against her like a cat on a warm furnace vent in the dead of winter.

"I can hear your heart beating."

"It beats for you. Get some rest." Hanna kissed her forehead. "I'll be right here when you wake up. Maybe I'll rest my eyes too." Within minutes, her blinks grew longer and longer until she too drifted off.

CHAPTER THREE

Jordan stepped out of the convenience store with her mostly eaten hotdog in one hand. A gust of wind swept around the corner of the building, pelting her with dust and discarded litter. She didn't turn away quickly enough, and an empty candy wrapper stuck in the dab of mustard on her last bite. She plucked the paper off, tossed it in the nearest garbage can, and stuffed the rest of her gas station dinner into her mouth. It was a tad grittier than the first few bites had been, but she was too tired and too hungry to care.

Before getting back on the road, she checked the weather radar one more time. The storm had already traveled through the lower counties, currently drenching a large swath of central Wisconsin, and based on the dark red shades on the screen, it was intensifying. So far, it continued to track north by northeast and was gaining on her location. It would likely catch up to her on the road since she was still about forty-five minutes away from her rental cabin. She would've stopped in Minocqua for the night if it hadn't been for the no vacancy signs flashing all along the road. The area had always been a popular destination on Memorial Day weekend.

Her phone buzzed in her hand and displayed a severe thunderstorm warning. The air felt heavy and already smelled like rain. She'd been on the front edge of the storm ever since she'd seen lightning streak the sky just before pulling her boat. Had that only been a little over three hours ago? It was best if she got moving. Hopefully, she could get to the cabin she'd reserved on the water's edge before this beast hit.

Within twenty minutes, large raindrops intermittently pelted her windshield. Moments later, the winds whipped, and the sky let loose. The deluge made driving nearly impossible. The swirling wind tried to push her truck and boat trailer off the road. She had a mind to pull off, but there wasn't enough of a shoulder on this one lane path to get her rig safely out of traffic from either direction, not that she'd seen another car in quite some time. A blinding flash of lightning caused her to momentarily squeeze her eyes shut, then the ground-shuddering boom that followed had her eyes popping wide open once again.

"Hold on to your hat, we're not in Kansas anymore," Jordan said and gripped the steering wheel tighter.

She kept a white-knuckled grip on the wheel. The rain battered the truck in drenching, wind driven sheets that came at her sideways, as if she was driving upstream through a swiftly flowing river. There were moments when she wasn't entirely sure she was still on the road, but then the wipers would sort of catch up and show the faint transition of asphalt to dense ferns and grass just ahead of the right front tire.

Another brilliant flash of lightning lit up the sky, and when her eyes readjusted to the darkness, Jordan noticed the faint red glow of taillights a few car lengths ahead of her. She'd happily follow as long as the leader stayed on the road. Another exceptionally powerful gust of wind tried to pull the steering wheel out of her hands. At the same instant, the car in front slammed on the brakes. Jordan did the same and stopped a few feet from the car's bumper with a strong, jarring recoil.

She flipped a switch, and the light bar above the cab illuminated the scene as best it could through the driving rain. A downed tree sprawled across the asphalt in front of the car. She pressed the button for her hazard lights and flipped another switch, engaging her flashing blue emergency lights. She didn't need anyone slamming into the back of her boat. From what she could see through the wind and rain, the driver of the car was quite animated in the front seat.

Well, now, what's going on up there?

She snugged her baseball hat onto her head, hoping to keep some of the rain out of her eyes, and gripped the door tightly to keep the wind from ripping it out of her hand. Good thing too because the wind tried to take it off its hinges. The early spring rain might as well have been sleet or ice, given how cold it was upon contact. Her clothes were soaked through as soon as she stepped out of the truck. She approached the driver's side, staying back to remain out of sight, and tilted her Maglite into the driver's window from above to illuminate the erratic movement of the occupant. The rain continued to fall in swirling bucketfuls. The car's windows were fogged up, making it difficult to determine any specifics.

She knocked on the glass. "Are you all right in there?"

From her vantage point, there didn't seem to be any damage to the car. As for the roadblock, at least the wind hadn't taken a huge tree. Her smaller chain saw should make quick work of clearing the road.

The driver's window rolled down about an inch. "Evening, Officer. Hell of a storm. I'm good, just trying to see a way around the tree." The driver was a Caucasian female with hazel eyes, smeared mascara, likely from the rain, and wet hair, which was dark, without an identifiable color. It was all Jordan could make out through the small opening.

"You were waving your arms. Are you sure everything's okay?"

"Yeah, I'm fine. Like you, I'm soaked from being out in the rain, and I was trying to get my sweatshirt on. That's all."

"Understood." At least the explanation of her movements made sense. Putting a sweatshirt on was a hassle when sitting behind the steering wheel, especially over wet skin. She'd been there before.

"Nothing illegal, I promise." The woman's eyes crinkled in the corner, indicating a smile.

Again, lightning struck close by, followed by a loud crack of thunder that shook the ground. Standing still on this lonely stretch of road made both of them sitting ducks, just daring another tree to topple. Jordan didn't smell alcohol, smoke of any kind, or anything else that would warrant a call for assistance from the sheriff. No sense in making trouble where there wasn't any. The only scent she picked up was the floral perfume her mom used to wear, Beautiful by Estée Lauder. Not only was the fragrance far too flowery for her taste, but the memories associated with that specific scent turned her stomach.

She stepped back. "I'll grab my saw out of the back of my truck and see if I can't give us a path through. Why don't you hang tight?"

"Thanks."

"If you could engage your high beams, it'd help me see what I'm cutting."

"Will do." The bright lights flipped on. "Thanks, Officer."

Jordan dropped her tailgate and pulled a chain saw case out of a side compartment. It was always fueled and ready to go. She made her way to the front of the car, eager to figure out her plan of attack. Thankfully, it was a younger tree whose top was blocking the road and not its main trunk. Three cuts would do it, keeping the limbs manageable to get to the side of the road. She turned to face the driver and gave a thumbs-up.

Jordan heard a bloodcurdling scream just as she pulled the cord for the saw. *What the hell?* She killed the two-cycle engine. Lightning flashed, briefly illuminating a female figure standing next to the open driver's door.

"You? But, how? No...No way. It can't be, I...I—" The woman's screechy voice cut through the storm. She stayed in the shadows behind the headlights.

"Excuse me?" Jordan took a step closer. She pulled her flashlight from a side pocket in her pants and took aim. The beam of light reflected the falling rain more than it revealed details of the woman standing by the car.

"Stay back! Get away from me." The driver's door closed, and the engine roared to life.

Another streak of lightning splashed across the sky, and thunder shook the earth. Jordan caught movement in the flashes of light as the car tires cut slightly to the left. A lightning bolt reached down to earth in jagged electric fingers. Loud pops and cracks of a tree being struck signaled the dangers of being caught in this storm.

The woman gunned it. Instinct kicked in, and Jordan darted off to the side as the car plowed right through the treetop.

Rain cascading from the bill of Jordan's hat made it almost impossible to see anything beyond what her truck lights touched. The car disappeared into the night. She made a mental note of the make and model. The Wisconsin plates started with RHR-1, but that was all she could see through the driving rain. She'd call it in but say what? The woman hadn't been stopped. She wasn't even fleeing the scene of an accident. The tree had fallen and blocked the road with no damage or injuries. *What the hell was that about?*

Another streak of lightning, followed by more rumbling thunder, made her realize she was standing in the middle of the road, drenched from head to toe. The cold that settled in and chilled her to the bones made her wish the rain would let up. Tomorrow, she'd document everything and share it with the sheriff in the morning, but at the moment, she had to deal with this tree.

It took a little over fifteen minutes to clear the road, which revealed a broken piece of the white bumper from the car. Once on the road again, Jordan traveled the last few miles, finally arriving at the lodge from her youth. She had requested cabin seven. It was the same one she'd stayed in with her dad and sisters for two weeks each summer those first four years after the divorce. Those vacations, eight short weeks of her life, were some of her best childhood memories.

The porch light was the same off-yellow color that was supposed to keep bugs away, but instead, it seemed to attract them and all their little flying friends. She found the key under the mat, right where the owner said it would be. Standing there, wrestling with the lock, an image came to mind of her dad doing the exact same thing twenty-some years earlier, only without the pouring rain. Hell, maybe it was the same brass knob after all those years. The key ring certainly looked the same. A thick, red plastic oval with a white number seven painted into the flat. Both the oval and the number were marred and scarred, showing the years of use. Memories of time with her dad were like a bittersweet hug since his death a decade ago.

Finally, the lock released. With a flip of the light switch, Jordan found herself transported back in time. She'd hoped the room would look similar to what it had back then, but she'd never expected it would be exactly the same. Yet, there she stood, staring at that same avocado green ceramic lamp, including the tear in the lampshade that had once been mended with Scotch tape, now yellowed and cracked with age. The lamp sat on the same tiny wooden table next to the same dark orange sofa bed where she and her two younger sisters had squeezed together to sleep each night of vacation.

On the other side of the room was the double bed her dad had slept in, including the matching orange and green floral bedspread. Beyond that was the door to the bathroom with the half-broken ceramic doorknob. To her right sat a dresser with a newer flat-screen TV on top, and to the left, there was a tiny kitchenette with a newer microwave. No wonder this lodge was so much less expensive than the others she'd seen online, but then again, it was the nostalgia that had her longing to return.

She'd been just shy of her eleventh birthday when her parents' divorce was final. Both of her parents had loved to smoke and drink and argue…oh, how they'd loved to argue. Her mom had taken partying and sleeping around to the next level after her dad had moved out, which had left Jordan with the weight of the world on her young shoulders. Or so Dr. Knoedel would later help her understand.

Without her dad around, she'd been left to keep things going when her mom was too blitzed out to even know who was in the room. She'd been the one left to clean her mother up after she'd passed out in the driveway and had gotten sick all over herself. She'd been the one who'd had to cook dinner each night so her sisters, Sarah, who'd been eight, and Chloe, who'd been just six, had something in their stomachs before they had a bath and went to sleep. And so it went, day in and day out, until late July that first summer after the divorce.

Her dad had pulled into the driveway in a newer model car. It was the first time she'd ever seen him clean-shaven, with his shoulder-length hair trimmed neatly above his collar. She might not have recognized him if he hadn't spoken.

"Hey, Jo-Jo, how about you go pack up some clothes for you and your sisters? Make sure you bring enough of everything for a couple of weeks. I'm not doing laundry, and don't forget bathing suits."

She'd stood there and stared at him. There were so many questions. Why? Where were they going? Were they coming back? But she knew better than to question him, especially if it meant they were getting away from her mom for a bit. So she'd run inside and did as he asked, all while her parents had stood in the front yard, screaming at each other for all the neighbors to enjoy. They were still yelling when she'd emerged, a Hefty garbage bag slung over her shoulder like a tiny little Santa Claus, and her two younger sisters in tow. Her dad had taken the bag from her and tossed it in the truck.

"Jo-Jo, really, a trash bag? What, you couldn't find a suitcase, or did your mother pawn them off too?"

She hadn't dared to tell him that he'd taken all the suitcases when he'd moved out. Instead, she'd kept her mouth shut. Being compliant was her norm back then. Rather than say anything, she'd quietly urged her sisters into the back seat.

The car was silent for the first three hours after they'd left Mom standing in the front yard screaming and sloshing her drink all over the grass. After a while, Chloe had started whining that she had to go to the bathroom. Jordan had tried to shush her and begged her to hold it for just a little longer. Her dad was known for his quick temper and an even faster backhand. Like always, she would take the impact to keep either of her sisters from being struck.

Instead of swinging and screaming, her dad had pulled off at a McDonald's and urged them all inside. When their bladders were empty and their tiny hands were all washed, Jordan had tugged on her sisters, trying to herd them back to the car. Fast food had always been out of the question, and yet, there was Dad, standing at the counter, ordering cheeseburgers, fries, and orange Hi-C for each of them. A twilight zone moment, for sure.

An hour after that, he'd pulled the car into the Waterdance Lodge and checked into cabin seven. He had even kept his cool while fighting with the lock that wouldn't release. Back then, she couldn't overlook the possibility that aliens had taken over, and he was some kind of patient imposter.

They'd stayed for two full weeks that first summer. And for those fourteen days, Jordan didn't have to be the adult. She didn't have to worry about dinner or homework or bath time. Instead, she'd been able to play outside with kids her own age. Her days became about fishing, swimming, and enjoying s'mores by the campfire. It had been the best two weeks she could recall. The four of them had returned for two weeks each summer over the next few years. Well, at least until her dad was arrested. She hadn't been back since but always thought about coming back up to the flowage and how'd she stay in cabin seven. Now that she was there, with the twenty-some-year-old furniture and the funky smell assaulting her senses, she wasn't so sure that it was living up to its nostalgic hype.

Chilled to the bone, she stripped off her wet clothes and stepped into the tub, hoping for a steaming hot shower. She wasted far too much water waiting for it to get hot, but it never achieved much more than lukewarm, better than nothing. She pulled the button to switch the water from the tub faucet to the shower and hoped for the best. There was some gurgling and sputtering, and then water sprayed every which way from the neck of the showerhead. Within seconds, the ceiling was soaked, the walls were soaked, and water was puddling on the floor. She tried to tighten the head, only to have it shatter in her hands. At least the water was no longer spraying the entire room.

Perfect. Just perfect.

Jordan stood beneath the tepid stream flowing from the pipe sticking out of the wall. She had the added treat of cold water dripping onto her from the ceiling. It was too late to go somewhere else now. She quickly soaped up and rinsed off as best she could with the pathetic pressure. Hopefully, her experiences of the evening weren't a bad omen of her future in the Northwoods.

CHAPTER FOUR

Hanna sliced a few nickel-sized pieces from the peeled gingerroot, then grated the rest into a large saucepan of water. Once the mixture was at a slow boil, she set the timer for twenty minutes. With any luck, the ginger tea would help settle Aunt Dottie's stomach. When the timer went off, she strained some of the hot ginger water into a cup and set the ginger slices on a small plate, carrying both out to the living room.

"Here, you can chew on the ginger slices like gum." She set the plate and cup on the rolling table next to her aunt's bed. "When you're tired of it or it gets tasteless, just spit out what's left on the plate. And this is ginger tea. It should help settle your stomach."

"Mmm. The fresh ginger tastes nice. I'll give it a go."

"Hopefully, it helps you find your appetite. Are you sure you don't mind if I head in with Auntie Ruthie today?"

"Go. Please. I'm begging you. She's so excited to have your help. The aides will be by soon to check in on me, so it's not like I'll be all alone. Besides, no one needs to watch me get a bath. It's humiliating enough that I don't have the oomph to do it myself."

Hanna bent and kissed her forehead. "Fair enough. Okay, I love you."

"Love you too, honey. I'm so glad you're here."

"Call if you get a hankering for anything, and I'll bring it home."

Dottie nodded, but the look in her eyes wasn't all that encouraging. She'd eaten little more than a few soda crackers since Hanna's arrival.

"Are you ready, kiddo?" Auntie Ruthie rested a hand on her shoulder.

"Kiddo?" Hanna smiled. "I'm forty-two, not twelve."

"I don't care how old you are, you'll always be my favorite kiddo." Auntie Ruthie squeezed Hanna's arm. She bent and kissed Dottie on the lips. "I love you, beautiful. Don't give your helpers too much grief today."

"I'll be good, I promise. I love you more." It was the strongest she'd heard her aunt's voice since she'd been back.

Hanna followed Auntie Ruthie out to the car. "Say, do Banjo and Chipmunk still work on cars in between fishing gigs?"

"Yep. Nowadays, they're the only automotive repair close by. Otherwise, it's an hour south to Minocqua."

"Do they still come into the diner every day for breakfast?"

"Seven thirty sharp, if they don't have a predawn fishing trip scheduled." Ruthie pulled her door closed and started the car.

"I need to see if they can take a look at Winnie. She barely made it here yesterday." Hanna pulled her seat belt across her lap and buckled it.

"I can't believe you're still driving that ol' rattletrap. It's seven years older than you are. Put her out to pasture. In the meantime, you can use Dottie's car. It hasn't been out of the garage in quite a while. Some miles would be good for it."

"Rattletrap? Winnie's a vintage classic."

"If you say so." Auntie Ruthie looked across the seat and winked.

"Ruthie, why didn't you call sooner? I could have been here to help. Dottie and the diner are a lot for one person."

"You know Dottie, she's a mule. She thought she could keep up with everything while also getting treatment, and she did, for a while."

"How'd you find out she had cancer?"

"Well, little by little, she lost her appetite. Then, she complained of stomach cramps and a persistent backache. Well, hell's bells, we work from four in the morning until four or five in the afternoon, keeping up with breakfast and lunch at the diner, then prep for the next day. It's par for the course to have some digestion issues when we inhale food whenever we have a free second, not to mention a backache after working day in and day out for God knows how many years." Ruthie sighed deeply. "Then, she complained about feeling bloated all the time and had to pee more often, but again, we're getting older. I have to pee more often, and I feel bloated if I eat too much crap food and not enough veggies. I told her to eat a salad and buck up. Jesus, I can be such an asshole." She looked across the front seat and grimaced.

"Like you said, those symptoms could come with working on your feet so many hours each day for all those years." Hanna gave her arm a gentle squeeze. "You can't blame yourself."

"I do, and I don't. It changes by the minute." Auntie Ruthie flipped on the blinker and turned left into the diner parking lot. She pulled around the back and parked the car by the back door but made no effort to get out right away. "It wasn't until she started bleeding again after having been in menopause for almost twenty years that we got a doctor involved. The results were a gut punch. Ovarian cancer is some sneaky shit at our age."

"It's sneaky shit at any age, I imagine," Hanna said. "It's not like it shows up on an annual exam."

Ruthie grimaced while popping her eyebrows up and down in acknowledgment.

"What's the prognosis? I need to know if she'll pull through. Stage three is bad, but from what I read, it's not the worst," Hanna asked.

"It spread more than they'd hoped but not to any other organs so that was good news. They removed everything they could, including a few lymph nodes, and did some kind of testing to make sure she received the most effective chemo for her type of cancer. At least it's the kind that has better odds of survival than the other, more fatal type. I'll take all the hope I can get. The treatments have been hard on her body. Right now, lying down is the most comfortable position, but I didn't want her isolated in the bedroom away from everything. That's why the living room looks the way it does." Tears fell from her sweet brown eyes. She covered her mouth with her hand. "Hanna, I can't imagine my life without her."

"She's a fighter, and we'll do whatever we need to help her win."

"Fighting will be difficult if we can't get some nutrients in her. The doctors say that she needs nourishment to help regenerate damaged cells and stuff. She's not eating. I've made all of her favorites, and I can't get her to eat."

"With any luck, the ginger tea should help. If it doesn't, I have other recipes to try. Is pot legal in Wisconsin? I've read that it can help with nausea and appetite."

"Nope, not legal here. It is in every state around us, but not here." Ruthie sighed.

"Michigan isn't far. A road trip might be in order." Hanna had made a stop already but didn't need her aunt worried that there was cannabis on the property.

"You and your friends can take care of that. I'm so glad you're home. I feel better just having you here."

Hanna reached across the car and hugged her. "You two were there for me when I needed you most. Let me be here for you. I owe you both so much." She couldn't keep the fresh round of tears from falling. "I'm here to help in any way that I can."

Ruthie nodded and pulled back. "People will start showing up soon. We should get inside and get some coffee brewing."

"I can't believe that you've kept the diner open with all you're dealing with."

Ruthie opened the driver's door and looked back. "We talked about closing it, but the normalcy keeps me from losing my mind. Besides, it gives Dottie time to rest without an overbearing caregiver underfoot."

"I didn't think about it like that." Hanna swiped at the tears on her face and drew in a deep, cleansing breath. She'd come up to be their strength, and it was time to dig in and get busy.

The diner hadn't changed all that much over the years. Sure, there'd been small updates here and there. A fresh coat of paint, updated tables and chairs, and new flooring, but all in all, it was still the same place she'd worked at every day after school and all summer during her last two years of high school. She and her aunts had enjoyed a rhythm back then, and she fell right back into it with Ruthie. She got busy at the front counter, making coffee and filling the neglected salt and pepper shakers, along with the almost empty condiments at each station. All the more evidence that the diner was too much for one person to manage. Meanwhile, Ruthie warmed up the friers and the griddle and started pulling out items for the breakfast crowd.

The bell above the door jingled.

"Good morning, Ruthie, I have your ord—" The word stopped midsentence, and a friend from so long ago stared at Hanna while the door swung closed behind her. "Quinn?"

"Here." Hanna smiled and held up her hand just like she used to at school. "Quigley?"

"Here." Carol hopped up and down with her free arm raised. "Well, I'll be a monkey's uncle. Hanna Banana, you're home! Hot damn, it's good to see you."

"You're a monkey's ass if you start calling me Hanna Banana again." Just the sound of Carol's voice offered an unexpected comfort.

Carol Quigley had been her first friend when she'd moved to the Northwoods at the tail end of her sophomore year. The common beginning of their last name often had them seated together in most of their classes. Back then, Hanna had been unruly and out of control, and Carol had been the perfect calming influence.

"Well, get on around that counter and give me a hug!" Carol lowered the hand truck and held out her arms.

Hanna sunk into her embrace. "Man, it's good to see you too. You have no idea how good."

"I'm sorry to hear about Dottie," Carol said and gave her an extra squeeze. "I'm glad you're home."

"Thanks, there's no place I'd rather be." The bell above the door kept jingling. Customers continued trickling in. Hanna savored the hug for a moment longer before she stepped back. "Can you stick around for a bit?"

"Sorry, not this morning. I have a shit ton of deliveries to make, maybe after work? Oh, here are today's pies, breads, and muffins. If I'd known you were coming home, I would have made your favorite. I can make some turnovers for tomorrow." Carol stacked the goodies on the counter.

"I'll look forward to it." Hanna transferred the baked goods behind the counter. "Everything looks so amazing. You're such a savant with floury things." Hanna turned to grab the coffeepot and a few empty mugs.

Carol caught her arm before she walked past. "Let me know if there's anything I can do."

"I will, thanks. We should get together and catch up." The bell jingled above the door again. It'd been a tough morning. The onslaught of patrons only added more pressure. Couldn't they just give her five minutes with her pal?

"Maybe this time, you won't get shit-faced and puke all over the hood of the sheriff's car." Carol winked.

Hanna shook her head. "Sweetie, you need new material. That was, like, three years ago, and in my defense, it was a devastating breakup. I've avoided love ever since."

"Yeah, well, you still owe me a do-over on the night out." Carol kissed Hanna on the cheek.

"I'd be happy just to get a cup of coffee," an older gentleman said while wiggling into a booth.

"Quigley, I'll see you tomorrow." Hanna squeezed Carol's arm.

"Definitely." Carol waved and pushed her cart out the door.

Hanna spun around to take care of the customers. Her head swiveled a half a beat behind her body, and she slammed into some poor unsuspecting stranger with a loud, "Oof." Two of the coffee cups slipped out of her hand and shattered when they hit the floor. "Oh shit, I'm so sorry. Are you okay?" Hanna's eyes caught sight of the shiny badge. Dammit, of all the things to happen right now was to run into the sheriff. Shards of porcelain crunched under the soles of her shoes. Had she heard them reminiscing about that awful moment in her life? This was not how she wanted to reconnect with the area. She was not a screwup. "I'm so sorry, Sheriff Reid. Are you okay?"

A steady hand landed on her shoulder. "No harm, and I'm not Sheriff Reid."

No, she certainly wasn't. There was something sexy as hell about a butch woman in uniform, and the woman standing in front of her was head-to-toe butch and smoking hot. She was tall, much taller than Sheriff Reid, with a stocky build, broad shoulders, and a friendly yet commanding presence. She wore her wavy, light brown hair short and shaved close around her ears and collar.

"For you, I'll forget I heard about that little thing that happened to the sheriff's squad car a few years back. Besides, I bet it's washed off by now." Her dark brown eyes crinkled in the corner when she smiled.

Wow, she had the best smile.

"Warden Pearce, but you can call me Jordan." She held out her hand. "If you tell me where a broom is, I'll clean up the broken mugs."

Hanna accepted her hand. "Hanna Quinn, but you can call me Hanna." *Okay, that sounded lame.*

"It's very nice to meet you, Hanna." Oh, there was that smile again.

"Hey, Deb, I have your breakfast ready to go," Ruthie called from the kitchen. She walked around the corner with a sack in one hand and a broom in the other. "Wait a minute, you're not Deb."

"No, ma'am. I'm Jordan."

"Warden Jordan? Now that's a mouthful." Ruthie chuckled. "Boy howdy, if you grew your hair out some and wore a ball cap, you could be Deb's twin. Do you work with her? Is she meeting you here for breakfast?"

"I'm Warden Pearce. Jordan's my first name."

Hanna realized she was still holding the warden's hand. She'd never been so instantly attracted to anyone like she was attracted to her. Butterflies, heart swoons, serious insta-love kind of attraction. She wasn't sure if she should pull her hand free or wait. The warden's hand felt calloused and warm. Her grip was gentle. Hanna felt eyes on her. She looked up into Warden Pearce's gaze and reluctantly released her. She'd daydream about holding her hand later.

"I'm covering her area for a spell. Do you know her well?"

"I know her well enough to know what she likes for breakfast and lunch, but that's about it."

"Understood. What's in the sack?"

"Sausage, egg, and cheese on a toasted English muffin," Auntie Ruthie said. "Best four dollars you'll ever spend."

"Sold. Can I get a large black coffee to go, too?" Warden Pearce asked.

"How long are you covering for her?" Hanna filled a to-go cup with coffee and set it on the counter. "I'm visiting too. Maybe we could hang out?"

"Undetermined, could become a permanent post."

"Is that so?" Hanna smiled. "If you get hungry later, come on back. We're open until two." *Way to sound like a schoolgirl with a crush.*

Warden Pearce nodded with a smirk that could melt an ice queen's heart. "I'll keep that in mind."

Hanna took the broom from Auntie Ruthie and started cleaning up the two broken mugs just to have something to do. When she had the mess pushed behind the counter, she grabbed a couple more empty mugs. The other customers were all staring at the group at the counter.

"It was nice to meet you, Jordan. I hope you come back by later." Hanna knew she had a goofy look on her face, but there wasn't anything she could do about it.

"And you, Hanna. Trust me, the pleasure was mine." The warden put a ten on the counter. "I'll swing by if I can. Keep the change. Sorry about the mugs. It was totally my fault." She nodded to Ruthie. "Thanks for letting me snag Deb's breakfast."

"Have a great day, Warden. Be safe out there," Ruthie said and disappeared into the kitchen.

Warden Pearce could be a wonderful distraction while she was in town. No doubt, the small flurry of commotion was just what Hanna needed to cope with her reasons for being back. She watched her walk outside and climb into her badass warden truck. They drove much sexier vehicles than the sheriff did. *I wonder if it has a bench seat? I bet I'd fit perfectly up against her body, riding shotgun.* Now, that was an image to keep her mind occupied during lulls at the diner.

CHAPTER FIVE

The trip out to the station house took much less time than Jordan expected. Donning latex gloves, she knocked on both the front and back door, and as anticipated, there was no answer, and each was locked. Next, a cursory exterior check. There were no visible signs of a break-in and no movement that she could see through the few uncovered windows. The station house, a single-story ranch with an attached two-car garage, wasn't all that far from the hustle and bustle of the eight businesses that made up the downtown.

Waterdance was a community nestled along a one-mile section of Loon Boulevard, which hugged the Turtle River, the feeder for the northern tip of the massive lake. Not at all coincidentally, and a favorite recently found fact, a water dance was also a term used for a grouping of loons. The community claimed to be the loon capital of the world. She could believe it since there were probably more loons in the area than there were people. It would be stretching it to consider Waterdance a tiny town, let alone the capital of anything. With just sixty-eight year-round residents, calling it an unincorporated village was a tall order. Still, there was something about the area that touched Jordan's heart and spoke to her soul.

She closed her eyes and listened to the distinctive, haunting wail of a loon out on the water, *oohhhhh oowhhh awh*, followed by another somewhere off in the distance. She could listen to them call back and forth all day long. The morning was cool and the air hazy with the leftover moisture from the previous evening's storm. The loon's songs continued to reverberate across the water. Their migration north was mostly complete, and the nesting season had already started. Within a month or so, she'd get to see the fuzzy little loonlets floating with their overly protective parents.

She could get used to this, already visualizing herself on the deck with a cup of coffee. More and more, this was looking like the perfect place to settle down, maybe even enjoy a normal life.

Before she could explore very much of the wooded property that Deb Ryder had called home for the last year and a half, a sheriff's cruiser pulled in and parked next to her truck. The woman who climbed out of the driver's seat appeared to be in her late fifties or early sixties. She was easily a head shorter than Jordan, with a slight, trim build, and gray streaked, dirty blond hair that dusted her shoulders. Her presence, her gait, everything about her screamed Holly Hunter. Jordan couldn't deny being a fan of the actress, having watched almost everything she'd ever performed in.

The sheriff's uniform wasn't all that different from a conservation warden's, other than the inverted colors. Jordan wore a light gray shirt and black trousers, whereas the sheriff wore a black shirt with a dark gray tie and trousers. Too bad the DNR uniform didn't include a tie. Jordan enjoyed wearing ties. The only other obvious difference was that Jordan's bulletproof vest was to be worn over her shirt, while the sheriff clearly had to wear her vest beneath her uniform.

Thank goodness her vest wasn't required in circumstances such as this. The protection was far too confining and smashed her 42D breasts.

"Mornin'." The sheriff waved. Hell, with the bit of grit to her voice, she even sounded like Holly Hunter. "I'm Sheriff Reid. If you get assigned to the area and stay in your lane, you can call me Ang." She stopped in front of Jordan and held out her hand.

Jordan accepted it with a mutually firm shake, thinking briefly about Hanna Quinn and her experience with the sheriff's cruiser, then the way she'd held her hand a tad longer than necessary. Hopefully, they could finish this up in time for her to head there for lunch. "Morning, Sheriff Reid. I'm Warden Pearce, but if I get assigned to the area, you can call me Jordan."

"Nice to meet ya. Are you familiar with this area at all?"

"Oh, absolutely, I love the Northwoods, especially this area. It's hard to believe that by building a dam and flooding sixteen lakes, it would create this incredible, massive body of water. Where else can you go camping on one of sixty-five private little islands? The Flambeau Scenic Waters would be the perfect post for me with all its undisturbed habitat and wildlife, especially the loons and the way they sing to each other." She tapped her heart. "Their calls touch me inside. Fortunately, the area's protected by the state, so generations to come will have the opportunity to experience the rugged beauty that it offers. To me, it's a magical place."

The sheriff crinkled her nose and curled her lip. "What are you, a walking Wikipedia?"

Jordan shook her head. "No, sorry, we used to vacation up here when I was a kid, and I fell in love with the area."

Sheriff Reid chuckled. "Yeah, well, next time someone asks… the second answer is the one you want to use."

The wind swirled between them, and that familiar floral scent haunted Jordan's nose and churned her stomach for the second time in as many days. "Sheriff, by any chance, were you out on Loon Boulevard last night during the storm, up where the road is a bit narrower?"

"Nope, I was snuggled up on the couch at home last night, drinking my after-dinner bourbon by candlelight. The storm took the power for about an hour. Why do you ask?"

"A tree went down and blocked the car in front of me. I didn't get a look at the driver, but she wore that same perfume. Beautiful by Estée Lauder."

"You've got yourself a good nose. I barely spritzed myself this morning. Popular scent for my generation. Shit, I think I just called myself old." She smiled.

"It was my mom's favorite fragrance."

"You're what, late thirties?"

"Forty-one."

"So your mom's in her early sixties?"

Jordan nodded. She didn't want to talk about her mom.

"See what I mean, old. Christ, I retire in just a couple of years." She rolled her eyes. "Let's get back to why we're here. I understand from your chief that Warden Ryder's resignation was unexpected, and her departure leaves some unanswered questions, so you'd like me to join you on a walk-through of the station house in case anything's hinky?"

"Yes, that's correct. Did you know Deb?"

"Just to say hi or assist on a call. She spent her summers out on the water and the other seasons keeping the hunters, off-road vehicles, and the snowmobilers in line."

"Does her resignation seem odd to you?"

"I've been on the job long enough that not much seems odd. Have you already checked out the house? Is it locked?"

"Yes. I knocked and walked the exterior. The inside was visible from several windows. The house is messy, but I saw nothing alarming. Last night's rain did a number, so there's not so much as a tire track in the gravel drive. From what I can see through the garage window, her assigned work truck is there but no other vehicle." Jordan walked next to the sheriff toward the house. "The locks are keyless. I have the master code, unless Deb changed it."

"Thorough assessment. I ran her through the system this morning and found a white 2017 Toyota Camry as the only vehicle listed in her name. If that wasn't in the garage, then it's a safe bet that it's with her."

"A white Toyota Camry was the same make and model of the car stopped by the tree in the storm last night. What's her plate number?"

Sheriff Reid pulled out her phone and tapped on the screen. "AQB-974. Does that match your car?"

"The plate from last night started with RHR."

"White cars are popular, they show less dirt, and if someone has a car anymore, as opposed to an SUV, it's likely a Toyota Camry or a Honda Civic." The sheriff whistled. "Man, I wish our department had housing for the deputies to live in while on the force. Imagine the money I could've banked toward retirement."

"Not all of us get to live in a station house. Trust me, something like this is a dream assignment. Hence, the concern about Warden Ryder walking away without notice. I mean, look, a gorgeous, five-acre wooded lot right on the water, and while the flowage is enormous, it's not half as busy as some of the lakes I patrol in the southern part of the state. What I wouldn't give to not have to trailer my boat to a different body of water every day. An assignment like this would be like winning the lottery."

"If everything pans out, you just might have won that lottery, then."

Jordan nodded and kept her wishful smile inside. Latex gloves felt suffocating on her hands, but if there were questions, it would be better not to have her fingerprints mess up any inquiry or investigation, should it come to that. Sheriff Reid followed suit. Jordan keyed in the six-digit code and let out a little sigh of relief when the light flickered green. She turned the dead bolt and opened the door. Once they verified no one was in the home by clearing each room, Jordan stopped watching for movement and started taking in the surroundings.

"Well, if the code hadn't worked, we could have entered through any of the windows; they're all unlocked, and that one's cracked open." The sheriff pointed over her shoulder at the sheer curtains blowing softly with the breeze off the water. "Are the station houses furnished?"

"From what I understand, no, but I'll have to verify. This is the first one I've been in." Jordan snapped pictures throughout the entire house.

"Sure looks like she left in a hurry. The bedroom closet and dresser are both empty, but there're hangers all over the closet floor, and a few of the dresser drawers are hanging open. Hey, do you know if linens came with the house? She didn't bother to strip the bed."

Jordan flipped on the light in the bathroom. "Similar scene in here. Stuff's missing, but it's a mess. Drawers left open. The linen cabinet is open, but she left the towels and linens behind." Jordan squatted in front of the empty sink cabinet. "Why take all the cleaning supplies from under the sink but leave the shampoo and conditioner in the shower?"

"Maybe she used them, and the bottles were wet, and she forgot to go back?"

"Yeah, maybe." Jordan couldn't escape the uneasy feeling in her stomach. She made her way into the guest room. Deb must have used it as an office. There was a full bed shoved into a corner. A desk sat to the right of the bed with dual monitors and cables. "She takes her computer but leaves the desk, monitors, and cables?"

"Could have had a laptop. Maybe she rarely used the monitors and forgot about them," Sheriff Reid said over her shoulder.

"If it were me, I wouldn't forget. I know that brand. They aren't cheap."

"You'd be surprised by what people leave behind, especially if they leave in a hurry. I could tell you some stories." The sheriff turned and headed back up the short hall.

Jordan followed. "That's what I don't understand. Why leave in a hurry? If the quiet was too much, why quit and not ask for a transfer? She could have moved south where the patrols are busier. Why not leave a forwarding address? Nothing about this makes any sense at all."

The sheriff turned. "It doesn't have to make sense to you. Could have been a violent end to an unhealthy relationship. Could be a family member became sick and needed help. There could be a hundred reasons why she bolted that you may never understand."

"I'm still not buying it. If there was a sick family member, she'd have access to FMLA leave. No one in their right mind walks away from a long-term career...from everything. Not like this." She opened the washer. It was empty. So was the dryer.

"Could be that she wasn't in her right mind, you never know. Maybe the solitude was a trigger. Mental issues can compound and sneak up on a person."

"Maybe, but Deb was always so positive and upbeat."

"People are masters at hiding what they don't want others to see." Sheriff Reid riffled through a pile of papers on an end table.

The sheriff wasn't wrong. Hell, Jordan kept all sorts of stuff close to the vest. "I guess so." She walked into the kitchen and opened the fridge. Other than a few condiment bottles in the door, it was empty.

From the kitchen, she could hear the loons continue to call to one another out on the water. Oh, how she'd love to get the assignment and live in this wooded paradise. *Keep looking.* No way did she want her desire to live on the property to be the reason she neglected some telling details. If anyone needed an objective advocate, it was the person who wasn't in the room: Deb Ryder.

Sheriff Reid interrupted her thoughts. "Trust me, plenty of people have left things much, much worse than this. I am not seeing anything that's throwing up alarm bells. I'd bet a week's wages that your friend had a nasty breakup, or something every bit as traumatic, and she did just what her email said...simply walked away. You'll see, she'll reach out when things settle down for her. I'll walk the perimeter with you, but unless I see body parts hanging out of a wood chipper, I'm not inclined to call this anything it isn't."

"Understood," Jordan smirked at the reference to *Fargo*. Still, her gut was telling her that something was off. Why was Sheriff Reid being so aloof? Shouldn't she trust Jordan's suspicions? Or was she simply too lazy to investigate? Hopefully, it wasn't the latter. It'd make working on future cases difficult.

They checked the detached garage. All off-road vehicles assigned to the warden: a long-track snowmobile that had been modified for duty, a similarly enhanced ATV, and a UTV matched up for registrations and were accounted for. Even the boat assigned to the property was elevated on the hoist, just as it should have been. Jordan had to admit that the sheriff wasn't wrong in saying that nothing looked nefarious, but there was still something gnawing at her, telling her that things weren't quite right. The Deb she knew from training wouldn't just walk away, not after so many years.

"Well, I see no reason to keep the next warden from moving in. If that's you, congratulations, I think you've got yourself a new post." She walked to her cruiser and opened the driver's door.

"Yep, looks that way. Thank you, Sheriff." Jordan looked around. "Say, by chance, did you run her financials? Have there been any transactions? Has she used her credit card for gas or anything?"

"Haven't run financials and I don't plan to. There's no probable cause for a warrant."

"Isn't the fact that she's missing enough probable cause? I'm telling you, she wouldn't up and walk away. Something's off."

"Now, see, we were getting along so well, and here you go, pissing in my sandbox. You're on the wrong force to be a detective. Stay in your lane, Warden. When someone quits their job, they're not considered a missing person. Even if they quit by email."

Law enforcement was law enforcement, plain and simple. Jordan hated the "stay in your lane" mentality. She had good intuition and trusted her gut, and her gut was telling her that something was off. What was crystal clear was that the sheriff would not be any help, so she let it drop for now.

"Is it wrong that I'm sort of excited? I mean, I feel bad for Deb and all, but just look at this place." She waved her arm at a stand of trees and the glistening water beyond.

"Not if it's like you said and the assignment feels like winning the lottery. Enjoy. You have yourself a good day now." Sheriff Reid waved out the window before she turned the car around and made her way down the driveway.

Jordan called Lieutenant Foley with the results of the search. She learned that while the station house wasn't supposed to be furnished, items had been left over the years to the point that it had become so, and the full kitchen cabinets, made beds, and linen filled closets weren't as suspicious as they might have been.

"I still can't make sense of this. It isn't at all consistent with the Deb Ryder that I've come to know for the past year and a half."

"I hear ya, Lieutenant, and I don't disagree. I had much the same conversation with Sheriff Reid. Sadly, she didn't see it that way."

"The chief told me that you've put in for a transfer for the post. I'm open to you getting the assignment permanently once I know what's going on with Deb. Would you lock up the house and leave it as is for now? That said, I'd still like you to stay on and fill in until we know all the facts. If she calls, saying life in the Northwoods isn't what she expected and quits, the post is yours. I just need to hear from her, not some vague email. You understand, don't you?"

"Certainly, Lieutenant. I'd like the same consideration if it were me. I'm happy to cover. I have my assigned boat and truck and can take over area patrols." She had hoped to move into the station house, but she could work from almost anywhere, and with summer kicking off, her work was on the water anyway.

"Thanks, Jordan. I appreciate your flexibility. If anything changes, please let me know."

Jordan agreed and hung up. Now to see the manager at Waterdance Lodge about a broken showerhead and some actual hot water. Either those two things had to be fixed or she'd have to find a new place to stay.

CHAPTER SIX

The bell above the door jingled. Hanna wasn't sure if customers were coming or going. *Can this day just be over already?* She'd love nothing more than to lock the door and close for the afternoon. Hell, close up period. She didn't understand why her aunts were working themselves to the bone to keep the diner open, but it was important to them, and they were important to her, so she'd do anything in her power to help.

She cashed out a few customers, refilled some drinks, then ran back into the kitchen, hoping the food on the grill hadn't burned to a blackened crisp. Thankfully, all was okay. Hanna lifted the basket of fries from the oil, gave it a good shake, and poured them onto a lined tray. The smell of the food cooking on the grill caused her stomach to complain about having skipped lunch. The kitchen area was about the same temperature as her aunts' house, if not hotter. Sweat beaded up on her brow and trickled down her back.

Melted cheddar cheese dripped from the top of the bacon-covered burger patties when she lifted them with the spatula. She slid each onto a toasted bun, added a crisp pickle spear, and a heaped a pile of fresh, thick cut fries alongside. How on earth Auntie Ruthie did all of this on her own day in and day out was beyond her. She'd had some errands to run that she'd been neglecting, and rather than make it an even longer day, Hanna had offered to tackle the lunch rush on her own and do the prep for the next day. Ruthie hadn't been gone for more than an hour, and she was already frazzled. She grabbed the two plates and made her way out to the dining room.

"Oh hey, Warden. I'll be right with you." Hanna almost stumbled but tried to play it cool. Jordan had actually come back for lunch. Okay, so there was a bright spot in her afternoon. She certainly couldn't deny being attracted to her. She'd spent much of the morning hoping she'd come back in. If only she'd known, she could have freshened up. Hanna shook her head. There was nothing she could do about her appearance now.

"No hurry." Jordan gave her a nod and that sweet smile. *Wow.* She really had the best smile.

"Here's a bacon cheeseburger with fries for you, Banjo." She set one plate down, then the next. "And the same for you, Chipmunk."

"Th...th...th..." He clicked his tongue and shook his head. "Appreciate it, Ha...Ha...Hanna."

Hanna had long ago become familiar with his stutter. It was much less pronounced when he didn't feel pressured to speak, and because of this, she made a point of not giving him the "what are you trying to say" stare. That, and after a stern talking to by Aunt Dottie, she never again attempted to finish a word for him. Like many afflicted with the condition, it disappeared completely when music was involved by lighting up an entirely different part of his brain. Put a banjo in his hands, and he could sing his thoughts clear as a summer's day, thus his nickname.

Banjo's other half, Chipmunk, had a pronounced overbite, and even though she was as skinny as a rail, she possessed some hefty jowls. Hanna had seen her stuff fourteen full-size marshmallows in her mouth, most of which were squirreled away in her cheeks, and she could still talk, clear as day. Hence, Chipmunk. Come to think of it, she couldn't recall either of their real names; she'd only ever known them as Banjo and Chipmunk, and they were always together, like peas and carrots.

"Thanks, Hanna. This looks fantastic. Say, we'll get out to your aunts' place soon to pick up your Winnebago. Don't you worry none. We'll figure out what's going on with it," Chipmunk said around a mouthful of fries.

"No rush. Whenever it fits in your schedule. I can use Aunt Dottie's car while I'm here."

"H…H…How's Dot…Dottie?"

"Hanging in there as best she can. Now to figure out how to get some calories in her. Cancer sucks, man."

"Yes, it d…does."

"Is there anything else I can get either of you?" she asked.

With full mouths, they shook their heads. Good, because a dashing warden was waiting at the counter.

"Twice in one day. You must really like the food here." Hanna plopped down on the stool next to Jordan. "Or maybe it's the outstanding service?"

"Perhaps it's—" Before Jordan had a chance to finish her sentence, the door burst open, ringing the bell above it for all it was worth.

"Quinn, you fucking shithead. I'm a fixin' to kick your ass!"

Without a word, Jordan spun around and stood in front of Hanna in a swift, fluid motion. She motioned for Hanna to stay behind her. Protective without being pompous or boisterous. *Wow, okay, that's hot.*

Hanna stood and looked around her. "Yeah, Marky Mark, you think you've got what it takes?"

"There's no need to escalate this," Jordan said. "Let's tone it down and take a breath."

"Hey, Badge, this doesn't concern you, so stand down."

Hanna touched Jordan's arm. "It's okay, she's a friend," Louder, she added, "A hell on wheels bitch…and a dear, dear friend."

"I know you've got that right."

Hanna stepped around Jordan and wrapped her friend up in an enormous hug. "Ah, Bobbie Rae, hot damn, it's been far too long."

"How long have you been back? And why haven't you come by the bar to see me?"

"I got in yesterday afternoon. I haven't made the rounds, Aunt Dottie's—" Hanna choked on the rest of the words. Everyone knew, so why did they all have to keep asking?

"Shit, man, I know. I'm sorry." Bobbie Rae held her tightly. "It's good you're here for them. You've been missed." She smelled like the bar, like booze and smoke and all in hard-ass attitude, and holding her again felt like, well, like being home. She was that one friend, the one person who no one could ever replace.

Hanna shivered in her embrace. "I've missed you too. It's been too long," she said into her neck. "It's hard seeing Aunt Dottie so frail. I'm glad they called me home. There's nothing I wouldn't do for them."

"Stay this time, eh, just stay. Grow your weeds up here," Bobbie Rae whispered in her ear.

"My weeds?" Hanna laughed. "You're a goof."

"It isn't the same without you. I know I keep saying it, but damn, woman, it's so good to see you."

"I hear ya. It's good to see you too." Hanna gave her an extra squeeze, then stepped back.

"I'm sorry, are you Bobbie Rae Marks?" Jordan asked. "You used to live with your mom in the apartment above the Drunken Loon Saloon?"

"Duh. Everyone knows that." She stood there defiantly. "What's it to you, Badge?"

"You probably don't remember me. We were eleven years old or so when we met. My dad and sisters called me Jo-Jo. You and I became fast friends on my first visit up here. Hell, we were inseparable. We laughed, talked about everything and anything, and spent most of our waking hours down by the river."

Bobbie Rae took a step closer. "I remember every minute of those days. Jo-Jo, is it really you? I've always wondered—"

"It's really me. Ask me anything."

"What'd we hide behind the log down by the dock?"

Cackling laughter from the booth behind her: Chipmunk. Hanna almost forgot there were other customers there.

"A pack of Camel cigarettes, no filter. We stole them from my dad after he'd passed out, but it rained that night and ruined all four left in the pack."

"Wait, what?" Thoroughly confused, Hanna looked from Jordan to Bobbie Rae.

"Holy shit, it's really you! Damn, look at you, all grown-up." Chipmunk cackled a delighted laugh and slapped Banjo's back. They were having a lively conversation, but she didn't have the wherewithal to figure it all out, not with this new development. Bobbie Rae and Jordan had history.

"Yeah, luckily, we don't stay eleven forever. You can't know how much I looked forward to those two weeks each summer and how sad I was when they were over. Hey, do you remember playing that Sophie B. Hawkins hit on your big boom box over and over again? It was years before I really understood those lyrics, but I tell ya, that was a great song."

"*Damn, I wish I was your lover,*" Bobbie Rae sang the title. "I still play it all the time. It's my jam. Seriously, what happened to you? Every year for four summers, then you left and fell off the face of the earth. No more letters, no postcards, nothin'. I remember you saying you were going to move here when you were old enough. What kept you away?"

"Life got a little upside down, and it took a long time for me to get right side up again. You look good, just as wiry and scrappy as ever."

"I might be half the person you are, but make no mistake, I could still kick your ass." Bobbie Rae slapped Jordan's hand in a high five.

"Oh, I have no doubt. All I ask is that you make sure I'm not wearing my uniform when you do it."

Bobbie Rae laughed.

"Okay, hold the phone. You two know each other? Like… know, know each other?" Hanna turned to Jordan. "Didn't you just get into town? I thought you were filling in for another warden?"

"Correct. I arrived last night—"

"Yeah? For how long? Hopefully, at least a week or two. Where ya staying?" Bobbie Rae asked.

"Waterdance Lodge, cabin seven. Where else would I stay?"

"Seriously? Man, that place was so awesome back in the day, but it's a serious dive now. It's a shame," Bobbie Rae said. "The lodge sold to new owners, gosh, fifteen years or so ago. It's sad that they haven't done a thing to bring it back to life. Instead, they're just raking in all the money they can before it falls apart completely,"

Jordan grimaced. "Well, now, that doesn't give me great confidence that they'll fix the hot water or repair the broken showerhead before tomorrow morning."

"Yeah, good luck with that. Then again, you do wear a badge, so they might step up their game. Give them the same cop stare you gave me when I came in. That'll get their attention."

"Jo-Jo?" Hanna still couldn't believe that Bobbie Rae and Jordan were childhood friends. "I feel so left out. Can I call you Jo-Jo?"

"I prefer Jordan now. It's more professional, given the badge and all."

"Aren't you Warden Pearce at work?" Hanna bumped Jordan in the arm with her elbow. "I really want in on calling you Jo-Jo."

"Jordan? Ha, forget that. You'll always be Jo-Jo to me." Bobbie Rae gave her a thumb clasp handshake. "Listen, I gotta get back to the bar. Hot damn, I can't believe you're back. We've got so much catching up to do."

"It's good to see you too. I always wondered if you'd stayed in the area. I'll swing by once things settle a bit for me."

"You'd better 'cause the bar is, like, fifty feet from your cabin."

Seeing the exchange was like being in the Twilight Zone. "What? Jo-Jo's back, and now I'm chopped liver?"

Bobbie Rae shot Hanna a cocky-ass smile and held out her arms. "Aw, Quinnie, you know you'll always be my favorite of the three musketeers."

She'd lost that spot long ago, and she knew it. Carol had taken over being the favorite because she'd stuck around, whereas Hanna had left and only came back for visits. Still, she stepped in for another hug that only Bobbie Rae could give. "Thanks for coming by. It really is so good to see you."

"I know your focus is on Dot right now, but I'm here if you need to blow off a little steam. Just say the word, and I'm yours." Bobbie Rae kissed her on the cheek before stepping back. She was an obnoxious ball of fire, but if push came to shove, there was no one else Hanna would rather have in her corner. "Banjo, Chipmunk…I hope I didn't disturb your lunch too much."

Thankfully, they were the only two still in the diner, besides Jordan. Each of them waved her off. All the locals were used to Bobbie Rae.

"Well, Warden Jo-Jo, that was unexpected. What other surprises do you have up your sleeve?" Hanna motioned for Jordan to sit at the counter.

"What, like the fact that I've been out fishing with Banjo and Chipmunk? Whenever we were up here, I'd go out as often as they'd let me tag along. I'd clean the boat, gut and scale fish, fillet, anything they needed help with just to earn the middle seat. When I was twelve or thirteen, I caught the record walleye for that summer, twenty-nine and a half inches. It was almost ten pounds. That night, we had those filets for dinner over the campfire. Walleye is still my favorite freshwater fish." She looked over her shoulder and nodded to Banjo and Chipmunk.

Hanna shifted on her stool so she could be a part of the conversation.

"Sadly, your rec…record's b…b…been b…broken, but no… not by much."

"Yeah, summer after summer after your last visit, we kept hoping to see you standing on the end of the dock with your fishing pole and tackle box. Normally, I'm not all that excited when we get stuck taking someone else's kid out fishing, but you were an unexpected treat, quiet, with thoughtful questions and always so grateful to be in the boat," Chipmunk said. "Your sisters, on the other hand, wanted nothing to do with fishing, especially anything slimy. Funny how kids from the same parents can be so different. How's your family doing? Your dad was Jim, Joe, John—" She scratched her chin.

"Jack," Jordan said quietly. Sadness flashed across her face.

Hanna rested a hand on her arm. Hopefully, that wasn't too forward. She looked over at Hanna with a softened expression, including a hint of a smile and a soft nod. That was a positive sign.

"That's it, Jack." Chipmunk snapped her fingers. "How's he doing?"

"He's gone ten years now." Jordan's jaw muscles tightened.

"Sorry to hear that. You sure were good with your little sisters. That's what I remember."

"Look at you, all gr...grown-up. Conser...ser...conservation warden, huh? I can se...see th...that. Even as a kid, you knew the fishing regs b...better than I did. Always loved to know the rules."

"I enjoy the work, no doubt. I should let you eat before your food gets cold." Jordan gave a nod and turned to face the counter again.

"I'm sure we'll see you out on the water," Chipmunk said. "Welcome back to the area."

"Thanks, I'll be out there yet this afternoon. Need to see how the island campers weathered the storm," Jordan said. Her upbeat demeanor had certainly darkened.

Hanna felt bad for prodding. It was time to change the subject. "How about some lunch before you go back to work? I make a wicked buffalo chicken wrap."

Jordan nodded. "Sure, sounds good."

Hanna patted her shoulder before she made her way to the kitchen. She decided to make two and eat a little something herself. They could share a mounded plate of fries and onion rings. Her stomach growled with anticipation. As she rolled up the second overstuffed wrap, the bell above the door jingled. She looked up through the pass-through window to see Banjo and Chipmunk waving good-bye. Relief washed over her. At least it wasn't more customers coming in.

"Have a good afternoon. I'll see you two in the morning. I'll be running solo."

"We'll be here to help." Chipmunk held up a thumbs-up.

The digital clock on the counter read one fifty-eight. Close enough. Hanna lifted the three plates of food to the pass-through ledge and made a beeline to lock the door and flip the sign in the window. Finally, the diner was closed. A bit of prep work after her meal and she could call it a day.

"I'm sorry. I forgot the diner was only open until two."

"Yeah, we cover breakfast and lunch, then the bar takes care of the dinner crowd."

"I can take my order to go if you need to close up," Jordan said. "I don't need to be a bother. I should get out on the water, anyway."

"Here, I thought you'd join me for lunch. I haven't eaten, either." Hanna kept her voice hopeful. She certainly hoped to get some one-on-one time.

Jordan smiled. "Now that's an offer I can't refuse. The water can wait a bit."

Her smile was turning into a craving. "What would you like to drink?"

"Iced tea sounds good."

"It does, doesn't it? Okay, two iced teas coming right up." Hanna set the plates on the counter and filled two glasses to the brim. "Ranch? Ketchup?"

"Both, please. This looks fantastic."

"I'm not sure that Auntie Ruthie's version would be quite so stuffed, but I was starving, so you get the Hanna version. I'm a bit of a foodie."

"Here's to hoping I always get the Hanna version. I haven't eaten since I stole Deb's breakfast." Jordan took a big bite of her wrap. "Mmm...this hits the spot," she said around the mouthful of food.

Hanna wiped her mouth with a napkin after swallowing her first bite. "I'm sorry about earlier. It seems we both got into town yesterday, and everyone who knows me has been stopping by and sweeping you up in a loud, awkward kumbaya."

"It's okay. Says a lot about your character. Everyone missed you and is happy to have you back. I can see that."

"Apparently, they're happy to have you back too. Who knew this was once your stomping grounds?" Hanna laughed. "So you and Bobbie Rae?"

Jordan half laughed, half coughed. "Better yet, how about you and Bobbie Rae?" She had the best sideways glance, enhanced with a perfect smirk. "Am I crossing a line by being here? I don't want to give her the wrong impression. She'll take me out while I'm sleeping. The lodge isn't known for security."

"Naw, I'm sure you're safe. Once upon a time, we tried to be something, but I needed to leave, and she needed to stay. We quickly realized we were better off as friends. Me and Carol, the spaz from this morning, and Bobbie Rae considered ourselves the three musketeers. We did everything together during my last two years of high school. The three of us even went to our senior prom together. Bobbie Rae wore a tux and had Carol on one arm and me on the other, each of us in a sexy dress and heels."

"I would've loved to have seen that."

"We were quite the trio, smokin' hot, if I do say so myself. I was more petite back then. We were the talk of the school for the rest of the year. *Tres lesbo*, as I recall." Hanna laughed, vividly reliving a treasured memory.

"No doubt you were the belle of the ball. Sounds like the three of you had a great time."

"Oh, we definitely had fun. My dress was shimmery emerald green, which looked great with my ginger locks. Did you wear a tux to your prom? I bet you looked hot."

"I never went to prom, but if I'd gone, I would have been all in on wearing a tux. Much to my parents' dismay, I have never, nor will I ever, own or wear a dress."

Hanna laughed at the last part. She couldn't picture Jordan in a dress. At least the image that came up wasn't at all flattering. Jordan was hot in her uniform and would be even sexier decked out in black formal attire. She felt the heat in her cheeks and knew she'd better change the topic.

"I'm glad you came back and had lunch with me, Jo-Jo." Hanna tried out the nickname. It felt weird on her tongue. Jordan even looked like a Jordan.

"Jo-Jo?" She chuckled and shook her head. "Me too. Any nicknames I can be privy to?"

"Nope, just Hanna."

"We'll see about that. I'll have to swing by the bar later. I bet Bobbie Rae has some stories." Jordan shot her another sideways glance, this time with a wink. "So if you grew your weed up here, would I have to arrest you?"

Hanna laughed. "It's not what you think, I assure you. Although that specific weed has many beneficial merits. I'm a medicinal herbalist."

"Ah, herbs are fascinating. I carry both plantain and yarrow salve in my kit."

"See, I knew we'd get along. We should go foraging sometime."

"Is that herbal speak for a snipe hunt?" Jordan wiggled her eyebrows. She really had the best expressions.

"For that, you earn bonus points." Hanna leaned over and bumped her with her shoulder.

"Do you create remedies or teach or—"

"Lately, I've been traveling the country, teaching workshops."

"So where's home?"

"Home is wherever I park my Winnebago. How about you? Or are you a traveling warden?"

"I have a house just outside of Madison, but I wouldn't call it home. At least, it's never felt like home. With any luck, I'll be able to put that on the market and call Waterdance home."

"Seems like Bobbie Rae would like to have you back. Hey, what was eleven-year-old Bobbie Rae like?"

"Oh, I imagine much like she is now. She was a force to be reckoned with, that's for sure." Jordan stuffed an onion ring in her mouth. She chewed slowly, as if lost in thought. "Honestly, I'm surprised she even remembers me."

"Oh, I have a feeling there's quite a memorable person hidden behind that badge."

"That's sweet of you to say." Jordan half laughed. "She came into my life when I most needed a friend. Ink aside, if I'd seen her on the street, I'm not sure I would have recognized her. Given her reaction, I doubt she would've recognized me, either. Thankfully, you were here to reintroduce us."

"None of us looks like we did when we were eleven, especially Bobbie Rae. She loves ink. The sleeves were done years ago. Her chest and back were new the last time I saw her, and the neck designs happened sometime in the last few years. Inside, she's still the same ol' Bobbie Rae. She'll fight to the death for the ones she loves."

"Don't I know it." Jordan looked like she was reliving her own memories. "Is her mom still alive?"

Hanna wanted to dig but decided not to. Jordan seemed to close up when the past was brought up. Maybe she'd open up more as they got to know each other better. "No. She passed away, gosh, eight or nine years ago? She drank as much as she poured. Liver cirrhosis took her at fifty. Bobbie Rae took over the bar. You should go check it out. She's done a lot to bring it back."

"The only thing I remember about the bar back then was that they had these fried potato wedges called jo-jo fries. She told me they were named after me, which I knew was a lie since they were already on the menu when I first came to town. But the sentiment was sweet."

"See, there's no one like Bobbie Rae to make you feel special."

"Indeed. No one like Bobbie Rae." Jordan looked in the bar's direction, then turned back. "I'm sorry to hear about what your aunt's going through. I know you're an herbalist and probably have ten things better, but if she has no appetite and nothing sounds good, try some canned peaches in heavy syrup. Who knows why, but they seem to settle well and hit the spot. At his worst, it was the only thing my dad could keep down."

"Canned peaches, huh? I'll have to pick some up." For some unexplained reason, Hanna didn't mind Jordan bringing up Aunt Dottie. Her words and her expression were genuine and kind.

"Thank you for a great lunch and your amazing company. I think that just before two o'clock is my new favorite meal break time." Jordan put a twenty on the counter. "I don't think I'll need dinner, either. Can I help clean up?"

"That's way too much money, and you don't need to help me clean, especially when you have to go back to work," Hanna said the words, but she hoped Jordan would hang out longer, even if just to keep her company.

"I didn't offer because I felt like I needed to do it. I have an hour and a half for mealtime, and we listen to the same music," Jordan pointed at the speaker on the shelf. "Besides, it will get you home to your aunt sooner. So tell me what to do, and let me help."

Hanna leaned over and rested her head on Jordan's shoulder. "Okay, deal, but only if you put that twenty back in your wallet and let me buy you breakfast tomorrow."

Jordan shook her head and left the twenty. "My labor is free. Our lunch was not. Your aunts aren't keeping the diner open because it's fun."

"I see you're going to be trouble. Fine. I'll clean the bathrooms if you'll wipe down tables, sweep, and mop out here. Then, you can get back to work while I prep for tomorrow."

"I'm on it." Jordan stacked the three plates and carried them over to the bin of dirty dishes.

Hanna would take all the time she could get with her new favorite warden. If she had to cover the diner for her aunts, at least there was a very sexy side benefit.

CHAPTER SEVEN

While time seemed to have stood still in much of Waterdance, especially at the lodge, there had been noticeable changes in the twenty-seven year gap since Jordan's last visit. For starters, gravel no longer crunched beneath her boots in the parking lot at the nearest boat ramp, now paved and expanded. The tree canopy above was taller, fuller, and the tree trunks thicker than she remembered. Hell, she was taller, fuller, and thicker too. All of which begged the question Bobbie Rae had asked at the diner. If this tiny community was truly her favorite place on earth, why had she waited all these years to come back?

She hadn't been lying when she'd said that life had gotten a little upside down. Little did anyone know that upside down was the understatement of the century. She thought being back would offer the escape it had when she was a kid, but anymore, it was harder and harder to escape a past that demanded to be dealt with.

She couldn't dwell on that now. It was time to go to work. She shook off the haunting guilt from years long gone and made her way down to her boat moored on the dock. The river was high. Six inches of rain from the previous night's storm had created a strong, flowing current. Floating near the reeds, the loons seemed unfazed, watching for fish and calling out to one another.

Jordan kept her boat just above an idle and immersed herself in her first solo trip as a conservation warden on the Turtle Flambeau

Flowage. Above, wisps of clouds scalloped so perfectly that the sky looked like the intricate pattern of a box turtle's shell. The afternoon sun that filtered through the wispy canopy was warm on her skin. All in all, it had turned out to be a beautiful day.

Jordan navigated with the current and carefully steered her boat downstream toward the flowage. She'd already loaded the map into her boat's GPS and had a planned path for her first trip. There were seven campsites between the Sturgeon Bay boat launch and the dam, four of which were on the big island along the Turtle River. She hoped to check on each of the sixty-five remote campsites before dark. She had just over five hours to accomplish her tour.

The wind from the storm had been strong enough to drop a tree across the road and could do just as much damage on any of the islands, not to mention relocating untethered boats that would leave a camper stranded. She'd been tempted to take the afternoon off and do the tour tomorrow, but the water temperatures this early in the season were in the mid-sixties and would make swimming an unpleasant task for those attempting to retrieve a wayward boat. After an intense storm like that, checking on the most vulnerable was a duty she didn't take lightly.

Her GPS chirped as she approached the first site. A quick tap on the screen verified the coordinates. A man stood from a crouched position next to a smokeless fire ring near shore.

Jordan shifted her boat to an idle and waved. "Afternoon. How'd you fare the storm? Glad to see your boat stayed tied."

"Hey, howdy, warden. Oh, I did all right. Don't suppose you have a dry match?"

"As a matter of fact, I do." And just like that, she was reminded why she loved her career. She beached the nose of her boat on a section of sandy shore. Jordan kept a Ziplock bag of matches locked in dry storage on her boat. She had plenty for the afternoon tour.

"My little aluminum fishing boat flipped easily enough to cover my woodpile, but dummy me left the matches in my camp chair. Teach me to camp without a lighter. That rain was wicked. Everything's soaked. I was just about to pack up and head for the store."

"Happy to have saved you the trip." She hopped off the front of her boat.

"Awesome, thanks." He accepted the small matchbox. "The sheriff that was by earlier wouldn't even acknowledge my presence. It's chilly without a fire, and my meals became a toss-up between raw eggs or raw meat. Neither seemed all that appetizing, so thanks for these."

Jordan loved the smell of a freshly struck match. The scent was like an appetizer for the campfire smoke that would soon follow. "When was the sheriff by?"

"Oh, a couple of hours ago. She was running the far shore at a decent clip. Not so much as a glance my way, and trust me, my voice carries. I waited a bit to see if my matches would dry out, but now you've shown up and saved the day." His kindling took, and the fire crackled to life.

"Well, happy I could help. There are sixty-four other campsites that I need to check on, so unless there's anything else, I'll be on my way."

"Thanks, I'm all set. The breeze should dry out my gear, and now I'll have some heat to warm my bones and cook some food."

"No problem. I should be back this way before dark if you need anything else." She started her boat and made her way downstream. She called in for a radio check and was happy to get a response from dispatch. At least she hadn't missed a call. She couldn't figure out why else Sheriff Reid would be out on the water.

Her encounters were similar at the next thirty-three campsites, at least the fifty percent that were occupied. Time and again, she found campers drying out wet gear, warming by a fire, and only a few were in need of matches or some dry kindling to get a fire going. So far, so good.

She couldn't ask for a better afternoon. Pleasantly warm with calm winds. This time yesterday, she'd been chasing Mr. Knowles on a crowded lake full of boat traffic, and today, she had the pleasure of checking in with soggy campers who were grateful to see her. Not to mention, twenty-four hours ago, she hadn't yet had the pleasure of meeting sweet Hanna.

Jordan hoped to get to know her better. They'd only just met, and already, she felt a connection, an attraction, that she couldn't deny. Hanna had an infectious, irresistible presence.

Enjoying thoughts of her, Jordan hugged the shoreline, in and out of numerous coves, inspecting the bank of the larger islands that held multiple sites, just to be sure nothing was missed. It was her first tour, after all. Although at this pace, she'd be lucky to finish before nightfall. With so many islands, the flowage was a colossal maze, and she was grateful for her GPS.

After checking on the forty-fifth site on her list, Jordan carefully navigated through a tight maze of tiny islands, all of which were too small for camping. The area was littered with stumps and rocks just below the surface. The depth finder had already saved her prop from a few close calls.

She glanced at her watch. Wow, it was after seven in the evening. There was no way she'd make it to the rest of the sites on the southernmost section of the flowage before dark. She shook her head. The thought of even one camper stranded without a boat or fire for warmth kept her going. She'd stay out for as long as it took.

She came around the back side of a small island and caught sight of something red bobbing in the reeds. An upside-down kayak offered a deep plastic thud with each wave that pushed it into a log floating against the shore. Alone, the kayak wouldn't have been too alarming. It could have easily floated offshore, given the relentless wind and several inches of rain, but seeing the paddle hung up in the reeds about fifty feet away was another story. Alarming indeed.

"Hello? Kayaker?" Jordan called. "Can you hear me? Anyone?" She flipped the kayak over and pulled it into the boat. There was a tether connecting the paddle to the boat; it was hung up on something underwater. Some kayakers used tethers in case they flipped, or the paddle floated out of reach. Scanning the area, she didn't see a person in the water or an empty life jacket that boaters often preferred to rest against rather than wear, but she did eye the largest snapping turtle she'd ever seen. The beast lumbered off the edge of a rock and entered the water with a great splash. She had zero interest in getting into the lake with that monster.

Jordan continued to call out as she slowly made her way over to retrieve the floating paddle. Once collected, she shifted her boat into neutral and waited to see which way the breeze and the current took her boat, then slowly backtracked, hoping to find the missing kayaker.

She keyed her mic. "1409 to dispatch."

"Hey ya, Jordan, you've got Dave here. What's up?" He sounded like a radio host.

And Jordan? Badge 1409 belonged to *Warden Pearce*. She shook off the informality. "Have there been any calls about a missing person out on the flowage south of Fisherman's Landing?"

"Nope, not a one. No missing person anywhere."

The radio informality of the Northwoods would take some getting used to. "I've located a kayak and paddle about a hundred yards northwest of site R-19, bobbing in the reeds of a smaller island between old Sweeney Lake and old Baraboo Lake without a paddler." She referred to two of the sixteen lakes that were flooded when the dammed river created Turtle Flambeau Flowage. "I've pinned the location into my GPS. No response to callouts and no body that I've found so far."

"I'll mark the location. Probably blew away from a site in the storm."

"I don't do probably. Besides, the paddle strap is still attached to the side which means the paddle was likely in someone's hands. I'll expand my search and report."

"Okey dokey, roger dodger."

What was Dave, twelve? She rolled her eyes.

She searched the area thoroughly, then searched it again for good measure. Not so much as an empty life jacket, let alone one filled with a person. She idled for a moment and opened the storage compartment of the kayak. Sadly, just some waterlogged snacks, a set of keys, including a car fob, and a full water bottle. Water dripped out of the car fob, indicating that the chip was likely damaged. Nothing that would identify the boater without fingerprints, at least not right away. She took photographs and documented the scene with verbal notes recorded on an app on her phone. Times like these, she wished kayaks and any nonmotorized boats less than twelve feet in length required a boater's registration. Not that it would help her find the person, but at least she'd have an idea of who she was looking for.

"Hello! Anyone?" she called.

Crickets, figuratively and literally, and it was getting dark. Jordan kept at it up and down the shoreline and around the many small islands littering the area. She turned on her docking lights and used a powerful spotlight once darkness covered the landscape. "1409 to dispatch. Is the sheriff's department still on the water?"

"Hey, Jordan, I don't show the sheriff's department being on the water today."

Well, now, that was odd. "Can you contact Sheriff Reid and get a twenty?"

"Do you need assistance? You're new, but you should know, Sheriff Reid seriously doesn't like to be bothered in the evenings unless it's absolutely necessary."

Jordan had already annoyed the sheriff once that morning. No sense in getting on her last nerve before her first day came to a close. "No assistance needed at this time. Cancel the request. I've already followed the current from the dam up to Fisherman's Landing and searched the area between old Mud Lake to Sweeney Lake. There are forty-three islands in that area, and I've circled them all. Repeated calls have gone unanswered. I've already searched everything around old Horseshoe Lake, as well as up the Flambeau River all the way to site R-40. The last area for me to explore is the area south of the dam and Mud Lake, which includes campsites R-3 through R-15. This boat belongs somewhere, and I'm sure the owner wants these keys."

"Roger that. Probably a fool's errand. Like I said earlier, I bet it blew away in the storm. We'll get a call when they figure out it's missing."

"Thanks, Dave. I'll report back at the end of my tour." If Dave could be informal, so could she.

She had plenty of gas in the boat and two spare batteries for the spotlight. It was a good thing she'd had a large lunch, although that had been over six hours ago, and pangs of hunger had her digging in her kit for a granola bar. Running just above an idle, she continued her search in the dark, circling each island, hoping to find the missing boater sitting on a rock, shivering. Instinct told her to keep searching, and she would, even if it took all night.

This section of the flowage was a vast area, with several clusters of islands. On a bright day, it would be difficult to see from one shore to the other, making a search a time-consuming task, especially in the dark. The inlets were tighter, and at times, the water was less than five feet deep, sending her depth finder into a panic laden series of beeps until she silenced the alarm. Still, she pressed on, scanning every inch of shore, scanning the water for waving arms or a life jacket, and inspecting the shoreline around each island. This wasn't how she'd expected her first tour on the flowage to go. She shook her head at the selfishness of that thought, and pangs of guilt washed over her. It probably wasn't how the kayaker expected things to go, either.

Campers at the occupied sites were mostly friendly, but every so often, she'd come across someone who didn't appreciate a spotlight scan of their temporary home away from home. Most became less vulgar about their invaded privacy once she engaged the flashing blue emergency lights and identified herself as law enforcement. Watching an indignant camper snap to attention at the sight of a badge and suddenly become a civil human being never grew old.

Another two hours of fruitless exploration passed before she came across an occupied site without a boat. This had to be where the kayak belonged.

"Hello, occupants of site R-9? Can you hear me?"

There was no response. She'd half expected as much. Still, she'd hoped it was as Dave suggested, and the kayak blew offshore in the storm. She flipped every switch on the light panel and lit up the landscape with various spotlights and the blue flashing lights. Sand and small stones scraped against the hull of her boat as she beached on a section of shoreline. Jordan hopped off with her mooring line in hand. She wrapped it around a tree and clipped the line to itself.

"Hello," she called out again, scanning the area with her handheld spotlight. The rain had pounded the sand with such force that it had erased any footprints. There was a small red Igloo cooler on the picnic table, a toppled camp chair by the dormant firepit, and a small orange tent.

Pointing the spotlight at the tent, she walked completely around the tiny dwelling. Situated on higher ground, it was closed up with the rain cover secured. Jordan kneeled in front of the main entrance and carefully unzipped the flap. She illuminated the interior as soon as the opening was big enough. There was a backpack on the floor next to an empty sleeping bag and a fluffy, unused pillow. Disappointment washed over her. She'd expected as much, but in the same breath, had held out hope that the camper was fast asleep. She retrieved the backpack and pushed aside female clothing, hoping to find a wallet or a small purse, anything that would provide identification. Nothing. The cooler didn't offer any clues either, other than that the camper enjoyed turkey burger, turkey bacon, and organic eggs. No ID, not so much as a first name written on a piece of masking tape. This was no longer a runaway boat.

"Dave, it's Jordan."

Silence.

She spoke a little louder. "Badge 1409 to dispatch."

"Hey, Jordan, I'm here. Was resting my eyes for a spell. What's up?" The mic caught Dave's loud yawn before it clicked off.

"I'm at site R-9. I need you to call the sheriff. It looks like we have a missing person."

"No shit. You mean to tell me you've been out there all night?" Annoyed, she shook her head. It wasn't like she'd gone home and taken a nap. "Yes, all night. I found the campsite without a boat or a camper. Call it a hunch, but I think the kayaker was staying here. Still no body."

"I'll be damned. Let me get the sheriff. Be right back to ya."

The line went dead for a long several minutes. Jordan turned in a slow circle, scanning the area for movement.

Her radio crackled. "Hey, Jordan, I'm back. Sheriff Reid asked that you stay on site until she gets there. She'll launch from Fisherman's Landing and get to you as soon as possible. She should be there by daybreak. I asked her to bring you a cup of coffee."

Jordan looked at her watch. Just after five o'clock in the morning. How on earth had she been on the flowage for more than twelve hours? The breaking dawn offered the first hint of color in the sky. "Coffee would be great. Thanks."

"No, thank you, Warden. Thanks for not listening to me and calling it a night. I hope you find your camper alive. My bad." He sounded sincere.

Jordan created a timeline of events with locations while she waited for the sheriff to get there, noting everything from the moment she'd spotted the kayak.

CHAPTER EIGHT

Hanna woke up early, tiptoeing quietly with the hope of not disturbing her aunts. She made a fresh batch of ginger tea for Aunt Dottie to sip while getting treatment in Woodruff. She couldn't be sure if it was the ginger or the canned peaches, but her aunt had actually eaten a light dinner. Last night had been good. A pleasant evening filled with fun conversations and laughter. Given their afternoon appointment, her aunts were still sleeping when she left to open the diner.

Faint hints of pink and orange barely teased the horizon when she pulled in. Hanna unlocked the door, but voices carried from inside as she pushed it open. She had locked up last night, hadn't she? If not and something happened, Aunt Ruthie would be pissed.

Her heart hammered in her chest. "Hello, is someone there?"

The inaudible murmurs continued as if she'd said nothing at all. She forced herself to be brave. She flipped the light switch on and stepped inside. The brief static, followed by an electronic step-up tone and a click, was her first clue. Hanna released her held breath and sighed with relief. Ruthie loved to listen to the emergency scanner, which was silent ninety-nine percent of the time. She must have forgotten all about it when she'd closed yesterday afternoon. Granted, she'd been slightly distracted by a certain warden. The speaker crackled to life again, spewing out a bunch of code speak and gibberish before she recognized any actual words.

"Dispatch, who reported the missing camper?" Wait, was that Sheriff Reid's voice? Hanna always thought she sounded like Holly Hunter.

"The new conservation warden, um, Jordan Pearce, badge 1409."

"What's she doing on the water at this hour?"

Static for a moment, then the step-up tones followed by the click. "Dave says she's been at it all night. Found an inverted vessel southwest of Fisherman's Landing at 1900 hours, then located campsite R-9, devoid of both camper and boat at approximately 0500 this morning. She only had eight sites left to search in all the flowage."

"Doesn't mean the two are related. Jesus, people set up empty tents to call dibs on campsites all the time."

"Warden reports a cooler full of food, low on ice. Backpack in the tent along with a sleeping bag. No foot traffic since the rains. If the boater was caught in the storm, well, the timeline fits."

"Ten-four. Have her remain on-site and wait for me. I'll launch from Fisherman's Landing. That's the most direct route down. Should be there within the hour. Oh, and alert the volunteer search to meet up at that same launch by seven. I'll send the warden back to coordinate."

"Ten-four."

Hanna waited for more, but there wasn't. She wondered what frequency the DNR communicated on. Had Jordan really been out on the water since yesterday after lunch? She stood there wondering what to do next. Should she open the diner or...or what? What could she really do to help? Jordan was coming back to coordinate. The least Hanna could do was bring her some food and coffee. Maybe she could join the search?

She rolled her eyes. They'd just met yesterday. Yeah, but that didn't mean there wasn't a connection. Whether or not she was avoiding love, relationships, and commitment, there was definitely a connection.

If the locals were being called to search, then she was about twenty minutes away from being slammed with to-go orders. She'd seen her aunts deal with a similar scenario before. She flipped on the rest of the lights, turned on the grill and the fryers, and started a pot of coffee. Just before she unlocked the front door, she made a point of turning up the scanner just in case there was an update on the missing person. The coffeepot gurgled out its brewing grand finale. Hanna moved the pot to a decanter warmer and got another pot started. She was in the back cracking eggs next to spread out sausage patties and bacon strips that she'd precooked the prior afternoon when the bell above the door jingled.

Hanna peeked out the pass-through window. Sheriff Reid. "Morning, Sheriff. What can I get you?" She was the last person Hanna had expected to walk through the door. While the transmission wasn't all that long ago, she'd assumed the sheriff would go directly to the boat launch.

"Mornin', Hanna. Wondered when you'd be back. Sure sorry to hear about Dottie. Can I get two cups of coffee to go?"

"Appreciate that. I got back the day before yesterday. Heard the news on the scanner." Hanna filled the two large cups and secured the lids. "I hope you find the missing camper."

"Thanks. What do I owe you?"

"On the house. Be safe."

"Will do." With a cup in each hand, the sheriff nodded and disappeared out the door.

A short time later, the bell above the door never stopped jingling. Hanna hadn't been wrong about the rush. Thankfully, she had over three dozen breakfast sandwiches made, wrapped, and waiting beneath the warming lights when the locals started rolling in asking for something warm to eat on the boat. It was difficult to keep the coffeepots full and fill the food orders, but she somehow managed, all the while keeping an eye on the clock. Jordan would be at the landing by seven.

For almost an hour, Hanna ran around in a flurry of insanity, and then, just like that, the diner was a ghost town. She wrapped the last few sandwiches and filled a large thermos with coffee and another with ice water. Finally, she shut everything down and locked up. She'd come back later and clean. A handmade sign on the door explained the diner was closed for the afternoon to help with the search.

❖

The parking lot at the Fisherman's Landing boat launch was bumper to bumper. Hanna parked her aunt's car behind the bathrooms on the grass, grabbed the bag of food and the thermoses, and ran for the dock. Hopefully, she wasn't too late to catch Jordan. She'd never been part of a search party and felt a burning desire to see the warden in her element, doing her thing.

Jordan's voice echoed through a loudspeaker over the whirling hum of countless outboard engines. Good, she was still there somewhere. Hanna jogged to the end of the dock but couldn't pick out Jordan on any of boats bobbing on the water. She spoke again, thanking everyone for coming out to help, and the engine hum became a low roar as boats began to disperse.

Staring at the sterns of at least forty boats, Hanna called out as loudly as she could, "Jordan, wait."

As the boats spread out, one remained idling in the back of the pack. When the area was clear of traffic, the boat turned around and aimed for the dock. Jordan. She drove standing up and looked hot as hell doing so. The engine went down to an idle, coasting the last bit until the boat brushed alongside the dock.

"Hey, you." Jordan smiled that smile that lit up Hanna on the inside. Not many people had ever had that effect on her. Certainly not so quickly. "What are you doing here?"

"You haven't slept, and I'm betting you haven't eaten." Hanna held up the sack of food and the thermos. "I thought I could help. I can look left while you look right."

"What about the diner?"

"Closed. Hell, the whole town's on the water. Whaddya say? Permission to come aboard?"

Jordan's expression softened, and her eyes crinkled in the corners. Hanna had seen that same hint of a smile yesterday when she'd offered food instead of more questions about her dad. She could already tell that Jordan kept things close to the vest. Hanna wasn't sure if that was because of her life experiences or her training or a bit of both. But for a split second, Hanna saw an emotional side of Jordan that she imagined most didn't get to experience. There was kindness and openness and appreciation all rolled up in a sweet and tender look.

Hanna accepted her extended hand while stepping down into the boat.

Jordan squeezed it before she let it go. "Permission granted. I'd enjoy your company." She looked like she wanted to say more but focused on pushing away from the dock instead.

Hanna sat in the passenger seat while Jordan backed the boat out and spun them around. Soon, they were again part of the search party. Hanna unwrapped one of the breakfast sandwiches and held it out.

She accepted it and took a bite. "Mmm, hits the spot. Thank you."

"My pleasure." Starving, Hanna pulled another sandwich from the bag. "Do you have any idea who you're looking for?"

"The missing boater is most likely female. Based on how the foot pegs were set in the kayak and the clothes I found in her pack at the campsite, I put her around five-five or so and roughly a hundred and sixty pounds. Hair in her brush was shoulder-length or longer and light brown to blond. That's my best guess."

"You just described me, except for the hair color. I can't believe you got all that from a backpack of clothes and a kayak? Impressive. I'm guessing this isn't your first missing person case."

Chewing, Jordan shook her head.

"Were the other searches successful? Did you find the missing people alive and okay?"

"Not always. Let's focus on this one, all right?"

Hanna nodded and didn't prod. "So where do you think she could be?"

Jordan slowed the boat, then shifted it into neutral. "I found the kayak over in that cluster of tiny islands. I wasn't sure how long it had been in the water, but I now believe it's been out here since before the storm."

"What makes you think that?"

"The campsite. The rain erased all the footprints, and no one had been there since. That night, the wind was coming from the southwest, with gusts of at least forty miles per hour." She opened a glove box and pulled out a folded map. "If I haven't said it, I'm glad you're here with me."

"Me too."

"Talking this through helps. Otherwise, I get stuck in my head." She opened the map, spread it on her seat, and held her finger on a spot. "If our missing boater was on the water before the storm hit, it wouldn't have been the river current and yesterday's gentle wind that nudged her boat along. More likely, it was the wicked wind from the storm, and that vastly expands the search area. Hell, she could have been south of her campsite, as far south as Beaver Creek or anywhere along this entire section of the flowage. Her kayak could have easily blown that far. There's a lot of open water in that southern portion. It's the biggest section of the lake."

"I don't understand. Is everyone searching in the wrong place?" Hanna asked.

"No, not necessarily. Most of the search party has fanned out and will slowly crawl south from where I found the kayak. But I think we should grab a few volunteers and start at the southernmost point and work our way north along these two shorelines." She pointed to a spot on the map where the last campsite was located. "I'd like to start with site R-15. I haven't checked on these last few sites yet. She could've been down in this area when she lost her boat. The wind from the storm could have easily blown it this far north."

Hanna heard an approaching boat and looked up from the map. "Bobbie Rae? Carol? Since when are you two members of the volunteer search party?"

"Well, well, look at who we found and with the warden, no less." Bobbie Rae cut the engine on the old Lund fishing boat. That old aluminum fishing boat had been tied on the dock behind the bar for as long as Hanna could remember. It looked the same as it had the last time she rode in it. "I believe we joined about the same time you did. This morning. If Jo-Jo needs help, I'm all in."

Carol sat in the passenger seat. "I saw your sign on the diner door when I stopped to drop off the baked goods. After a few calls, I found out about the missing camper. So I woke up Bobbie Rae, and here we are. How can we help?"

"Is your boat gassed up?" Jordan asked while folding the map. "Full tank."

"Here, take this radio. It's set to communicate directly with my boat. How about we start down by Beaver Creek? I know you know these waters, so you set the pace."

"Hell, yeah, let's do this." Bobbie Rae hit the throttle. Carol squealed as she slid off the edge of her seat and grabbed the side of the boat. Hanna couldn't help but laugh.

Jordan followed in the smooth waters just outside the wake. The morning was warming up, and the wind felt good in her hair. Hanna couldn't remember the last time she'd been on a boat. She hadn't been in the flowage since high school. She couldn't remember what Bobbie Rae and her mom had fought about, but their afternoon on the water had become a release of all sorts of pressurized emotions and made for one scary ride in that same old boat.

Riding with Jordan at the helm felt much safer. She looked comfortable and relaxed behind the wheel. She knew this trip wasn't a joyride, still, Hanna enjoyed getting to see Jordan in her element.

While she'd rather stare at Jordan, Hanna knew she'd volunteered to help search. She forced herself to scan the area for movement as they made their way south. She watched for waving arms or flashes of color or anything that could possibly be a stranded boater. By the time they made it to their starting point, Hanna hadn't seen anything helpful. Hopefully, the boater was safe and sound.

"Okay, how about you two take the eastern shoreline, and Hanna and I will take the west? If you could check in on the four sites on that side, I'd appreciate it. I didn't get to those campers last night."

Carol had a confused expression on her face. "What are we checking for? Like, drugs or something?"

Jordan laughed. "I was thinking more like, are the sites occupied? How'd they survive the storm? Did their boat stay tied? Do they need dry matches? Stuff like that."

"Yeah, I suppose that makes more sense." Carol flushed and rolled her eyes. "You can tell I don't get out of the bakery much."

"Your help is appreciated." Jordan handed her a handful of small boxes of matches.

"Hey, Jo-Jo, do you remember the time that we built that badass raft out of driftwood? Your sisters pushed it out to play on and ended up being swept away in the current? They were long gone before anyone knew what happened. I think a search party like this was called back then too. Man, you got whooped good over that one."

Jordan stiffened, and her jaw tightened up. "Yeah, I remember," she said through gritted teeth.

"Hey, is that why you became a warden? Because it was a warden who saved your sisters?"

"Bobbie Rae, can we focus on finding our missing kayaker?"

"Oh yeah, gotcha. I'll call you on the radio if we find anything." Bobbie Rae pressed a button and talked into the radio. "Testing one, two, three."

Her voice boomed out of the speakers in Jordan's boat. Hanna about jumped out of her skin. She was glad to see it startled everyone else too. Well, except for Jordan. Was she always so calm, cool, and collected?

"I have the volume set to hear it over the engine and the wind. I'll turn it down since we'll be slow going."

"Good to know it works. Well, we're off to find a missing kayaker." Bobbie Rae gave her boat a little gas, and they disappeared into a cove on the eastern shoreline.

Jordan gave her boat some gas, and they also were off. "Nothing is insignificant. A flash of color, a hat in the water, movement. If you see something, let me know, and we'll check it out."

Hanna watched the shore while Jordan seemed to watch everything. Every once in a while, when Hanna was least expecting it, Jordan would yell, "Search party, kayaker, call out." She tried to hide her startled surprise, but the harder she tried to be prepared, the more it startled her when it happened. Maybe if they talked, it would help.

"If you don't mind my asking, what was the pull for you to come back up here after being away for so long?"

Jordan kept on scanning the area. Her dedication to the task was both impressive and mildly annoying. After a few minutes, Hanna gave up on an answer and went back to watching for movement herself.

"I don't know how to explain it. I find myself at a point in my life where I'm looking for something or searching or—"

"What are you searching for? Or do you mean, like, soul-searching?"

"I guess you could call it soul-searching. A place where I not only fit in but I belong." She glanced at Hanna before searching the shoreline again.

"You're looking for your community, your people."

"Yeah, that's a good way to describe it. My people. I'm not sure I've ever felt that kind of connection."

"I totally get that. I've been traveling the country trying to find my place too. Looking for that place where it hurts too much to leave."

"You don't have that here?" Jordan asked.

"The Northwoods check most of the boxes but not all of them. Not yet." She smiled. "I'm sorry. I didn't mean to take over the conversation. Let's get back to what you were saying."

Jordan was quiet for a long moment. "Have you ever felt like you weren't part of your family? Like, there had to have been a mix-up in the hospital because no matter how hard you tried, you just didn't fit in?"

Hanna couldn't get over the question. She turned to fully face Jordan. "Um, yeah, like every single day of my life until I moved in with my aunts when I was fifteen. My brother's the golden child, and I never measured up. How about you? What made you feel that way?"

"It takes so much energy to deal with my family. I swear, they consume all the air in the room. I was always so busy trying to keep the peace, trying to stop the fighting, trying to fix what was broken, and please everyone that I lost sight of fact that I'm an adult, and I don't have to live like that anymore. What a bunch of wasted effort. The only place I ever felt a hint of freedom from the responsibilities was up here. I hope I still feel that as an adult." Jordan's jaw was tense, and her chin quivered. She swiped at something on her cheek. "I'm sorry. That was probably way more than you wanted to know. I haven't slept, and my stop talking button must be on the fritz."

"Honesty is exactly what I'd hoped for. It explains your reaction when Banjo and Chipmunk brought up your dad. You tensed up, much like you're doing now while talking about your past."

Jordan's eyebrows furrowed, and she stared ahead.

Hanna turned to see what she had spotted. "Speaking of Banjo and Chipmunk, isn't that them up ahead? Their boat is so pretty. I've always loved that ruby red. Did you call them and share your idea about starting down here?"

"I don't think I needed to." Jordan waved. "They know these waters better than anyone, including the currents and storm patterns."

"Good morning," Chipmunk said. "Made sense to start down here. I see you thought the same thing."

"Good morning. Has anything caught your eye?" Jordan asked.

"Not yet," Banjo said. "We've co…covered everything from R-7 around old Rat Lake down to here."

"Circled all the islands too," Chipmunk said, nodding. "Been listening to the scanner since last night. The lack of footprints at the campsite was a good catch."

"Um, Jo-Jo, you'd better get over here." Bobbie Rae's voice boomed through the speaker. "We're in front of that little cove between R-10 and R-12, and there's something going on in the water in front of the tiny island over here. I'll wait for you before I get too close. Hurry."

"On our way." Jordan cut the wheel and hit the throttle. Banjo and Chipmunk followed alongside. Bobbie Rae and Carol came into sight within a few seconds.

Jordan slowed the boat and coasted past them. Hanna sat up taller to see what was happening. The lake churned as if there was a current in just that small spot. Then, there was a bit of splashing, as if someone had thrown a handful of fish food into a koi pond, but it wasn't fish creating all the commotion.

"Are those…turtles?"

"Looks like a couple of large snappers." Without looking away, Jordan pressed a button, and two metal arms on the back of the boat folded out, each extending a metal shaft down into the water. Hanna had never seen anything like it. The boat jostled slightly just as Jordan released the switch, then the boat seemed to lock in place and no longer bobbed in the waves. Next, Jordan opened a hatch on the side of her console, pulled out a bucket, and handed it to Hanna.

"Just in case."

"Just in case what?" Hanna asked.

Jordan walked to the front of the boat and lifted a pole with a hook on the end from a long cubby along the side.

"Hey, Jo-Jo, do you have another gaff hook?" Bobbie Rae asked.

"Sadly, no."

Jordan used the long tool to pull turtles away from the craziness in the water.

Hanna leaned over the side to get a better look. "What are they doing?"

"F...Feeding. Snappers don't share. They're fighting over the food." Banjo locked his boat in with a similar device to what was on the back of Jordan's boat. He lifted a long-handled net and pushed at an especially large hissing turtle.

Hanna tried to be cool. She wanted to impress Jordan. "Feeding on what?" She had no sooner gotten the words out than a mangled human hand floated to the surface. In an instant, a huge turtle surfaced, chomped on the hand, and pulled it back beneath the water.

"I ain't the only one who saw that, right?" Bobbie Rae asked.

Stunned and numb, Hanna shook her head while Jordan and Banjo kept pushing the turtles back. She heard a splash and looked over. Bobbie Rae used one of her oars to push another turtle away. It hissed at her from the water and locked on to the tip of the oar. "Ha, I'll keep you occupied. Eat wood, fucker."

Jordan pulled a CB mic from her shirt and pressed the button on the side. "1409 to dispatch"

"Go ahead, 1409."

"We've located a body between sites R-10 and R-12. I'll pin my location in my GPS after retrieval. Send the sheriff and the medical examiner."

"Copy that."

Jordan put her pole deeper in the water to push the turtles away. "Damn it, I'm hung up on something." She used both hands and pulled.

What came toward the surface could best be described as something out of a horror movie. There was some hair and a head, but where a face should have been was not much more than flaps of meat, strips of skin, and a dangling eyeball. The back of the neck was just as mutilated and disgusting. Thankfully, there wasn't blood, just pinkish, gray-looking chunks of flesh.

Hanna's stomach heaved, and she ran for the other side of the boat.

"Bucket! Use the bucket." Jordan wrapped an arm around her waist and held her in place. "Everyone, try not to puke in the water. It will contaminate the scene. Back away if this is too much."

Hanna forgot she'd been holding a bucket. She held it up just in time to catch the contents of her stomach. So much for keeping her cool and impressing Jordan.

"Shit, she's going back down. She's tied to something. Jesus, there's a rope tied around her."

Hanna spit in the bucket and lifted her head to see what was happening. Jordan pulled on the pole until the hooked rope was at the side of the boat.

"Hanna, in the cubby next to my seat are a pair of leather gloves. Can you bring them to me?"

She set down her bucket and bent over the driver's seat. The gloves were right there on top. She grabbed them and rushed to the front.

"Hold the right one out so I can put my hand in it."

Hanna's hands shook violently. Still, Jordan managed to slide the glove in place. She repeated the process for her left hand.

"If your stomach is still queasy, you'll probably want to go to the back of the boat and stare at the engine for a minute, okay?"

She nodded and went to the back. Regardless of how many times her stomach flip-flopped, she couldn't look away.

With her gloved hand, Jordan grabbed the rope and dropped the long pole to the floor. From what Hanna could see, the body was bigger than Jordan. How on earth was she going to get it in the boat? Using her knees as bracing, she leaned far over the edge and reached deep into the water. It looked like she was groping around beneath the body. Was she searching for something? One of those big turtles couldn't pull her in, could it?

"Got it." Jordan held a thick rope in her hand. Water streamed off her soaked sleeves as she drew the line taut and readied her feet for what looked to be a desperate game of tug-of-war. She leaned back and heaved. And heaved some more. It didn't seem like anything was happening. Jordan grimaced as she gave it her all again, tugging against a relentless, invisible force. The tendons in her neck seemed like they were going to pop from the effort she was exerting.

Then, it freed.

Jordan stumbled a few steps backward but quickly caught her balance. Hand over hand, she pulled a huge anchor out of the water. It landed on the flat bottom of the boat with a loud thud. She perched her hands on her hips, almost satisfied, as if that was humanly possible in this moment.

"That's some hefty evidence."

The body floated alongside the boat like shark bait. Jordan squatted and stretched over the side to get it. She tucked both her arms around the torso. The lifeless arms on the corpse ducked and bobbed in the disturbed water. It was surreal to think that, in different circumstances, those arms would be clutching to life and reaching out for help. With a good grip, Jordan thrust herself backward, and the body came mostly out of the water. The head tilted at an awkward angle and thumped against the upper edge of the side of the boat. Seaweed tangled in her hair and around that dangling eyeball.

Hanna's breath caught, and her stomach clenched. Jordan's effort didn't seem to be enough to get the body in the boat. Not by a long shot. Jesus, she was tough, but this seemed like a lot to ask of one person.

"I'm losing her," Jordan said through gritted teeth.

Hanna couldn't move, but she thanked God for Banjo. In a flash, he was standing on the edge of his boat, then stepped into Jordan's. He rushed to her side, grabbed the legs, and helped pull the mutilated body into the boat. When it landed, some air bubbled out of the mouth or stomach or from somewhere. It was a weird gurgling sound. Water seeped from the corpse's soggy clothes onto the deck like discarded wet rags. The body was puffy and grotesquely swollen. Lifeless. Horrifying. Hanna screamed before she could cover her mouth. Others screamed too, but she didn't know who. Then, the smell hit her. Oh, it was putrid, utterly indescribable decay. She pulled the fabric of her shirt over her nose, but it trapped the stench, maybe even amplified it. Her stomach lurched again. Luckily, the bucket was close. Hanna heaved, but nothing came up. Even with the heaving, she couldn't stop staring at the corpse.

"I d...don't think th...that's the k...kayaker," Banjo said.

Jordan shook her head. "Definitely not."

"Oh dear, look at the patch on the sleeve. Is that who I think it is?" Chipmunk asked.

"I believe it is." Jordan removed her glove and reached for her mic. "Dispatch, keep the search going. We still have a missing kayaker."

"Rodger that. Wait, what d'ya find then? Do you still need the sheriff and the coroner?"

"Affirmative. Send the sheriff and a medical examiner, not the coroner."

"The only M.E. this far north is three hours away. Sheriff is bringing the coroner."

Jordan shook her head, as if upset by the information. "This wasn't an accidental death. I believe we've just recovered the body of Conservation Warden Debra Ryder. It appears she was murdered. Her body was weighed down."

CHAPTER NINE

Jordan stared at the body on the floor of her boat. "How long do you estimate she's been in the water?"

The turtles had done a number on most of her, but there was no mistaking that uniform. It was identical to the one Jordan wore day in and day out. Luckily, a few fingers had survived the feeding frenzy. Hopefully, they could confirm her identity with fingerprints. She didn't need any test to know that the munched-on body had once been Deb Ryder. Clothing, gender, hair color, and body type...everything matched. Both her badge and gun belt were missing. So far, neither'd been found in the lake. What was she doing down here in uniform without her gear and her boat? None of this made any sense.

"Oh." The coroner scratched his chin. "I'd say she's been in a good couple three days."

"A good couple three days? Seriously?" Her tone was harsh, but she was too tired to care. "Not much for specifics, are ya?"

How she wished the medical examiner had taken the lead instead of the local coroner. For starters, coroners didn't have near the training that medical examiners did. The M.E. from her region in the southern district of the state would have already run her prints using a portable scanner and would've narrowed in on a time of death instead of some vague guess with a plus or minus factor of seventy-two hours.

"Warden, I know you're upset. Hell, we all are, but cut Daniel some slack. He hasn't had a hot minute to figure anything out. I don't know how often this sort of thing happens where you're from, but it's not every day we pull a body from the flowage." Sheriff Reid snapped the gum she'd been chomping on.

Jordan caught another whiff of her perfume. Between it and the stench of the body, it was all she could do to keep her breakfast in place. Yet, the anger bubbled. "Still offering a week of your wages that Deb just walked away from it all?"

Sheriff Reid rested her hand on the butt of her pistol. "Your point's not lost on me. Not that the outcome would've been different had we started the search yesterday morning."

After a plethora of photographs, the coroner and his assistant bagged the body and moved it, along with the rope and anchor, to the sheriff's boat. Even with the body gone, her boat still smelled of death. She looked at her soaked clothing. She also reeked of rotting flesh.

"We've got everything we need from your boat," Sheriff Reid said. "You've had a hell of a couple of days. Why don't you go get some rest? I've got lead on the investigation. We'll get justice for your friend."

Sleep? Like she could sleep now. Though the adrenaline overload was quickly wearing off. Jordan's eyes stung with fatigue. Hell, her whole body ached. She stood and stared at the wet spot on the vinyl flooring where the body had been. Sure, she'd been skeptical that Deb just walked off the job, but she'd never expected this. She never expected to find her anchored below the surface and left for the carnivores and carrion feeders.

"Hey, Warden, you okay?"

Everyone was staring at her. Apparently, she'd been standing there longer than she thought. "Yeah, I'm fine. Call me when you have a positive ID and let me know if you find the kayaker before I resume my search. I'll be in touch later this afternoon if I don't hear from you."

She started her engine and retracted the hydraulic shallow water anchors that had locked her boat in place. What a day it'd been already, and it wasn't even ten in the morning. She gave the boat a little gas and looked over to the seat Hanna had been sitting in just an hour or so earlier. It'd been such a treat to see her standing at the end of the dock, all too eager to help with the search. Jordan hadn't missed the way Hanna had leaned back in the seat, enjoying the wind and the sunshine. The vision of that moment had her wishing Hanna was still on the boat.

She'd offered to stay, even after the body was out of the water. She'd insisted she wanted to be there, but Jordan could tell the sight and smell were a bit too much. Hell, it was a bit too much for her, and she'd already experienced it a few too many times in her career. She'd understood when Hanna had changed her mind and decided to return with Bobbie Rae and Carol. It was for the best. She didn't need to stare at Deb's body for another hour while photos were taken and the water was searched for items not yet recovered. What the group had already witnessed was more than anyone should have had to see.

On her way to Sturgeon Bay Landing, where her truck and boat trailer were parked, Jordan tried to call both Chief Grace and Lieutenant Foley. Each call went directly to voice mail. Leaving no specifics, she left messages asking for a callback, stressing the importance. It was probably a good thing they were busy with the conference. All she could offer at this point was pure speculation since Deb's identity hadn't yet been positively confirmed. Hopefully, she'd have some specifics by the time they called back.

Thankfully, there was a high-pressure sprayer at the boat ramp. Early in her career, Jordan had made it a habit to keep a spray bottle of Simple Green all-purpose cleaner on board after a stranded group of sandbar partiers had made a gut-wrenching mess of her boat. She used the entire bottle now, scrubbing until her hands were raw, and her arms ached. Once her boat was cleanish and secured to the trailer, she spread a towel on the seat of her truck and headed for the lodge.

Traveling northbound on Loon Boulevard thinking about nothing and everything, she approached the driveway to the station house, the same five acre parcel she'd walked through the morning before with Sheriff Reid. Jordan hit the brakes hard and pulled into the driveway. She hadn't planned on stopping there, but something deep inside told her she should.

Donning a new pair of latex gloves, she keyed in the master code for the lock once again. It was time to look at things from a new perspective. Based on the condition of the body, Deb clearly hadn't packed up and moved out. Someone else had cleared out the house to make it look like she had bolted. Likely, the same someone who'd sent the resignation email. Room by room, Jordan considered what had been taken and what had been left behind. Maybe the person who'd packed up had been looking for something. Maybe they hadn't found it, so they'd taken everything, hoping to find it later. Touching as little as possible, Jordan evaluated each room, each drawer, each cubby. Nothing jumped out at her except for a pegboard with a bunch of keys.

Not sure what key was for what, she collected a handful and went outside. Since the warden had been found in the flowage, Jordan inspected the boat first. The overwhelming scent of bleach hit her the moment she lowered the cradle on the hoist. Why hadn't she done this yesterday when Sheriff Reid was with her? It would have given credence to her claim that Deb wouldn't have just walked away. She hated making mistakes and was mad at herself for doing so. Still, she lowered the boat and searched for clues.

There was nothing unusual beneath any of the seats or in the glove box. But Jordan didn't keep her citation book in either of those places. There was too much effort involved to grab the handheld binder when she needed it. Instead, she kept hers shoved in a hidden nook between the console and the side of her boat. There, it stayed dry and out of sight but was easily accessible.

Lady Luck was shining down on her because it would appear that Deb had the same philosophy.

Jordan flipped the citation book open and leafed through Deb's work. All in all, she wrote out very few tickets. When she did, it was for fishing without a license or exceeding the catch limit. Nothing odd or unusual. Her notes were another story entirely:

May 6th, 3:43 p.m.
Approached another rental boat to check licenses. Renter asked if they had to pay me too. Claims a female sheriff was going to ticket them for exceeding the catch limit unless they gave her one hundred dollars cash to forget she'd been by. Fishing license was valid. Catch was legal and within limits. Boater refused to give a statement because the sheriff had their personal information.

Jordan counted fourteen notes with the similar pattern. Dates on the notes occurred mostly on the weekends over the past three weeks. Using her phone, she took pictures of each note, including the tourist's name and fishing license, which linked directly to an address, and driver's license number. Time and again, the description of the sheriff was a female with a slight build and light brown or hazel eyes. It couldn't be Sheriff Reid, could it? The description matched, but she was close to retirement. Why would she risk her pension for a little bit of cash?

Things in the Northwoods were getting weirder and weirder. Once she'd reviewed and photographed all the warden's notes, Jordan put the citation book back where she'd found it. Investigators should be by to go through the property with a different lens now that Deb's body had been found. It was time for her to put the keys back and get out of there. Her agency could only be part of the investigation if their assistance was requested. Sheriff Reid had certainly not requested any assistance, and the sheriff or the state investigators wouldn't look kindly on what could be considered tampering with evidence.

❖

After a blissfully hot shower, which included a new and functioning showerhead, Jordan dressed in civilian clothes. It wasn't her day off. Or maybe it was by now. Either way, she just couldn't bring herself to put her uniform on. No doubt the news had spread, and she didn't want to be bombarded with questions if she wore the same uniform as the victim.

Sleep would probably do her some good, but she was to wound up and wired to rest, especially after finding Deb's notes. It was just after one, and as if on cue, her stomach growled. A quick walk through the woods had her at the diner only to find it dark, Hanna's note hung on the door explaining why it was closed. Okay, time to try the other side of the lodge.

There were two cars in the parking lot at the Drunken Loon Saloon. At least it was open, and based on the smell in the air, the deep fryers were up and running. She stepped through the door and waited for her eyes to adjust. The sights and smells were so familiar that she half expected to see Bobbie Rae's mom behind the bar and her dad seated on a stool opposite with a handful of empty shot glasses, each shadowed by a matching empty beer bottle. Her sisters would have been on competing sides of the Pac-Man game with a fistful of quarters. Their electronic babysitter had, at some point, been replaced with a few brightly colored video slot machines.

"Well, well, would ya look at what the cat dragged in?" Bobbie Rae's expression held that same smiling look of recognition that Jordan had loved to see each summer after that first visit, as if a mere glance shouted, *I missed you,* and, *there's my best friend in the entire world.*

"I feel like I've gone a few rounds with something bigger than a cat."

"I can't even begin to imagine." Bobbie Rae used a remote control and lowered the volume on the music.

"Wait, is that Shakira singing 'Back in Black' by AC/DC?"

"Good ear." Bobbie Rae nodded, cranked the music back up, and grinned. "See, now that's why we became friends. You have great taste in music."

"I kinda feel like it's my new favorite cover of that song. She has the best growl."

"You should see the YouTube video. She's so fucking hot."

Jordan bobbed her head along with the music. She tried to match Shakira's growl and Colombian accent. "Okay, that was awesome. Where are the other two musketeers?"

"Man, that was some freaky shit out on the water. While you and Banjo were the only ones to actually wrestle the corpse, we couldn't shake the stench and parted ways to get a shower. I'm not sure if Carol will swing back by or if she'll just get a jump on tomorrow's baking, but Hanna planned to stop by the diner to clean the place up quick before she comes back for a drink. How about you? Thirsty?"

Jordan nodded. "I'm off duty. Yeah, I'd take a drink. Probably should eat some lunch too. What a day."

Bobbie Rae scribbled some stuff on a pad before ripping the sheet free and clipping it on a spinning wheel at the pass-through window. She rang a bell, then turned back to Jordan. "What's your poison?"

"You're the expert. You tell me." Jordan leaned back into the comfy barstool. She was glad it was just her and Bobbie Rae. They really hadn't had a chance to catch up. The connection they shared was still so strong, even after all these years apart. A bond beyond any standard friendship. They shared a childhood that not many experienced, or at least, Jordan hoped not all kids had to grow up so fast.

Bobbie Rae stepped back and stared for a moment. "Rum? No, wait…whiskey but not any whiskey, Tennessee Fire Whiskey."

"Nailed it. My favorite. The perfect amount of cinnamon but not as sweet as Fireball. You've earned your bartender's badge."

"I'd hope so. I do own the bar." Bobbie Rae wiggled her eyebrows. "Your eyes gave you away. You looked in that direction for a split second, probably to see if it was even on the shelf. You didn't react when I mentioned the top-shelf rum at the end of the row, so it had to be Tennessee Fire."

"Ol' number seven is my favorite with a mixer, but for sipping, I do like a good cinnamon whiskey."

"Rocks?"

"A few, just to give it a chill."

Bobbie Rae poured two and walked around the bar, sitting on the stool next to Jordan. "Here's to no more dead bodies. May they find the missing kayaker alive and well."

"I'll drink to that." Jordan tapped her glass against Bobbie Rae's and took a sip.

"Speaking of the body, do they know if it's Deb?"

"Yeah, the fingerprints were a match. It's definitely Deb Ryder. I broke the news to the brass just before I came over. How well did you know her?"

"Not all that well. She rarely came in here, and I don't get out on the water much. The bar keeps me pretty busy. Any idea what happened to her? Ya know, other than the turtles. Do they have any information yet?"

"I really shouldn't discuss it."

"Aw, come on, Jo-Jo, it's just us in here. Jimmy's in the kitchen with all the fans and fryers. He can't hear shit. It's a safe zone."

"You know how it is. It's an ongoing investigation and all that." Jordan swirled the ice in her glass. "At least, that's what I was told."

"Which really means that Sheriff Reid told you to stick to what you know. Wouldn't be the first time she's said that to a warden. I've seen her blow a gasket when she thinks y'all are trying to tell her how to do her job. She doesn't like to be challenged. Between you and me, I don't think she respects what y'all do."

"I can't say I disagree."

"Now, as far as how the warden died, I'd bet money it had something to do with the bullet hole in her shirt." Bobbie Rae held out her shirt and pointed at her heart where the hole had been. "The bloodstain around it was the big clue. Probably dead by the time she hit the water. A shot like that will drop a deer, even at a full run. I'm bettin' it's the same for a human. Was there an exit wound? Or do they have the bullet for ballistics?"

Jordan raised her eyebrows and shot Bobbie Rae a questioning expression.

"What? I dig crime shows and listen to a true crime podcast. I know things."

She wasn't wrong about any of it, but Jordan didn't offer specifics or confirm her suspicions. "You should've been a cop."

"Only if cops can ride a Harley. A woman has her standards." Bobbie Rae walked behind the bar and retrieved two plates overflowing with deep-fried appetizers. Jordan spotted the jo-jo fries and smiled. It smelled amazing. She added squeeze bottles of ranch, buffalo, barbecue, and ketchup. Jordan's kind of lunch.

"Okay, detective, here's a question. Have you heard any customers complaining about being taken for cash by someone with a badge out on the water?"

"Actually, yeah. I overheard a couple of tourists in here last weekend bitching about being taken for a hundred bucks each. When I offered to call the sheriff so they could report it, they waved me off and said it hadn't happened to them, just something they'd heard on the water. Do you think Deb was crooked?"

"Not Deb. I think she was on to whoever was extorting the tourists. I'd even bet it has something to do with her death. Now, I just have to figure out how to prove it."

"If not the warden, then the only other badge in this neck of the woods is the sheriff's department. Well, that really narrows it down." Bobbie Rae stared at her. "Whoa, dude. You've got big ol' brass ones if you're accusing who I think you're accusing. Mighty Mouse pretty much runs this town."

"Ha, Mighty Mouse, that's a good one. I'm not accusing anyone without plenty of proof. I may not be able to investigate Deb's murder, but I can investigate an issue involving tourists who are being extorted while fishing on the flowage. That falls within my purview. Keep it under your hat though, would ya? What's said here stays here between us. Otherwise, it might be my body that's shot and fished out of the lake."

Bobbie Rae nodded and stuffed a breaded mushroom in her mouth.

Silence hung for a long moment. Jordan couldn't think of a better time to bring up the topic. "I was sorry to hear about your mom."

"Thanks. It's been a hell of a ride. Watching someone die from liver cirrhosis is brutal. I don't recommend it."

"I've seen the effects blended with lung cancer 'cause why not go big? Remember, we both had parents cast from similar molds."

"Who was it for you? Your mom or dad?"

"Dad. Surprised me that he got it and not my mom. She smokes and drinks around the clock. I'm sorry you had to go through that alone." It had been a lot for Jordan to deal with her father all alone.

"Thankfully, I wasn't alone. Hanna came back. Carol's here. Dottie and Ruth brought me some home-cooked food. The community up here is pretty tight."

While Jordan was happy to hear how much support Bobbie Rae had, it didn't stop a twinge of envy from settling in. No one in her life had stepped up to help. Not that she let that many people in. Even her girlfriend at the time had bailed. What she wouldn't give to have a community that cared about her.

She shook the envy away. "I wish I'd known. I would've liked to have been here for you too."

"Aw, that's kind of you to say. That sentiment goes both ways. Hey, did you hear that I almost lost this place? I knew we owed on the bar, but Mom had it financed to the hilt. She owed a bunch to the food and liquor distributors too. Everything was delinquent. I debated just walking away from it all. Seeing what the world had to offer."

"How'd you manage to save it?"

"Banjo and Chipmunk, of all people, put together a save the Drunken Loon Saloon benefit. The timing coincided with peak tourist season. The area was packed. This is still the only bar on the flowage with slips for boats to dock. Those out fishing seem to dig coming over by boat to grab lunch and then get right back out there. People came from all over. It made all the difference too. I was able to bring everything current, make some upgrades and repairs, and refinance the bar for a more manageable rate and payment. A few more years and it should be paid off."

"It's funny to hear you talking about refinancing for a better rate. Look at us, all grown-up." Jordan chuckled. "Is that what kept you here?"

"Yeah, after everyone helped out like that, I couldn't just up and walk away. I didn't want to, either. I'd miss everyone too much." Bobbie Rae dipped an onion ring in ketchup. "Your turn. Spill your guts. What happened that kept you away?"

Jordan rubbed her eyes. "Things got a little upside down."

"You said that already. I want specifics."

"Apparently, Dad hadn't been paying child support for some time before we made that last trip, ya know, when Sarah and Chloe took off with our raft. I guess he'd lost visitation. We weren't supposed to be up here with him at all. They called it parental abduction, three counts. I remember it was odd that he picked us up from school instead of the house, and we came up without luggage, but he made excuses, and we didn't ask questions. We never asked questions."

Jordan drew in a deep breath and let it out slowly. "After Sarah and Chloe were rescued and I got my ass whooped, thanks for reminding me of that, I guess they ran dad's name. The police showed up later that night and arrested him. Mom was too blitzed out to drive up and get us. We waited at the police station in Minocqua until the next afternoon when Aunt Kathy made the trip after work."

"So that's why you vanished without a trace? Whoa, that sucks. I can't believe your mom had your dad arrested. See, now you know why it doesn't bother me that my sperm donor bolted."

"An issue of his own making, I'm afraid. He spent some time in jail. Got out and the cycle started all over again. He'd refuse to pay child support. Insist he wasn't going to pay for her drinking and drug habit. Said none of the support went to us, anyway. The courts didn't care why he'd hadn't paid, just that he hadn't."

"He couldn't get custody?"

"I honestly don't know that he asked for or wanted full custody. You remember how me and my sisters fought?"

Bobbie Rae nodded. "Especially your sisters. Like vipers."

"I think he liked being the weekend dad and the vacation dad. Not the parent-teacher conference dad. Anyway, they'd start fighting again. Oh, how they loved to fight. She'd take him to court. He'd lose visitation only to show up at school and pick us up. Each time he went back to jail, he'd have to stay in longer. By that time, I was fifteen or sixteen and got a job after school. Sarah was skipping school and always in trouble. Chloe was sneaking booze and smoking pot. Mom had different men at the house all the time. It was rough. Things sucked for a long time."

Bobbie Rae walked behind the bar and refilled their glasses. "I missed your letters. You just disappeared."

"I thought about you often. I wrote. Even made my own envelopes out of paper from school because Lord knew we didn't have any stationery supplies at home. Before I was old enough to work, I'd find some change in the couch, hoping to buy a stamp and end up buying ramen noodles instead because there was nothing to eat in the house."

"I wrote to you too. But the letters came back stamped 'not at this address.'"

"We moved…a lot. More than once, we'd gotten evicted and lived out of the station wagon."

"Man, that sucks. I bet you bolted the moment you turned eighteen."

"You'd think. Looking back, I should have, but instead, I went to community college and worked, trying to keep a roof over our heads. I thought I could give Chloe and Sarah some stability and a chance at a normal life. It didn't work out that way despite my efforts."

"What are your little sisters up to these days?"

"Chloe's now my mom's mini me. They go partying together and get creepy dudes to support their habits. She's been arrested a host of times, and we almost lost her to an overdose a few years back. Sarah ran off with a carny and is who knows where, peddling fake fortunes. Hell, I'm not even sure she's alive. We couldn't find her to let her know about Chloe."

"Seems you turned out okay. How'd you escape the madness?"

"A little scarred but I'd like to think so. Over the last few years, I've had to tap out to save my sanity. I'm done rescuing them from themselves. And you? How'd you escape?"

"Time and time again, my mom taught me what not to do. That's how I see it, at least." Bobbie Rae swirled the ice in her glass.

"That's a good way to think about it."

"How'd you find the strength to turn your back on them? No matter how much I wanted to ditch my mom, I couldn't just up and walk away."

"Honestly? Years of counseling. I'm sure I've paid for a semester or two of college for at least one of Dr. Noodle's kids."

"You're getting therapy from someone named Dr. Noodle? Seriously?"

"Well, her name is really Dr. Knoedel." Jordan sounded out her last name. "But over the years, she tolerated me calling her Dr. Noodle. Going's been good for me. Helped me break the cycle of being the fixer and the peacemaker and the giver. It's one of the reasons I put in for the transfer up here. It's time for me to do something that's just for me."

Jordan caught the sweet scent of lavender. Then, arms wrapped around her shoulders, startling her.

"You weren't kidding when you said that dealing with your family was tough," Hanna whispered softly and leaned her head against Jordan's. "We'll be your people, right, Bobbie Rae?"

"Well, no doubt I'll be, but who knows how long you'll stick around?" Bobbie Rae wadded up a napkin and threw it at Hanna.

"How long have you been here?" Jordan hadn't planned on sharing her past with anyone but Bobbie Rae and only because she already knew much of it. They shared a similar past. They'd helped each other through a lot over those four years.

"For a while. I heard everything after how Bobbie Rae was able to save the bar. I didn't want to interrupt, so I sat by the door and waited. But hearing about all you've been through, I couldn't sit there and wait anymore. I really wanted to give you a hug. Oh my God, what are you wearing?"

"Flannel and jeans."

"Not your clothes. You look hot, by the way. I'm talking about this amazing scent. If you tell me soap, then I'll need to know what kind."

"I'm wearing Citizen Jack Absolute. I'm told it goes well with flannel."

"Holy hell, let me be the first to say it would go well with anything and everything." Hanna emphasized the last word and snuggled even closer. Jordan felt her lean in and inhale against her neck. As expensive as it was, Jordan would wear it every single day to get this response.

She relaxed into Hanna's embrace. At that moment, she was grateful that Hanna had heard about her past and about the counseling. Her childhood wasn't something she had ever been willing to share with anyone. Bobbie Rae was a kindred spirit and already knew about her past, and now Hanna knew some of it too. Maybe that wasn't such a bad thing.

CHAPTER TEN

People trickled in two and three at a time. Soon, the bar was packed with unsuccessful searchers who were obnoxiously vocal about being both hungry and ready for a cold drink. Bobbie Rae, along with her staff, rushed around, catering to everyone's needs. It was every bit as busy as the diner had been for Hanna earlier in the day with coffee and warm food, if not busier. Buzz of the recovered body quickly filled the room and became the topic of conversation. Jordan looked wiped out and grimaced when incorrect details were discussed and perpetuated. Hanna knew enough to know Jordan couldn't clarify or set the record straight. She suddenly understood her reason for being out of uniform too, beyond simply enjoying a drink at a bar.

"Hey, Bobbie Rae has plenty of help. She's got this. Come on, let's get out of here." Hanna tugged on Jordan's hand. "You've got to be wiped out. I'll walk you to your cabin. If you're nice, I'll tuck you in."

"While very tempting, I feel like I should get back out on the water. There's still a missing kayaker. I know it in my gut." Jordan put some cash under the edge of the plate and waved to Bobbie Rae.

"Behave, you two. Don't do anything I wouldn't do." Bobbie Rae returned the wave. "Catch up with you tomorrow."

Hanna nodded and gave Bobbie Rae a thumbs-up. "You can't keep pushing yourself. You've done so much already."

"I hear you, but the focus has become about Deb, and no one is out looking for the kayaker. What if she's hurt? What if she's in that small section we haven's searched yet?"

"Everyone with a boat's been out there for six hours searching and calling. You were out there all night. Someone would have found her if she was able to answer. I heard Donny say that a bunch of them are going back out to keep looking after lunch. You'll be of no use to anyone tomorrow if you don't get some rest today."

"But—"

"Please, no buts. You're exhausted. If you don't want to sleep, how about you spend some time with me?"

"Do you need to get home to your aunts?" Jordan asked when they were outside.

"No, they won't be home from Woodruff until late this evening."

Jordan offered her hand. "Before you tuck me in, would you join me for a short walk?"

"Any place in particular?" Hanna smiled and intertwined their fingers. She smiled when Jordan didn't pull away once they were walking.

"Come on, I know just the spot."

Hanna followed her behind the bar and down to the sandy river's edge. The foliage on the riverbank was thick and lush and hung over the water in places like a living arch. Seemed early in the season, but the spring had been unseasonably warm. The area really held a beauty all its own. The sound of the water burbling over the exposed rocks that protected the shoreline around the tiny islands sounded like something from a very expensive meditation tape. Somewhere off in the distance, a loon called out and was answered with a similarly whimsical response. Ever since she'd first heard the birds, so famous in the Northwoods, Hanna had fallen in love with their call.

"Are you taking me foraging? Or is this the infamous snipe hunt you promised? Mind you, I'm not opposed to either," Hanna asked playfully. She was rewarded with a side glance and the best smirk. Her heart swooned.

The path was wide enough that she could wrap her arm around Jordan's waist and snuggled closer when Jordan wrapped her arm around her shoulders. Heaven. Absolute heaven. Hanna inhaled another lungful of cologne. The scent had her wanting to shove Jordan off into the thicket and take her right there on the sandy shore. She settled for hooking her thumb into the waistband of Jordan's jeans and letting her imagination run wild. So much for swearing off love. How could she be falling for this woman so quickly and so deeply?

"When I was thirteen or fourteen, I'd checked out the VHS tape of *Fried Green Tomatoes* from the library. Shortly after, we moved, and I never did return it. Instead, I watched it over and over until the VCR ate the tape. Even then, I mended it and kept watching it through the static-laden section and the missing part. I loved how Idgie Threadgoode dressed, and I adored how she looked at Ruth. Idgie's expressions were better than a thousand words. Serious heart melt moments. Have you seen the movie?"

"Of course I've seen it." Hanna knew exactly what Jordan was talking about. She loved how Idgie looked at Ruth and had long ago enjoyed illusions of a life with someone who would look at her that way, though so far, the illusion had proven to be just that, time and time again. "Your expressions are just as effective."

"Really? You think so?" Jordan wiggled her eyebrows. "That movie cemented the fact that I could be me. That it was okay for me to be attracted to women. That it was okay not to wear dresses and to climb trees. So if I remind you of the picnic scene with the bees and the honey, you can picture it in your mind?"

"Absolutely." Hanna swung around and walked backward. "Are you taking me on a secret picnic, Warden Pearce?" For fun, she added a little bit of the Alabama twang to imitate Ruth's character. She was rewarded with that distinct, sweet, sexy smile.

Jordan turned them to the right, following a trail deep into the woods. Perfect. Some privacy away from the shoreline and boats. Until then, moments of flirtation had been supervised in the diner and on the lake. Her attraction to Jordan was undeniable, and if they didn't kiss soon, Hanna would implode or explode…a dramatic notion, but the deprivation was real. At least the trail was still plenty wide for them to walk arm in arm.

"Hopefully, it still looks the same. I mean, it's been twenty-seven years." Jordan stopped and touched an almost-healed carving in an old oak tree. Hanna watched her trace the letters with her fingertip. J.P. "This is it. Follow me."

She followed Jordan into a very large, very dense patch of staghorn sumac. Along the way, she held branches aside for Hanna to step over and pass without being scratched. Every little thing she did made her more and more irresistible.

"The clearing is a little smaller than it used to be. The saplings and smaller trees weren't here back then, either, but this is it. This is really it." Jordan held the last of the scrub off to the side until Hanna stepped into the clearing. "See." She walked around and held out her arms. "Soft prairie grass and here's the big shade tree, and over there's the broken, hollow oak, though that one didn't have a hive in it the last time I checked. Sounds silly, I know, but back then, I always dreamed about replicating that scene and bringing someone special here for a picnic. That last trip, before my dad was arrested, I came out here with my beach towel and spread it out like a blanket. I closed my eyes and got lost in that daydream for hours."

"So you haven't had a chance to make that dream come true?" Hanna wrapped her arms around Jordan's waist.

Jordan shook her head. "You're the first to set eyes on this spot besides me. Not too many people explore through a stand of sumac. I found it toward the end of our third year up here. I was hiding from my dad. Can't remember what I did to make him mad. It didn't take much, but I knew I didn't want to be found until he cooled down. Then, I saw the movie and kept this little spot secret." Jordan pulled her closer and wrapped her arms around her back. Hanna had read about smoldering eyes, but looking up into Jordan's eyes brought the expression to life. There was no masking her desire. "May I kiss you?"

Hanna paused for a split second. She'd never been asked before. The sentiment, while unneeded, was sweet and touching. She could only think of one response: "Please."

Jordan cupped her face and bent down to her. At first, her kiss was soft and gentle. Her lips pressed against Hanna's without pressure for more. Hanna wasn't feeling quite so patient. She'd been hot for Jordan since the moment they'd met. She parted her lips and teased Jordan's lips with the tip of her tongue. Rewarded with a moan, she felt Jordan pull her closer and deepen the kiss. *Heaven. Yes. More.* Hanna responded with everything she'd been feeling since they'd met that first morning. She stood on her tiptoes and cupped the back of Jordan's head. Pulling her down, Hanna kissed her with all the desire that had been building over the last few days.

"Is the grass soft?" she breathed into Jordan's mouth.

Breaking the kiss, Jordan sat and patted the spot next to her. Hanna had a better idea. She straddled Jordan's legs and kneeled until she was sitting on her lap.

"Hmm, this works too." Jordan pushed a few windblown strands of hair out of Hanna's eyes. "You're so incredibly beautiful."

"Thank you. And you're the sexiest woman I've laid eyes on."

"I'm glad you think so."

Hanna tugged on the collar of Jordan's shirt until their lips touched again. She explored Jordan's back with her hands. It was so broad and strong. Jordan's kiss ignited something deep in her core and set her body on fire. After a few minutes, Jordan pulled back and lifted Hanna's hair off her neck before exploring from her earlobe down to her collarbone. Hanna tilted her head and savored the attention.

Jordan's hands left her shoulders and slid down her back and rested on her hips. Hanna moved her hands onto Jordan's shoulders, then slid them down her chest just above her breasts. Jordan's breath caught, and she softly hummed.

"Is this place private?" Hanna unbuttoned the top button of her own blouse. "I'll try to be quiet."

"Oh God, I hope so." Jordan unbuttoned the next two buttons and kissed the top edge of her breast, up to the hollow of her throat, and along her neck before lifting her face enough for Hanna to steal her lips for another kiss. Jordan released the last few buttons on Hanna's shirt. Her hands were warm on the bare skin of her waist. She felt a slight tug, and her bra was unclasped. Jordan's touch on her breasts was teasing, with just the perfect amount of pressure. Hanna cupped her hands over Jordan's and pushed into her touch. A gentle pinching on each of her nipples sent an electrical rush to her core. *So good.*

"How do you know just what I like?"

"Your body is so responsive. I can't help myself."

Hanna stared into Jordan's eyes while she unbuttoned her flannel shirt and pulled it free from her waistband. Jordan wore a black sports bra with a zipper in the front, as if her ample breasts were trapped behind a fortress. Oh, fun. Hanna unzipped the zipper and freed the center clasp. She pushed Jordan back until she was lying in the grass. She bent and teased one of Jordan's nipples with her tongue. It hardened beneath her touch. Jordan cupped Hanna's ass and lifted into her.

"Oh yeah, that's it. Just like that." Hanna pressed her hips forward and pushed into the pressure. She tucked her splayed fingers into Jordan's hair and kissed her with even more passion. "Touch me. Oh, baby, I need you. I want to touch you."

Jordan held Hanna against her and rolled until they were on their sides. She barely touched her waistband, and her jeans were unbuttoned. Even less effort had her jeans unzipped. *Whoa, wow.* Hanna's breath caught. Jordan's touch inside her lace underwear was just what she needed. Her hand was warm, and her fingers were firm and teasing without too much pressure. Pure bliss. Hanna wrapped her leg over Jordan's hip and pushed into the pressure. She knew how wet she was. She could feel it. Still, it excited her to hear Jordan moan into her neck when she first felt her. Her touch was everything Hanna had dreamed it would be, and oh, so much more.

She unbuckled Jordan's belt. It took longer than it should have, but my, oh my, Jordan knew exactly what she liked, and it was difficult to focus. Finally, she released the button on Jordan's jeans and unzipped them. Hanna slid her hand inside her fitted boxers. Jordan bent her knee and shifted her leg for better access. She was wet too. Soaked. It felt amazing to feel Jordan push into her hand. Why hadn't they gone to her cabin? At that moment, she wanted Jordan naked. She wanted to experience her without the risk of peering eyes or uninvited guests out in the open beneath the clear blue sky. She'd have to wait for another time. Hanna certainly didn't want to stop things now and head back. Jordan pushed inside her slightly, then pulled back. It was too much and not enough all at once. It was pleasurable perfection and sexual torture all at the same time.

"Oh, baby, inside. I need to feel how much you want me." Hanna didn't recognize her own voice. It was husky and rough. Hell, she felt husky and rough and so needy.

Jordan filled her with deep, penetrating gratification. Hanna pushed a few fingers inside her too. Jordan rolled half on top of her and pressed her thigh between Hanna's legs, which made it even more intense. Jordan lifted her head and kissed her. Everything combined was orgasmic blissfulness. Jordan matched the rhythm of Hanna's hips and applied pressure from deep within. *More, she wanted more.*

Jordan's kiss was pure passion. She wrapped an arm around Hanna and held her close, which made her feel adored.

"Amazing. You. Feel. So. Good." Hanna gasped for air.

"Come for me, sweet Hanna," Jordan whispered in her ear. "Come for me."

It was all the encouragement she needed. She had already been so close. Electricity emanated from deep within. She thrust her hips into Jordan's hand to match the rhythm of the charge. Deep. Hard. Thrusts. One more. Maybe another, or three, and then fireworks erupted. An explosion from within. Jordan was right there too. Hanna felt her shudder inside and push into her with each climatic wave.

Hanna saw flashing lights from behind closed eyelids. Her heart thrummed in her chest on double time. She couldn't catch her breath. She pushed her hips hard into Jordan's hand and held herself there, circling ever so gently as to keep the amazing pleasure from ending. At long last, she held herself still against Jordan's hand and savored in the electrical aftershocks. She tucked her forehead against the side of Jordan's neck and breathed in her scent. Seductive bliss. That was what she'd call Jordan's cologne. Seductive bliss.

She relaxed into Jordan's embrace and snuggled in close. "Hmm, lovely. I wonder if Idgie and Ruth had this much fun under their shade tree?"

Jordan held her tightly. "For their sake, I sincerely hope so. Being with you is incredible. Amazing."

Hanna pulled her hand from Jordan's jeans. She shuddered when Jordan did the same and instantly missed her touch. She sank into Jordan's arms. The kisses on her neck were tender. The beat of Jordan's heart was soothing and felt like somewhere she could get lost in. And she did. Her blinks became longer. Jordan's breathing had already changed, becoming a slow, deep rhythm. Sleepy. She felt extremely satisfied and very sleepy.

Voices. Hanna blinked against the brightness. Daylight. Shit, she was half-naked...and outside. She sat up, startled. The voices were getting closer. Fumbling, she pulled her bra in place, clasped it, and buttoned her shirt quickly before leaning back and lifting her butt off the ground to pull her jeans and underwear up.

"Voices are coming from the river." Jordan had a sleepy smile on her face. "It curls around." She pointed behind her head.

Hanna rolled on top of her. "Did we fall asleep?"

"Safe bet. A brief recharge after you used the last of my energy reserves." Jordan traced her finger across Hanna's forehead. "Holding you in my arms felt wonderful. Thank you for following me into the woods."

"Hmm, thank you for showing me your hidden meadow." Hanna winked. "Win-win in my book. Best snipe hunt ever." Hanna leaned forward and kissed her.

Jordan returned the kiss. "We start this again, and we'll be sleeping here tonight. You're irresistible."

"The feeling is mutual." Hanna nibbled on her earlobe. "Our next time together needs to be in a bed, somewhere we can both be completely naked. I want to savor and enjoy all of you."

"Hmm. That sounds perfect." Jordan lifted some loose hair out of Hanna's eyes. "Your eyes are the most beautiful shade of green."

"I love how your compliments are always matched with the sweetest expression. There's no poker face with you, is there?" Hanna trailed her fingertip along Jordan's jaw.

"Apparently not where you're concerned. I have a practiced cop face for work that's proven effective."

"Oh, I've seen it. It's effective." Hanna sat up and stretched. "We should head back before it gets dark."

"Probably not a bad idea." Jordan stood and turned her back to Hanna.

When she turned around, her shirt was buttoned and tucked back into her jeans. Modest. For some reason, Hanna expected nothing less of the warden.

"Our exit is this way." Jordan pointed to the opposite side. "We'll join up with the Loon Lake Trail. From there, I know a shortcut through state land that'll take half the time to get back."

"I trust you to get us back safely." Hanna followed her through more of the dense sumac stand. "For having spent just eight weeks spread out over four years some eons ago, you sure do know your way around these woods. I lived here for two and a half years and have never been on these trails." Hanna wrapped her arm around Jordan's waist again once they were out on the wider walking path.

"I've always loved the woods. Exploring the area helped me find some calm and stillness in the insanity of my life. I don't know how else to explain it."

"Oh, I think you've explained it perfectly. Trust me, I understand the need to find calm in the insanity." Hanna leaned into her.

"Yeah? Care to tell me about it?" Once again, Jordan's expression and words held such sincerity.

Hanna had always dreamed of being with someone who was genuinely interested in what she had to say. Instead, she'd had a habit of dating the self-absorbed bad girls. *And look at how that turned out.* She'd ended up alone with a broken heart. Things with Jordan already felt different. Especially considering how Jordan treated her. Words like considerate, adored, and treasured came to mind. Bonus, she was an incredible lover, even out in the elements.

"We don't have to talk about it if you don't want to." Jordan's voice pulled her out of her thoughts.

"No, no…I'm happy to talk with you about anything. You've shared so much. I'm sorry, just got lost in my thoughts."

"No worries. It's been a day."

"You can say that again. So what was your question?"

"What prompted your need to finish high school up here?"

"Short answer, me and my undiagnosed ADHD. My mom and I have always butted heads. My dad was always indifferent, and my older brother, Conor, set the bar way too high for me to reach. He was the perfect child. Altar boy at our church. He got the top grades, was the president of the student council, the quarterback of the football team, and didn't misbehave in school." Hanna drew in a deep breath before confessing her truth. "I was none of that. In fact, I was the opposite of all that. My entire life, I heard, 'why can't you be more like your brother?' I was kicked out of daycare for being out of control. Banned from the bus in kindergarten because I couldn't follow directions and had my own desk in the principal's office throughout grade school because I was inattentive and disruptive in class. No matter how hard I tried, I couldn't stay out of trouble. I spent most of my childhood grounded in my room."

"I'm picturing a redheaded Tasmanian devil." Jordan shot her a smiling sideways glance.

Hanna couldn't get enough of that look. "You're not far off."

"Ah, lots of siblings are polar opposites. Look at me and my sisters."

"Yeah, but in your scenario, you're the golden child, whereas I'm the very spastic Sarah, skipping school and getting into trouble. Luckily, I have yet to run off with a carny. Give me time. I'm known for epically bad decisions." Hanna squeezed Jordan's waist and winked. "Oh, and let's not forget the icing on the cake. I came out as a lesbian the summer before my sophomore year. Came out because my mom caught me having sex with a classmate in my bedroom. A cute little butch from the swim team." Hanna shook her head. "Let's just say that having a lesbian daughter wasn't as cool in the mid-nineties as it is now."

"So what happened? Clearly, you're not a spastic rebel, or you're very good at concealing the spaz."

"My teachers kept sending notes home with me about being tested. Mom said it was a bunch of hooey, and I just needed more discipline. She threatened to send me to a special reform school, as in, school the craziness and the lesbian out of me, kinda school. I wasn't sticking around for that. I emptied my savings account and bolted."

"Does your family live close by? Where'd you bolt from?"

"Would you believe…the Upper West Side of Manhattan?"

"Seriously? New York? How'd you manage to get up here?"

"I took the subway to the bus station and bought a bus ticket from Manhattan to Wausau, the northernmost stop in Wisconsin. Once I was at the Wausau station, I called Aunt Dottie and begged her to come pick me up. Who knew Waterdance was two hours away?" Hanna shook her head at what she'd put her aunt through.

"I'm sure she was happy to be there for you," Jordan said.

"I'd only met her one other time before that day."

"Seriously?"

"Yep. I met her for the first time at my grandma's funeral, and we totally clicked. We had this connection that I'd never had with my parents. Auntie Ruthie was there too. I loved how she stood by Aunt Dottie's side no matter how rude or nasty the family was. Righteous assholes. I heard the whispers about them being 'that way.'" Hanna used air quotes. "So I figured they'd know what I should do. And Aunt Dottie had grown up with my mom, so she'd have to know how unreasonable she was being. If nothing else, maybe she could talk my mom out of sending me to that place."

"What happened?"

Hanna laughed. "Aunt Dottie and Auntie Ruthie drove down and picked me up. They called mom to let her know I was safe, but rather than send me home, they asked to have time with me. I mean, I was there, listening to their side of the conversation, and that was how they put it. They offered to enroll me in school and let me finish out the year."

"Was that when you were diagnosed?" Jordan asked.

Hanna loved how well Jordan listened. She's shared this story a thousand times. Okay, less than five. Even so, no one else had ever asked questions. "My parents agreed to let me stay. Once up here, the school had me tested. Back then, they called it hyperkinetic impulse disorder. Now it's classified as ADHD. Aunt Dottie said she noticed I was calmer if I had a couple of cups of coffee. I guess caffeine helped level me out. At first, I tried the standard medications but had an adverse reaction, and some side effects concerned Aunt Dottie. She and Ruthie looked into natural remedies. They found a study where Vitamin B6, along with a quality magnesium supplement, could help balance out the brain chemicals associated with ADHD. It took time, but it worked for me. To this day, I still take those two supplements. Don't get me wrong. Modern medicine is invaluable. It's giving Aunt Dottie hope. And there's a lot to be said for nature's remedies too. I firmly believe they work hand in hand."

"Is that what inspired a career as an herbalist?"

"Yes, it had a lot to do with it."

"How does one go from a life in Manhattan to a life in the Northwoods to a life in a Winnebago?"

"Easy. Life in my Winnebago because I have also been looking for my people. I wouldn't have been able to put it into words until our conversation this morning." Hanna squeezed her waist.

"I agree. Sounds to me like you had some angels in your—" She stopped mid-sentence. She stopped walking too.

"What is it?" Hanna snuggled in closer. "What's wrong?"

Jordan lifted her arm from around Hanna's shoulder and stepped forward. She looked left up a steep hill, then right down into a valley. "Looks like a car went off the road. Look down there. The back end of a car." Jordan pointed at the tracks. "Come on. Someone might be hurt."

Staring down the hill, Hanna could barely make out the crumpled back of a car at the bottom on an odd tilt. She wasn't so sure she was up for two bodies in one day, but she'd rather be down there with Jordan than up on the trail wondering what was happening. With cautious steps, she followed Jordan down the steep incline.

CHAPTER ELEVEN

Jordan used trees to slow their pace on the steep hill, hoping to keep them from tumbling ass over teakettle. As they worked their way toward the wreckage, more and more contents from the vehicle's tumbling descent were strewn about: one shirt, then what looked like a drawer full of shirts. Several pairs of jeans and a suitcase, colorful clothing dispersed like confetti, starkly contrasting with the forest floor.

"Hello? Call out if you can hear me." Two days of repeating that phrase was two days too many. Debris from the car now mixed with the contents as they got closer. Bathroom cleaning supplies lay near part of a bumper and glass from a window. Jordan slowed her pace and focused on any movement in the debris field. "Hello? Call out if you can hear me."

"What can I do?" Hanna asked.

"If you'd like to keep searching this side, I'll go check the passenger side. The car doesn't look stable. Steer clear of the front."

"I can do that."

Jordan worked her way around the back of the car. The plate was still fastened to the rear bumper, RHR-137. Was this the car from the night of the storm? The back window was busted out. Items from the back seat were hanging half out of the opening. She wasn't sure what the car was balancing on, but it was certainly tilted at an odd angle. Its perch was so peculiar that she wouldn't have been surprised if the slightest bump or nudge sent it deeper into the valley.

"The driver's window is closed, and I can't get the door open," Hanna said from the other side. "I don't see anyone behind the wheel. And there's no one on the ground anywhere over here that I can see."

"Sounds good. I'll check this side."

The windshield and passenger window were both shattered but intact. Jordan used a sturdy stick to poke a hole through the cubed glass in the passenger door. She kneeled and looked inside. The potent scent of Beautiful by Estée Lauder assaulted her senses. She didn't see a body, but it was too dark inside to be sure. She pulled her phone out and shook it to engage the light. No one in either of the front seats. She noticed the Toyota emblem on the steering wheel. Seemed odd to see it. Then, it dawned on her. Typically, the airbags deployed in an accident like this. She checked the back seat. While littered with clothing and an open cooler already raided by hungry wildlife, it was devoid of any bodies.

"There's no one in the car, and no evidence that anyone tried to get out." Using the stick to extend her reach, Jordan pressed the car's start button. The dash came to life, prompting the need for a car fob before the car could start. "Neither of the airbags deployed."

"What's that mean?" Hanna asked from behind her.

"It means the car was powered off when it was pushed down the hill. Today's air bags don't deploy if the car is off. Also, there's no blood." Stick in hand, Jordan popped open the glove box, revealing the vehicle's registration. Not wanting to contaminate the scene, Jordan found a discarded T-shirt and wrapped it over her hand like a glove. Without touching the car, she slipped the paperwork out of the cubby. "I was afraid of this."

"Afraid of what?"

"This is Warden Ryder's car. I bet if we run that plate, it comes back stolen. It definitely doesn't match what's on the registration."

Jordan walked around the car and took a picture of the VIN number through a small hole in the windshield. It matched the registration.

"Someone pushed her car down the hill?"

Jordan nodded. "That'd be my guess. The same someone who was driving it the night of the storm. That night, a tree went down and blocked the road. I'm certain this was the car that was in front of me. I still have part of a broken bumper in my truck." Jordan ran her fingers through her hair. "Deb's killer could've been behind the wheel, and what'd I do? I offered to clear the path." Frustrated, Jordan leaned against the car. It creaked, and something underneath it popped. She stepped away quickly.

"At that point, did you have any way of knowing Deb was in trouble?" Hanna asked.

"No." Jordan stared off into the woods. "As far as I knew, she'd quit."

"You can't blame yourself for any of this. All you can do is figure out what happened and who did it. Right?"

"You're right, of course." Still, Jordan couldn't shake the guilt.

Rather than call the sheriff's department directly, she decided to run the call through the DNR dispatcher, just to have a record of the find. Things, law enforcement things, were getting more and more convoluted in the Northwoods. At the moment, she wasn't so sure who she could trust. An issue she'd never before encountered in her career.

She didn't have her radio with her and would have to use her cell. Jordan opened the app that worked like her radio with the DNR dispatch office. "Badge 1409 to dispatch."

"Go ahead, 1409."

Dave must have had the day off. "Be advised, vehicle found"—Jordan tapped away to her map app—"east-northeast of Kyle Pass, north side of Loon Boulevard, down in the valley. No bodies, no injuries, no driver or passenger, ample debris. Send recovery tow and requesting the crime scene response unit."

"Say again, crime scene response unit? Confirm single car, no bodies, none injured?"

Jordan smiled. Day shift was a tad more formal. "Affirmative. Requesting the crime scene response unit."

"Nearest CSRU is in Wausau. I'll convey the request to the sheriff's office, but I doubt they'll come all this way for a car dump."

Just like not having the Medical Examiner earlier, this was yet another resource that Jordan had taken for granted in the bigger city. "CSRU because vehicle identification number is connected to deceased warden, Deb Ryder. Plates currently on the car, Wisconsin RHR-173. Plates do not match registration found in the glove box. All evidence and prints are pertinent to the murder investigation."

"Wisconsin RHR-173 registered to a Zoey Mitchell. Licensed vehicle, blue 2013 Toyota Camry of Taylor County, Wisconsin. Will transmit details."

"10-4 dispatch. Any local reports of stolen plates?"

"Negative."

Jordan pinched the bridge of her nose. "Who are you, Zoey Mitchell? And how do you fit into this mess?" So many more questions than answers. Where was the blue 2013 Toyota Camry? Better question, did it belong to the soaked car fob of the missing kayaker? The possibility couldn't be overlooked. Too bad the sheriff's office had the car fob. That didn't mean she couldn't look for the car.

"Are you up for a climb?" she asked. "We should be up there on Kyle Pass to meet the investigators and the tow truck."

"I had no idea being a warden was so intense. You work around the clock and deal with the ickiest things."

"It's not always this intense, but the motto 'expect the worst and hope for the best' has proven effective. Because of our patrol environment, wardens are seven times more likely to experience violence in their career than other law enforcement officers. That sobering fact is baked into our training. We are always prepared, always aware, and always ready."

"That was a fact I didn't need to know. Why are you more likely to experience violence? What's different?"

"Take the sheriff's department. If they pull someone over for speeding, the likelihood that they'll encounter an armed driver is a single-digit percentage. Granted, it's greater if it's in an urban area known for drug violence and gang activity. But a conservation officer has the opposite statistic. There's a small, single-digit percentage of encounters where a weapon *isn't* readily available: hunting, fishing, or those simply off-roading. Typically, our encounters include at least one weapon, often several, between guns and knives."

"I never thought about it that way." Hanna's breath became labored with the steep climb. "Jesus, why can't all land be flat? This is ridiculous."

Jordan laughed. "All in a day's work. Climb up, scurry down, climb up again from late summer to early spring. Now you know why boating season is my favorite. It gives my legs a break."

"And here I thought being in a boat all day was what made your legs so strong, balancing on the waves." Hanna turned back and looked at her. "I'm dying up here." She gasped for air. "Totally out of breath and you're cruising along like it's nothing."

"I'm cruising along like it's been my job for almost twenty years."

"Is your job always this intense? Please tell me that what you've experienced these last couple days is a one-off."

"Believe me, this is an exception, not the norm. I came up here to enjoy a slower pace. My life in Madison was much calmer than it's been here so far."

For years, Jordan had hoped to find a place that felt like home. A community where she belonged and was a part of things. Beyond her connection with Hanna and her friendship with Bobbi Rae, at this point it was difficult to know if her request to transfer to Waterdance was the right call. *Look how it turned out for Deb.* There weren't even services available to run a proper investigation. Had she been wrong to crave the smaller community? Had she been wrong to come back?

❖

Billowing plumes of dust announced the speeding first responder well before the red and blue flashing lights came into view. Jordan recognized the sheriff's car just before it skidded to a stop about ten feet from where she stood.

The driver's door flung open. Sheriff Reid stepped out, walked around the hood, and peered over the edge into the valley before sauntering up to stand in front of Jordan. "Here I thought you were going to get some rest. Have you slept at all?"

"I'll sleep tonight."

"Gotta be running on fumes by now. You keep making the damnedest discoveries. The kayaker. The warden's body. So where's the car?"

Jordan caught another whiff of her perfume. The hairs on the back of her neck stood at attention. She turned and pointed. "It's about fifty yards down there. It's the same car I told you about the other day. The one that was in front of me when I came into town the night of the storm. All that stuff that's missing from the station house is scattered everywhere down there. I called for a crime scene response unit. Maybe there's prints or DNA or some evidence that will lead us to Deb's killer."

Sheriff Reid nodded. "Yep. Dispatch conveyed the request. And to show you what a good sport I am, I called over to Wausau to see if the team could pop over. Problem is, they're out on another high priority call, a missing child. There's a chance that she's still alive, so that case takes precedence."

Jordan took a step closer. "Seriously? Don't they have more than one truck? We're talking about a murdered law enforcement officer."

Sheriff Reid leaned against the side of her car. "I'm well aware and perfectly capable of running the investigation. While it doesn't happen often, this isn't my first murder case. None of us are taking this lightly. Daniel's had some CSRU training. He'll take a look-see once the vehicle's towed to the lot behind the office."

"Daniel? The coroner? Mr. A Good Couple Three Days, Daniel?" Jordan was beside herself. "Evidence could be lost in the tow or destroyed in the collection."

"It's the best we've got for now, and since I'm the sheriff in these parts, I'm calling the shots. Understand, Warden, this is my case, my scene. Unless, of course, you have forensics training to go with that shiny gold detective's badge you keep wanting to pull out?"

Jordan ignored the dig. Regardless of the force, she was a law enforcement officer. "Would you trust Daniel with the evidence if it was one of your deputies I'd pulled out of the lake? We should contact Wisconsin DOJ and have the criminal investigative unit come up. They have the tools and resources to find the evidence."

Sheriff Reid didn't respond to the question or the suggestion. Instead, she walked to the edge and looked down the hill. "Have you remembered anything new about the driver from that night? The slightest detail could be relevant."

"You mean other than the fact that she was soaking wet, slight of build, and wore the same perfume you're wearing right now? Go on, check it out. The car still reeks of it."

Hanna gasped. Shit, Jordan had been so caught up in going toe to toe with the sheriff that she'd almost forgotten that Hanna was standing right there.

The sheriff slowly turned and glared at Jordan. "Yeah, other than that because I know I've not been in that car. Guaranteed the evidence is on my side."

"Especially if Daniel collects it. Because what's a little evidence tampering among friends?" Jordan couldn't stop herself.

The sheriff stepped forward with the speed of a striking cobra. She collected a fistful of Jordan's shirt in her hand and yanked on it until they were almost nose to nose. Instinctively, Jordan whipped her arm up and broke the sheriff's grasp, quickly returning to her full height. If looks could kill, she had a feeling they'd both be dead.

"I hear that lack of sleep can distort a person's perspective, so I'm gonna cut you some slack. Don't you have a missing kayaker to look for? Seems to me, that's the only open investigation you've been invited to assist with." The sheriff's tone was curt. She held Jordan's glare. Any other time, Jordan would've admired her gravitas. She never flinched, nor did she blink.

Neither did Jordan.

She'd long ago developed a tough edge. At times, it was useful, especially when almost all of her encounters involved someone who was armed and doing something wrong. She'd never needed to be arrogant or be the know-it-all cop, but having a confident demeanor in the situation had always gone a long way. "If you ask me, these cases are all related," Jordan said. She almost suggested they should work together to solve it. She almost mentioned Deb's notes. Luckily, she came to her senses and quickly decided against it.

"Funny, I don't recall asking you." Sheriff Reid snapped her gum.

"Sheriff, can't you see? The timeline for each of the events is right around the day of the storm?"

"Isn't that about the same time you came to town?" Sheriff Reid raised her eyebrows as if making a profound point.

"Ah, flip the cards to divert suspicion?" Jordan could play the same game. All. Day. Long.

Hanna's hand tucked into hers with a slight tug. "Maybe we should get going."

Shit, Jordan needed to swallow her pride and bite back her comments. Hanna shouldn't have to see any of this.

The sheriff turned her attention to Hanna. "Shouldn't you be checking on Aunt Dottie? I'm sure you'd be far more help to her than you can offer here."

Jordan didn't like that one bit. Sheriff Reid could be as curt with her as she wanted, but she shouldn't take it out on Hanna. Again, defenses flared.

Hanna must have felt her bristle, because she tugged on Jordan's hand. "Let's go."

Jordan nodded. "Yeah, we've still got a bit of a hike." If it wasn't for Hanna's warm fingers in her palm, she probably wouldn't have given in so easily. She flashed one last glaring look in the sheriff's direction before she relented to Hanna's pull toward town.

They'd walked for about ten minutes when Hanna spun around and stopped directly in front of Jordan. "You mind telling me what all that was about?" she asked, pointing back toward Kyle Pass. "Do you really think the sheriff is involved in Warden Ryder's death?" Her eyes held a hint of fire, like she was ready to argue her point.

Jordan had zero qualms about pushing the sheriff's buttons. There'd been a reason for it. But that wasn't at all how she wanted things to be with Hanna. She deserved honesty, not an argument. "Yes, no, hell, I don't know. I have good reasons to be skeptical. I don't know what to believe right now. My words back there were more to rattle her cage, but she didn't respond like I expected her to."

"How'd you expect her to respond?"

"Defensive. I expected her to deflect and not make eye contact. She did the opposite, which throws my Spidey senses all off whack. Everything is pointing to her being somehow involved, but I must be missing something. If she's not involved, why is she freezing me out of the investigation?"

"If you accused me of being involved, I'd freeze you out too. Things are a little different up here in the Northwoods. Folks are protective of their own, and you're the stranger in town. I've no doubt that Sheriff Reid wants to find out what happened to Deb. She was part of the community. Trust me. I wasn't always from around here, either. You'd fare better to offer a little honey instead of spit and vinegar."

Hanna's expression softened, and in an instant, Jordan's defenses deflated. She didn't want to alienate the one person she already cared so much about.

"If you want this to become your home, you've got to become part of the community. You can't stand on the outside looking in, judging everyone's moves, and expect anyone to want your opinion. Complaining that things don't operate up here like they do down in the city doesn't help much either. Trust me, I've been there and done that."

Hanna's words stung, but she wasn't wrong. Overwhelmed and frustrated, Jordan blinked back tears that were threatening to spill over. Aw, shit. She might have really screwed this up. She needed to get a grip.

"Listen, you've had a tough couple of days. You haven't slept, and you haven't had a minute to process the fact that just this morning, you pulled your friend's body out of the lake. It's bound to make anyone a little edgy." Hanna tugged on her hand. "I like you, Jordan. Like, really like you. I'm begging you, get some sleep. Reset. If you still think things are upside down tomorrow, then I'm all ears. In the meantime, I've got enough on my plate with Dottie. I don't need any trouble with Sheriff Reid."

"I really like you too." Jordan nodded. "Yeah, you're right. I'm sorry. Okay." She couldn't think of anything else to say. She was too emotional, too fried, and too worked up to say anything of value. The lodge was just around the next bend and across the road. She wrapped her arm around Hanna's shoulder and enjoyed her company for as long as she had it.

CHAPTER TWELVE

The house was empty when Hanna walked in. After such a roller coaster of a day, she was grateful for the bit of solitude. She should have run out and gotten the last of her things out of the camper so it was ready when Banjo and Chipmunk came by to pick it up. But she was way too spent to do even one more thing.

Standing in front of the open refrigerator door, Hanna looked for something to make for dinner. She ended up eating two slices of cheddar cheese, a few pieces of ham, another slice of cheese, and three Spanish olives before deciding that nothing sounded worth the effort of actually cooking. She settled on a slice of buttered bread and ate it while watching her favorite episode of *Gilmore Girls* through the Netflix app on her phone. A perfect way to zone out and ignore the craziness of the day, both good and bad. The messenger app popped up, pausing the show.

Auntie Ruthie: *Out back. Need help.*

Hanna popped out of her chair, so grateful she'd gotten home in time to be there for them. She left the phone on the table and ran out the back door. Ruthie had parked right next to the newly installed ramp.

"She slept most of the way home, but it's been a rough go since she woke up."

Aunt Dottie sat in the passenger seat, slumped over a wastebasket. Hanna opened the door and squatted so she could be close to her. Dottie heaved nothing but a spittle of bile into the bin. Hanna could definitely relate. She'd done that several times earlier and now realized that her stomach was much stronger when a dead body wasn't involved.

"Hey, Auntie, how about we get you inside?" Hanna asked.

Dottie sort of shrugged and toppled against her. Hanna put the trash bin on the ground, pulled her aunt into her arms, and carried her into the house. A sack of rice weighed more. There was nothing to her. She didn't need to pinch her skin to know she was likely dehydrated. Using the glow of the kitchen light to illuminate her path, Hanna made her way into the living room and lowered Dottie onto the hospital bed. Having already added an electric blanket to the pile of bedding, Hanna tucked her in and switched the controller to medium.

"I'll be right back." Hanna kissed her forehead. She rushed outside and helped Ruthie carry a few things inside.

"Thanks, honey. I'm so glad you're home. There's no way I could have done that." Ruthie collapsed in her comfy chair next to Dottie's bed. "I'm pooped, and I wasn't the one getting chemo."

Hanna walked up behind her and bent down, wrapping her arms around Ruthie's shoulders. "There's nowhere else I'd rather be. Have you eaten? I could cook something."

"Don't bother, I'm too tired to eat." Ruthie leaned back until her chair's leg support flipped up. "Ah, that's the ticket."

Aunt Dottie coughed into a napkin. Her eyes seemed more sunken than normal. As if there was a normal for cancer.

"Did she get any of the ginger tea in?"

"She tried, but the effects of the treatment hit her hard and fast. It's stronger than the last round, and it's her first one since the surgery. She was still so weak from the previous cycle. The few calories we got into her last night weren't enough to give her the strength she needed. I should have pushed it off for another week."

"Would she have tolerated the dose any better given another week?"

Ruthie shrugged. "Who knows? Likely not."

"Did they give her a patch for the nausea?"

"Yeah, she has the little pod thing on her arm. She's had them before. They don't seem to do much for her, but it's better than nothing. She'll feel a little better by the time we have to go back. Cancer sucks."

Cancer totally sucked. No arguments there. "She's so dehydrated. We've got to settle her stomach. Otherwise, she's going to end up in the hospital hooked to an IV. I'm not sure they could find a stable vein."

Ruthie reclined the back of her chair, raised her arm, and covered her eyes. "I'm open to ideas, my little herbalist."

"Hang on, I might have just the thing." Hanna turned for the back door. "I'll be right back."

After she'd rushed out of Branson, Missouri, she'd read enough about cancer treatments at each gas station stop to know that nausea was a big issue. If the pods weren't helping, she had to try something a little more powerful than ginger. A pit stop at a medicinal dispensary in Illinois had offered a host of options. Hanna found the box right where she'd hidden it, in a cubby beneath her bed in the camper. She grabbed it and rushed back to the kitchen.

"Is cherry still her favorite flavor?" Hanna set the box on the side table next to Ruthie's chair. She pulled out a bag of cannabis gummies.

"Like candies taste like anything but fruity sugar. How is candy going to help her stomach?" Ruthie leaned forward and looked in the box.

"Ah, these aren't just candy." Hanna picked up a pair of scissors and cut the bag open. She pulled out a red gummy, cut it in half, and went to Aunt Dottie's side.

"Don't chew this, okay? Just tuck it in your cheek and let it dissolve. I'm hoping it helps settle your system."

Aunt Dottie opened her mouth. Hanna tucked the gummy in.

It made her smile to see her aunt move the candy from side to side with her tongue.

Her brow furrowed. "It's spoiled or something. It tastes weird."

"It's not spoiled. I promise. Try to keep it in your cheek."

It would act much quicker if it could dissolve rather than if it was swallowed. What she wouldn't give to see her aunt get some relief.

"Can I have one?" Ruthie asked. "If you're going to get my wife stoned, I should be able to float in the clouds with her. Wait, if she gets one, shouldn't I get two or maybe three? Hey, Dot, you're right. They taste like crap."

"I only gave Dottie half." Hanna grabbed the bag. "How many did you take? Please, not more than one. Jeez, I can only handle one incapacitated aunt at a time."

"I totally think I could handle two. Ya know, I smoked a joint or two back in the day." Ruthie popped a second one in her mouth before Hanna could say anything.

"Two will knock you on your ass." Hanna shook her head. "At least chew and swallow them and give me time to take care of Dottie first."

The way Dottie was clicking her tongue and poking it between her lips hinted at the THC getting into her bloodstream. Hanna hoped it would help calm her stomach and let her get some fluids in.

Ruthie spit a half-chewed gummy back into her hand and finished chewing the other. "Fine, bossy lady."

Hanna grabbed the spittle-covered candy and popped it into the trash can before Ruthie could change her mind. "I can see you're going to be trouble." She folded the package and clipped it closed. "I'm hiding these."

"Where? In the bottom of your closet behind the fake wall panel? Or under the floorboards beneath your bed?" Ruthie winked and smiled. "Just in case Dottie needs the other half."

Hanna laughed. "You knew where my secret hiding spots were?" Like she expected anything less from Ruthie.

"I make it my business to know all the things going on with the people I care about. I never found anything that concerned me, so I didn't bother calling you out on it. You had enough people telling you how to act and what to do. The least I could do was give you a bit of freedom."

"Aw, Ruthie, see, I always knew you were a big softie. I love you." Hanna hugged her.

"I love you too."

"Could I interrupt?" Dottie pushed the button and inclined her upper body slightly.

"Absolutely. How are you feeling?"

"Better, thank you, and the blankets are warming up." She licked her lips. "I think I'd like a sip of water."

"Hallelujah." Ruthie popped up out of her chair and ran into the kitchen. She returned a moment later with an insulated bottle of water with a straw and the large Tupperware bowl. "Here you are, sweetie." She handed Dottie the bottle and set the bowl on the bed next to her. "Just in case your tummy isn't ready."

Hanna had a vision of Jordan handing her the bucket. Not the most romantic moment on a non-date date but certainly the most memorable she'd ever had. Never before had she had such an intense day with someone, from freakish to orgasmic to odd and confusing, only to part ways in the evening instead of crawling into bed and snuggling. While she would have loved to have stayed in Jordan's arms for the evening, this was where she needed to be. Besides, if she'd stayed, neither of them would have gotten much sleep.

Dottie nodded and took a sip. "Hmm, nice and cold." She lowered the bottle until it was resting in her lap. "Are there any of those peaches left?"

Hanna looked at Ruthie, who looked back at Hanna with the same shocked expression.

"Heck, yeah. I'll buy them by the case if that's what hits the spot." Hanna hurried into the kitchen. She pulled the covered bowl of peaches from the fridge, cut them into smaller pieces, and returned to her aunt's side. She scooped a piece onto the spoon and slipped it into her aunt's mouth.

"Mmm, that's nice." She chewed slowly and held her hands out for the bowl.

Hanna handed it to her. "There are plenty more."

"We heard about the missing person on the scanner this morning and about the recovered body on our way to Woodruff. I can't believe all that's happened today," Ruthie said.

"You don't know the half of it." Hanna pulled Aunt Dottie's reading chair over, creating a conversation triangle. She flopped down and propped her feet on the end of Dottie's bed.

"Do you know if they've identified the body?" Ruthie asked.

"Yes, it's Warden Ryder." Hanna focused on a loose string in the hem of her shirt. She had known her aunts would ask about it, but truth be told, she would have liked to forget the image of the warden's mutilated body being pulled from the lake, even if only for the evening. She hadn't known Deb, but if she'd been anything like Jordan, as Auntie Ruthie had already suggested, well, that was…just too much. Hanna hadn't known Jordan but a few days, and already, she couldn't bear the thought of losing her. Especially not like that.

"Do they have any suspects yet?" Ruthie asked.

Hanna thought back to the encounter with Sheriff Reid out by Kyle Pass. She trusted Jordan but hoped her instincts about the sheriff were wrong. Regardless, she couldn't share things she'd only kind of heard about, especially about events she shouldn't know about. "None that I'm aware of." Jordan hadn't had solid proof, so it wasn't really a lie.

"What about the missing boater? Have they found them?" Ruthie asked.

"Not that I've heard. The search crews have been on the water since early this morning, and nothing so far." Hanna sat and watched her aunts. Who knew where her life would have ended up if they hadn't stepped in? All things considered, they were doing pretty good for being in their early seventies. Well, except for the cancer.

Why hadn't she come home more often? She always had this weird sensation when she was there, as if she'd traveled back in time and was a teenager all over again. With it came the feelings of trying to be on her best behavior so they wouldn't send her back to Manhattan, not that anyone could tell her where or how to live now. Did everyone experience that when they returned to their hometown? Or was she the odd one out?

Jesus, she hadn't even had a gummy of her own.

"Are you sure there's pot in this candy? I don't feel a thing. God, the gnats." Ruthie swatted at invisible bugs.

Hanna laughed. "Oh, I'm pretty sure there's a little something in there."

"Have you seen Warden Jordan? How's she dealing with the loss of her friend?"

The image of the corpse from the boat sprung into Hanna's mind, assaulting her temporary reprieve.

"Could I trouble you for a few more peaches?" Dottie held her bowl out. Jordan's suggestion had certainly been a winner.

Hanna nodded and went to the kitchen. She refilled the bowl with a scoop of the diced fruit in sweetened syrup and returned to her aunt's side. "I'm glad you're feeling better."

"Me too." Dottie dug in, thoughtfully chewing each small piece. Seeing her enjoy food again was a treat all on its own.

Ruthie thrust her upper body back on her chair. It whipped back into the reclining position. "Whee!" She held her arms up in the air. She sat forward, and the chair returned to the sitting position. "Ooo." Ruthie thrust her torso back again. "Whee. Dot, look, a carnival ride." She leaned forward again.

"Oh boy. She's stoned." Aunt Dottie nodded toward Ruthie.

"You're not kidding. Thankfully, she spit the second one out. Can you imagine if she'd had two?" Hanna laughed.

"Whee!"

"She's a lightweight." Dottie yawned. "Thanks for the candy. It really helped. You're such a treasure."

"Ooo…whee!" Ruthie cackled with laughter.

"I'm glad it gave you some relief. The other half is in a dish on top of the fridge next to the bag, in case you ask Ruthie for more. Don't let her give you too much. It won't be pretty, especially if you try to navigate that walker."

Dottie laughed. It was so great to hear.

"Up and at 'em, Dot. We gotta get going," Ruthie said from her comfy chair, reaching for something behind her left shoulder.

"Ruthie, what are you doing?" Hanna asked.

"I'm trying to fasten my seat belt. What does it look like? It's like the thing is made out of air. I can't seem to grab it. Carnival's closing. We've gotta get going."

"Why do you need your seat belt? You're sitting in the living room."

"I am?" Wide-eyed, she turned her head from left to right in slow motion. "How'd we get home so fast? Where's the pizza I ordered? Oh, I really want pizza."

"You've been home for more than an hour. Sorry, there's no pizza."

Hanna pressed her lips together to keep from giggling.

"I'd like pineapple on my half," Dottie said after swallowing her peach bite. She looked at Hanna and winked.

"Instigator." Hanna poked her foot. "Is there a pizzeria in town now?"

"Hmm, I don't think so, but wouldn't it be great if there was?"

"It sure would because now I want pizza." Hanna shook her head.

"Maybe it's still in the car?" Ruthie tried to get up and fell to the floor. She lay there, flat on her back, laughing hysterically.

Laughing right along with Ruthie, Hanna helped her back into her chair.

"Oh, what about some eggs and ham and cheese?" Ruthie motioned from her chair. "Scrambled...oh, with potatoes and green chilies."

"Mexican scramble, coming right up." The evening was just the distraction she needed. It seemed to be just the distraction her aunts needed too.

CHAPTER THIRTEEN

Dark gray clouds hung ominously low in the sky, a stark contrast from the day before. Such a dramatic change that Jordan wasn't entirely sure if she'd slept through an entire day until she checked the date on her phone.

Preparing to tackle another shift on the water, she dressed in a clean uniform, taking special care to wrap the black mourning band around her badge before pinning it in place. When she was satisfied with her appearance, she tossed her rain gear into her pack, along with some granola bars and a few bottles of water. She dropped her pack onto the front seat of her truck before walking to the diner for some much needed breakfast.

Her chest tightened as she approached the diner's entrance. For reasons she couldn't quite put her finger on, she was nervous to see Hanna. The previous day had been such a whirlwind of events and emotions. The passion they'd shared in the afternoon had been incredible. Still, Jordan feared it was a one-off. She'd gotten the impression from Hanna's lifestyle in a Winnebago—and a few of Bobbie Rae's comments—that Hanna didn't stick around.

In the past, Jordan had been the opposite. Time and again, she'd stayed, with her family and in relationships, far past the expiration date, trying to fix the unfixable. Well, that was until Dr. Knoedel helped her see that she needed to break some bad habits and old patterns before she could expect anything different from a relationship. It'd been five years since she'd started that work, and she'd been single the entire time. But just because she had a history of falling too fast for the wrong woman—and had been incapable of tossing in the towel on the failed relationship that followed—did that mean she had to be single forever? God, she hoped not. Single was lonely. Besides, Hanna was everything her past girlfriends hadn't been. Or at least, that was Jordan's impression so far. She seemed incredibly independent. She was thoughtful and kind. Without apology, she was her own person. Jordan could go on and on. Did any of that matter if she packed up and took off the moment her aunt was better?

For a long moment, Jordan stood outside the door and watched Hanna interact with customers at the counter. Playful, light, and airy, her distinct laughter could be heard through the glass and instantly put Jordan's apprehension at ease. Hanna's eyes sparkled when she laughed, and her cheeks pinked ever so slightly. What Jordan wouldn't give to have some uninterrupted time with her. An afternoon, an evening, a day, a week, she'd take anything she could get, whenever she could get it. That said, she understood that they both had overflowing plates demanding their full attention.

"Are you going in? Or are you going to just stand out here and watch her?"

The vaguely familiar voice startled her. She turned to find Carol standing with a large crate of baked goods.

"Geez, sorry. Here, let me get that for you." Jordan took the crate.

"She digs you too. I haven't seen her this smitten in a long time." Carol pulled the diner door open. "After you."

She digs you too. Hearing that had Jordan floating on a cloud.

"Two of my favorite peeps." Hanna's eyes sparkled even brighter if that was possible. Jordan barely noticed the counter as she set down the crate. Her sweet voice was like a breath of fresh air. "Good morning," she said, and began transferring pastries, bread, and confections to a shelf behind the counter. "Did you get some sleep? How are you feeling?" She set a large cinnamon roll off to the side, white icing from the side of the container stuck to her hand. One by one, she licked the sticky glaze from her fingers. Jordan licked her own lips. She wouldn't mind a little sugar right now. Hanna raised her eyebrows. Crap, she was expecting an answer. Sleep. Had she slept?

"Yeah, I went out like a light. Thank you. Yesterday was, well, thank you for sharing your afternoon." Jordan couldn't wipe the goofy grin off her face if she tried.

"The pleasure was all mine." Hanna blew her a kiss, and her face turned scarlet red. Embarrassed looked adorable on her.

Jordan couldn't get enough.

"I got some sleep too. Thanks for asking." Carol playfully gave Jordan a shoulder shove. "Though I did have some freakish nightmares about our time on the water. Hanna Banana, I have time for a cup of coffee this morning if it's slow enough. I made your favorite treat to go with it too." Carol touched Jordan's arm. "Since you're here, I guess you can join us."

"Hanna Banana?"

"Nope. That's not going to become a thing." Hanna wiggled her finger at Jordan. "Do you hear me, Jo-Jo?"

"Truce." Jordan nodded. "What's your favorite?"

"Oh, Carol makes these cherry turnovers that are to die for. Would you like to try one?"

"Would you mind if I took it to go? I really need to get out on the water before the sky lets loose. The search party is still working." As much as she wanted to, spending some time in the diner with Hanna was not an option.

"They haven't found the kayaker yet?" Carol asked.

Jordan shook her head. "No, but I'm holding out hope."

"Hey, Warden Jordan. Could I interest you in another breakfast sandwich? I made it this morning before I realized what I was doing." Ruthie held up the paper sack. Small blotches of grease seeped through on the sides. "Sure am sorry to hear about Deb. Just the thought that something like that could happen up here in the Northwoods. It's heartbreaking. She was good people."

"Indeed, and she was. Thank you. It'd be an honor to have Deb's breakfast this morning." Jordan accepted the sack. Ruthie offered a solemn nod and returned to the kitchen. It'd been fun to snag Deb's favorite breakfast on that first day. Sort of a "see what you're missing" notion. But today, it was hard to reconcile that Deb would never get the opportunity to hear the bell jingle above the door and have a hot meal ready and waiting. To have her breakfast was definitely an honor. Jordan sucked up her wayward emotional thoughts and faced Hanna. "Could I get a coffee to go and if Carol made enough, a cherry turnover, too?" As much as she didn't like it, duty was calling, but taking as much as she could from the diner to be out with her on the boat felt comforting.

Hanna picked up a sack from beneath the counter and shook it open. She stared at it for a second, then set it down. "Carol, I'll be right back for that coffee break." Hanna pulled the bagged breakfast out of Jordan's grasp and set it on the counter. She tugged on her hand. "You, come with me."

Jordan complied as Hanna pulled her around the corner and into the woman's restroom. Given the mischievous glint in Hanna's eyes, Jordan would have followed her to the very depths of hell and regretted nothing.

When the restroom door closed, Hanna reached up and gave Jordan's shirt collar a gentle tug. She didn't need to be asked twice. Hanna's lips tasted sweet from the frosting she'd licked off her fingers. Her tongue was just as sweet. What Jordan wouldn't give to scoop her up and carry her out through the diner and over to cabin seven. One of these days, hopefully very soon.

Breathlessly, Hanna broke their kiss. "I've missed you."

"Hmm, I've missed you too." She leaned forward and kissed her again. "I'm sorry about yesterday afternoon, ya know, with the sheriff."

"Me too. I don't know all the specifics. I shouldn't have challenged you about your job." Hanna tucked her head into Jordan's neck. "I'm glad you slept. If Dottie's doing okay after dinner, can I see you tonight?"

Jordan felt like more should have been said about her confrontation with the sheriff, but Hanna seemed okay with dropping it, so she did. "Yes. Please." She rested her chin against Hanna's head. "I could come out and pick you up. Maybe I could meet Dottie if she's up for it."

"Sounds wonderful. I'll let you know how the evening goes. Last night was rough for her. Can I text you when we're slow? You don't have to answer if you're busy."

"I'd like that." The gloomy day on the water alone just got a little bit brighter. At least she had something to look forward to. Hanna had missed her too. Yesterday hadn't been a mere one-off of fun. She basked in the thought. The day had just got a whole lot brighter, indeed.

"Carol's waiting," Hanna said with a sigh. "I should go."

Jordan bent and kissed her gently one more time. "Enjoy your visit. I'll see you tonight."

"I'm already looking forward to it." Hanna opened the door, then turned back with a smile. "Come on, sexy. The sooner we get your day started, the sooner we can spend some time together."

Jordan couldn't argue with that logic.

Jordan launched her boat and raised the aluminum-framed Bimini top to keep her as dry as possible. So far, the rain had held off. After a quick call to the dispatcher, Jordan's tour officially began. She headed south, intent on searching three boat launches closer to the island where the kayaker had been camping. Unless the missing boater had been dropped off for her camping trip, she had to have a car out there somewhere. Deb's notes came to mind. Jordan kept her eye out for the sheriff's boat and any rented fishing boats. Maybe she'd get a more detailed description. Along the way, she continued to call out, each time holding her breath, hoping for a response. Sadly, no response ever came.

A heavy mist kept visibility low. Unlike the warm, clear skies of yesterday, there was a chill in the air, more aligned with early April rather than late May. Jordan unrolled the clear plastic front and side panels of the canvas top. Once each was snapped in place, she had a fairly dry, three-sided shelter to work in. Even then, with the slower speed, she shivered in the swirling damp air. Too bad she didn't have a heat source. She pulled her rain jacket out of her pack and put it on, zipping it all the way up. It helped hold her body heat and allowed her to go just a little faster. From Waterdance on the Turtle River to the southernmost point, there was a lot of lake to cover.

The first boat launch was a bust. Given the cloudy skies and bone-chilling temps, she wasn't surprised to see the parking lot devoid of any cars, let alone a 2013 blue Toyota with missing plates. Jordan returned to her boat and carried on. She was halfway to the second launch on her planned path when a camper flagged her down.

"Warden. Hey! Over here."

Jordan checked her GPS, campsite F-4. It was one of eleven sites located on the big island. She called in her location and lowered the throttle once she had the boat drifting closer to shore. "Morning. What can I do for you?"

"We were on the water all day yesterday looking for that missing kayaker, and when we got back, our camp had been raided."

"Sure am sorry to hear that. What kind of stuff was taken?"

"Oddly enough, what was left of my wives' clean clothes, including the backpack they were in, my heavyweight flannel, rope and a tarp that we brought to keep the picnic area dry in the rain, oh, one of our sleeping bags, and most of what little food we had left. We'd already planned on heading back today. It was too late, and we were too tired to pack up last night, so we got cozy in my bag. Anyway, I was wondering if you've heard of any other sites being robbed?"

Jordan took in the list of items that had been taken. Items a stranded kayaker would need to keep warm on a cold damp night. She'd been out in the elements at least three nights without a boat, and it would be difficult for her to get back to her site, even if she knew the area. If she was new to the lake, then navigating most anywhere would be difficult at best. These dense woods had a way of skewing one's sense of direction.

"There haven't been any other reports as far as I know, but my tour just started. You'll want to contact the sheriff, especially if you plan to file a claim on the loss."

"Aw, I don't plan on filing a claim. It's not like we brought our good clothes camping. The most expensive thing was the sleeping bag, and we've had these for years. It was just odd. You don't suppose that the missing boater is on foot and lost?"

"Given what was taken, the thought crossed my mind."

"Well, if it was, it takes the sting out of being robbed. I don't mind sharing if it was because someone was trying to survive. But why not just wait here for us to return? We'd have been happy to help."

Jordan had that same thought. Why not seek help? The lake had been full of boaters yesterday, each calling out to the missing kayaker. Why run from those? "Do you mind if I beach my boat and take a look?"

"Not at all." He waved her in.

Jordan hopped down to the sandy beach and tied her mooring line to a tree. "I'm Warden Pearce."

"Tim Oshner." He motioned to a woman sitting at the picnic table. "My wife, Natalie."

"Nice to meet you both. Sorry it's under these circumstances."

Nothing unusual jumped out at her. Natalie had her feet propped up and crossed on the ring of the firepit, and from what Jordan could see, the soles of her shoes matched many of the impressions around the site. Tim stepped closer, leaving a tread pattern of his boot that was clearly responsible for the other prints in the sandy loam. Jordan lifted the lid on the cooler. Four dirty fingerprints on the underside of the lid caught her eye, as if a hand had curled around it while lifting.

"Do you think these prints belong to either of you?" she asked.

"Doubtful," Natalie said. "We're both pretty good about washing our hands before going for the food."

Jordan took several pictures before she found one that showed several clear fingerprints when she zoomed in. She sent it off to dispatch.

Do these prints belong to you, Zoey Mitchell? Are you my missing kayaker? Why are you running? Fingers crossed, the person was in the system, and she'd get a name. She continued her look around, following several trails leading deeper onto the island. None of them gave her a direction of travel or a shoe impression different from Tim and Natalie's.

"Sorry, we looked all over the place for our stuff. Called out too. We probably trampled anyone else's footprints." Natalie shrugged.

"No harm. Well, if anything turns up, I'll let you know," she said after gathering the campers' contact information.

"Sounds great. Thanks for stopping. I guess we'll pack up and head home." Tim extended his hand.

She shook it. "Sorry again about the theft. Have a safe trip."

Below the camper's names, Jordan jotted some notes on the encounter and called her availability in to the dispatcher. She freed her tie line and hopped into the bow of her boat just as drops of rain gently fell from the sky. The pitter-patter on the canvas cover was a pleasant sound, conjuring up memories of sitting on the tin porch of cabin seven. Back then, she'd been a big *Nancy Drew* fan and had sat out there reading for hours when the rain kept her from exploring.

The weather forecast for the next several days was more of the same. Cooler temps and spotty showers. So it wasn't a surprise to see so many more vacant campsites as she made her way down the shoreline and around the islands. Within a half an hour, she made it to the second boat launch. From the water, she didn't have a clear visual of the parking lot. Bummer. The rain had picked up too. She'd have to dock the boat and walk up to see if there was a blue Toyota in one of the spaces. She flipped her hood up and snapped it around her chin before she stepped onto the slippery wooden dock.

There were two cars in the back corner, too far away to make out the model through the rain. But something felt off. With a heightened sense of awareness, Jordan approached the area cautiously, her right hand wrapped around the grip of her side arm. "Hello? Conservation warden, announce yourself." She hoped she sounded more confident than she felt at the moment.

Movement.

Jordan drew her weapon and took aim.

A doe popped her head up above the trunk of the second car. She had grass sticking out of the sides of her mouth. Two tiny fawns were at the wood's edge.

Jordan released her held breath and holstered her weapon. "You're safe, momma," she said softly.

The doe seemed unfazed by her presence. She flicked her tail and sauntered into the woods.

Jordan pulled her phone out and took pictures of each car, capturing the license plates. She stepped over to the second and noticed a third tucked back in the corner, obscured from her previous line of sight.

Pay dirt: a blue Toyota Camry with a kayak rack mounted to the roof. It had been backed into the space, the front plate still on the car, RHR-173. She walked around the back, and as expected, the plate was missing.

She tried to picture the white car from the night of the storm. The evening had been such a crazy series of events. Had the front and rear plates matched? Her attention hadn't been on the front. The high beams had kept her from seeing much of anything.

Who would have thought that the one car on the road during the storm had likely been driven by Deb's killer? Why had she taken Deb's car? Why pack up Deb's belongings and make it seem like she'd up and quit her job? Was it just to buy time? Or had she hoped the body would remained undiscovered? Why dump the car? Had there been damage from driving over the tree?

If only Sheriff Reid would work the case with her instead of shutting her out. Unless Sheriff Reid was responsible for the entire mess.

So how did Zoey Mitchell fit into all of this? That was the big question. Had she been the driver that night? Deb's notes in her citation book came to mind. They mentioned a sheriff hassling the tourists, not someone tooling around in a kayak. Besides, given the clothes in the kayaker's backpack, she wasn't of slight build. One thing was certain, Jordan had far more questions than answers.

She radioed dispatch and reported the find. She agreed to wait for the responding officer but really wasn't looking forward to another confrontation with Sheriff Reid. Hopefully, a good night's sleep had done them both some good. One way or another, this case needed to be solved. Otherwise, she wasn't so sure she wanted to move to an area filled with so much abrasive contention.

CHAPTER FOURTEEN

The big lunch rush had quieted down. Hanna cashed out the last few customers and cleared the tables. Finally, a moment to breathe. She flopped down at the counter and pulled her phone out of her pocket. Seeing the symbol for a new text message brought a smile to her face.

Jordan: *My office has sprung a leak. Rain is really coming down now. I would like to order a hot cocoa to go. Brr.* She added two snowflakes to the text.

Attached was a picture of Jordan. Her face was soaked, and her raincoat was beaded up with water. Hanna could even see little splashes on her shoulders where raindrops were landing. She had the best grimace.

Hanna: *Oh, I'm sure I could arrange something. I totally volunteer to help you shake the chill when your shift ends.* Hanna attached an emoji of a grinning devil smiley face, complete with horns and a pitchfork, along with two fire emojis.

Jordan: *I'm not sure if I should be excited or a little nervous.* She added a winky face.

"You've had that phone in your hands about a hundred times today. What gives? Got a hot date?" Ruthie asked from the back.

Hanna set her phone on the counter. Without a doubt, she'd checked it a hundred times throughout the day. Her heart did a little flip-flop of excitement whenever there was something from

Jordan. "Actually, I do…depending on how Aunt Dottie's feeling tonight. Jordan asked if she could pick me up later. She was hoping to meet Aunt Dottie before we take off."

"Sweetie, Dottie isn't up for meeting new people. Not the day after chemo." Ruthie said matter-of-factly. "Hopefully, your warden isn't stuck waiting on that tow all night. As far as I know, they still haven't dispatched a truck."

"Waiting on a tow?" Hanna asked.

"Yeppers. She found the car that was missing the back plate. She suspects it belongs to the missing kayaker."

Hanna stood and walked around the counter to the pass-through window. "How do you know all this? I've been texting with her all day, and she hasn't said anything."

"I doubt she would. Not over text. But it's perfectly legal to tune into the scanners, and they have been hopping like crazy again today. I brought the extra one in from my workshop. I have one set to the sheriff's frequency and the other set to the DNR's."

"You know the channel that the wardens talk on?" Hanna asked.

"Um…yeah. Cell phones are a newer technology, all things considered. There's nothing like a good two-way radio scanner or two to know the details of what's really going on." Ruthie wiped her hands on her apron and pointed toward the devices on top of the fridge. "I have a setup at home, one in the car, and one here. I always know what's going on. You just have to know what channels to listen to."

"Okay, so what all is going on with Jordan?"

"Well, let's see. Like I said, she found a blue Toyota Camry at Sportsman Landing, northwest of the dam. It was backed into the space, so the missing back plate hadn't been noticed when they cruised the lots. Not only that, but there was a kayak holder fastened to the top of the car, making the warden think the registered owner, Zoey Mitchell, is, in fact, the missing kayaker. She's also taken a report that a campsite had been robbed. The campers reported loss of a tarp, a bundle of rope, a sleeping bag, women's clothes, and the last of their food, which wasn't much. All while they'd been out on the water yesterday searching for the missing kayaker. Curious business, isn't it? Now, the sheriff's side's been considerably quieter. Not too much over the airwaves, anyhow."

"Holy crap. It's not always like this, is it?"

"Ha, hardly. Nothing like this ever happens up here. Normally, the scanner sits up there quiet as can be unless someone does a radio check."

"She's had to deal with the weirdest stuff ever since she got to town. Why on earth would she accept a permanent post given all this insanity? Why is all of this happening now?" Hanna threw her arms in the air.

"You really care about her, don't you?" Ruthie had been in her corner from the very beginning. Her advocate and cheerleader when everything seemed so upside down. She'd always been Hanna's confidant and a great judge of character.

"Yeah. I barely know her, but I see her, and I have the butterflies like a teenager. I can't explain it. These feelings…well, it's more than I've cared about anyone in a long time."

"Were you planning on staying with her tonight?" Ruthie asked.

Hanna must have had a surprised expression on her face.

"Oh, come on now. I remember what it's like to be hot for someone who totally lights your fire, and it's not like I expect you home by eleven. You're a grown woman."

Hanna laughed. "I hadn't made any definite plans, but it would be nice to spend some time with her that doesn't involve pulling a body out of the lake or finding a dumped car. Although, what we experienced between the two events was quite magical. The warden has some skills, let me tell you."

There were just a handful of people Hanna could be so bluntly honest with and one hundred percent herself. Curious, all of them lived in Waterdance. It was nice to have a safe space where she could speak so freely. More and more, Bobbie Rae's suggestion of staying and making her tinctures up here was feeling like the right thing to do.

"Well, thanks to the peaches, ginger, and your special candy, Dot's able to keep food and water down much better than she has in months. I've got things at home tonight and tomorrow morning. You go have some fun."

"Are you sure, Aunt Ruthie?"

"I am, if you don't mind opening the diner in the morning, that is?"

"I think I could handle that." Hanna couldn't wipe the smile off her face if she tried.

"I can finish the prep if you want to run out to the house and pack an overnight bag. No sense in her driving all the way out there to pick you up when you'll be coming right back here." Ruthie winked.

"All the way? The house is, like, three miles away, but I won't look a gift horse in the mouth." Hanna tucked her phone into her pocket. She walked around the counter to head out the back door where Ruthie's car was parked.

"Hey, kiddo. Take out that sack of trash to the dumpster for me, would ya?"

Hanna had been so lost in her thoughts that she would have tripped over it if Ruthie hadn't said something. "Yeah, no problem." She scooped up the knotted bag.

Jordan wasn't kidding. The rain was really coming down, and the dumpster was on the far side of the back parking lot, positioned in a concrete enclosure so the sanitation truck could easily empty it. Hanna sprinted across the lot, opened the gate, and stepped in, but the heavy plastic lid was already open. Odd. Typically, the lids were kept closed and latched to keep animals from getting into the trash. She tossed the bag into the side with the open lid and walked around the back to flip the lid closed. Three crates were stacked up like a set of steps.

She heard rustling coming from inside. Hanna grabbed the stick that they used to scare raccoons and carefully climbed on top of the crates to peek over the edge.

"I'm armed," she said, as if she could reason with a raccoon. A sudden movement startled her. She screamed and jumped down, but it wasn't a raccoon at all. It was a person, a woman. She swung a leg over the side and slid down the open lid into the small space behind the dumpster. Her hair and shoulders were soaked. Her skin and clothes were filthy, and her hair was a tangled mess. With cheeks stuffed full of food, she chewed on whatever was in her mouth, holding a fistful of fries. She tried to run around the other side, but the container had been dropped too close to the wall for her to get by. Hanna stood between her and the only way out. The women's eyes darted around, looking for an exit.

"Wait." Hanna tried to steady her voice. "If you're hungry, come inside. I can cook you something, anything. It's just me and my aunt in there."

The woman looked at the fistful of cold fries. She tossed them into the dumpster and wiped her hand on her filthy shirt. "I need to get back."

"Get back where?"

"Away from people."

"At least eat something before you go. It's cold and raining. Doesn't a warm meal sound good?" Hanna had no idea who this woman was, but no one should eat out of the dumpster.

The woman jumped up and hooked her hands on the top of the concrete wall. She tried to pull herself over but didn't seem to have the strength. Instead, she slowly slid back to the ground. Her eyes darted from side to side as if looking for an escape route.

"It's okay. I mean you no harm." Hanna held her hands up, hoping to calm the woman.

"Then let me out." Her chin quivered.

"Okay, okay." Hanna backed up. "If you're hungry, I have a chicken wrap inside. You're welcome to it."

The woman peered out from behind the dumpster until Hanna was halfway back to the diner. She scurried out of the opening and ran behind the enclosure. Hanna waited. After a few minutes, she peeked around the side.

"Something warm does sound good. I'll wait out here."

"It's raining. You're welcome to come inside where it's dry." Hanna stepped back and swung her arm toward the door in invitation.

"No, I'm okay here."

"At least wait under the awning." Hanna ran to the back door of the diner. "Ruthie, hey, Ruthie?"

"Yeah?" Ruthie called from inside.

"Would you hand me my chicken wrap? It's under the warming light." The lunch rush had been busy enough that Hanna hadn't had a chance to eat either. She'd stashed it beneath the warming light only to forget all about it.

"Sure thing. I thought you left?" Within seconds, Ruthie appeared at the back door with the basket of food in hand.

"Not just yet. I'll be right back."

Hanna carried the basket around the back of the building where they kept crates and other returnables under the awning. The woman watched her from the other back corner of the dumpster.

"Here, it's a chicken wrap and some fries. My name's Hanna. I just want to help you." Slowly, she snaked her way around trees, closing the gap between them.

The woman held out her hands and licked her lips. "Thanks. I'm starving." She picked up the wrap with her filthy hand and took a huge bite.

"Are you the missing kayaker? Are you Zoey Mitchell?"

She stopped chewing, and her eyes grew wide. She started backing up.

"Wait, it's okay. You're safe here. You can tell me."

Tentatively, the woman stepped back under the awning but kept a safe distance. Tears welled in her eyes, then trickled down her dirty cheeks. She nodded. "You didn't see me. I wasn't here. Please don't turn me in. I don't want to die."

"Wait, what? No one wants to hurt you. We've been combing the water looking for you. The entire community has been trying to rescue you. Come inside. The diner's closed. You can sit. I could get you something to drink, water, soda, coffee…anything you want."

Her jaw muscles tensed. She peered around Hanna, looking at the parking lot and beyond to the street. "I shouldn't. I'm not safe here. She knows who I am. She has my ID. She knows my car and where I live. She's looking for me. I gotta stay hidden until I can figure out what to do. Please, forget you ever saw me." Her words weren't making any sense. She looked terrified.

"Who has your ID? Who's looking for you?"

"The sheriff. It's not safe. Please don't tell her you saw me."

"Sheriff Reid?" Hanna was trying to take in every word. Was Jordan right about the sheriff? Was she involved? "Did you do something wrong?"

"No. Nothing wrong." Zoey shook her head. "I don't know her name. A lady sheriff."

"What's she look like?"

"About my height, real skinny, older than me, with hair like mine."

"Sounds like Sheriff Reid. How does she have your ID?"

"She stopped me. Said I had too many fish. I only had one. I kept saying I only had the one crappie. She wanted a hundred bucks to forget the whole thing. I didn't have it. I just wanted a few days in the woods away from my ex. She didn't care."

Hanna was trying to keep up, but none of this made any sense. Sheriff Reid didn't work on the water. Not unless she had to. "I know the warden. She's super nice. You can talk to her. She'll keep you safe."

Zoey emphatically shook her head. "The warden's dead. I saw it happen."

"No, the new warden." Hanna wished Jordan was here. "Wait. You saw it happen?"

Zoey shoved some fries in her mouth, chewed, and swallowed. "The sheriff took my wallet, my license, and was writing down my address, then the warden came along. The sheriff took off in her boat. The warden went after her and cut her off. They started arguing, so I got the hell out of there and hid. I saw everything through the reeds. The sheriff pulled a gun. There was a shot, and the warden fell. The sheriff tied her up and threw her body in the lake. She called out for me. Told me to come out. Said she knew who I was, and if I didn't come out, she'd hunt me down and kill me too. But I stayed in the reeds. After a while, she towed the warden's boat away. I was so turned around, I couldn't find my way back. Then, the storm hit, and I've been running ever since."

"You can't run forever. I'm telling you, the new warden will protect you. If you want, I can take you to her now. We've got a radio scanner. I know where she is." Hanna held up the keys to her aunt's car. "Apparently, she's in the parking lot next to your car."

"She found my car? I've been looking for it. Not that I have the fob. It was in the kayak, and the storm blew the kayak away."

Gravel crunched beneath car tires on the dirt road. Zoey ran to the far side of the dumpster enclosure and hid. Hanna turned toward the sound. She saw a grill guard similar to what's on the sheriff's car. Hanna's heart seemed to stop beating. She stood there frozen in fear as the vehicle came into view. She noticed a rusted red fender. Whew, it wasn't the sheriff.

"It's just an old guy in a pickup," Hanna said.

There was no response.

"Zoey? Come back. Jordan will know what to do."

Hanna walked around the enclosure and saw the empty basket on the ground. The food was gone, along with Zoey. She looked everywhere and didn't see so much as a swinging branch. Hanna had no idea which way she'd headed or where to begin to look for her. The rain was really coming down. Holy shit. What was going on around here?

Hanna picked up the red plastic basket and ran through the rain to the diner.

"That was quick. Did you remember your toothbrush?" Ruthie asked, her back to the door.

"I haven't left yet. Ruthie, the missing kayaker, she was in the dumpster. You won't believe what she told me. I have to call Jordan."

❖

Jordan's boat came flying up the river, throwing a tall rooster tail of water behind it. She slowed and coasted into one of the dockside spots behind the bar next to Bobbie Rae's old Lund. Like an acrobat, she hopped off the front of the boat and hooked her front mooring line to a cleat.

Hanna had seen people dock a million times, but she'd never seen someone maneuver a boat like that. Jordan was sexy as hell. Especially when she was behind the wheel of that boat.

Taking the steps up from the shore two at a time, Jordan ran until she was standing with Hanna beneath the awning behind the bar.

"You haven't told anyone about Zoey, have you?" Hanna asked. "She's totally freaked."

"Not yet, but I'm going to have to call it in. I can keep it off the radio and call my lieutenant directly. Can you show me where you saw her and where she ran into the woods?"

Hanna held Jordan's hand and led her to the back of the diner. "She was hiding back here when the truck drove by. When I walked around to tell her it was okay, all I found was the food basket. No Zoey."

Jordan spun a slow three hundred and sixty degrees. "Are there any cameras back here?"

"I don't think so. Let me call Ruthie. She had to run home to help Dottie." Hanna pulled out her phone.

Ruthie answered on the third ring. "How's it going?"

"Jordan just got here. Listen, are there any cameras around the back of the diner?"

"What, like, security cameras? Nope. I might still have a trail cam on a tree behind the dumpster. I don't know if the batteries are any good. We had a bear issue for a bit, and Deb wanted to know if it had a collar."

"Perfect. Thanks, Ruthie." Hanna disconnected the call. "Ruthie said there's a trail cam back there somewhere, but she's not sure it's on."

Jordan was squatting, staring at something on the ground. Hanna walked up behind her and leaned forward, trying to see what she was looking for. "Have you walked back here?" Jordan asked.

"Yes. I walked back there to find Zoey. She left the food basket at the back corner."

She pivoted slightly. "Can you show me the tread of your shoe?"

Hanna held up her foot.

"Thanks." Jordan stood but stayed crouched over. She used a stick to move ferns off to the side, slowly making her way along the garbage enclosure.

"Oh, look. There's the trail cam." She stepped around.

Jordan's arm shot out and blocked her path. "Stay behind me, please. I'm trying to find her shoe prints before the rain washes them away."

"Oh, sure. That makes sense." Hanna rolled her eyes at herself. She'd have made a horrible cop.

Jordan placed each step with great purpose and moved at a turtle's pace. Had it been Hanna's task, she'd have marched right in there, darting from spot to spot, probably trampling all over everything. It was obvious that even medicated, patience wasn't her strong suit.

"Okay, I found where her footprints overlap in each direction. The prints on top are headed out to the woods. You can grab the disk out of the trail cam now." Jordan unzipped a side pocket in her pants and pulled out a rugged cell phone-looking device.

"What's that?" Hanna worked to release the strap around the tree.

"You don't need to take it down. There should be a clamp on the side. Lift it, and the front panel should swing open."

"Oh, hey, you're right."

"Okay, inside, there should be an SD card like in digital cameras. It should release the same way, with a simple push."

"Got it." Hanna couldn't believe how proud she felt. She rushed to Jordan's side and held out her prize.

"This is a portable SD card reader. It's helped me solve quite a few cases. People forget that trail cams take pictures when you turn them on. There's usually at least one of the person who hung the camera." Jordan slid the disk into the bottom of the device. The screen came to life. Just like a phone, she used her finger to swipe right to go through the pictures.

"Hey, look. There I am, looking for Zoey. Oh, wait. There's Zoey," Hanna said excitedly.

"Let's see if we have a better shot of her face." Jordan flipped through a few more pictures. "Bingo. This one is clear enough that I can compare it to her ID." She powered off the device and tucked it in her pocket. "First, I want to follow her tracks before the rain washes them away."

"Can I come with you?" Hanna asked.

"It'd be better if you didn't. If what you said is true and the sheriff is tracking her, it could get dangerous. I'd offer you my truck, but it's at the boat launch with my trailer. Here's the key to my cabin. Go get a shower. Raid my suitcase if you need dry clothes. I'll send you updates. Okay?" Jordan's eyes pleaded every bit as much as her voice did.

How could Hanna say no? "Promise me you'll be careful and come back in one piece, alive and in one piece. That's an order."

"I'll do my best." Jordan leaned down and softly kissed her. "Besides, you have a promise to keep."

Flipping through recent conversations in her mind, Hanna wasn't sure what Jordan was saying.

"You promised to help me kick the chill." Jordan winked at her. "I'll see you later."

"You'd better 'cause I keep my promises."

Hanna watched her disappear into the woods. She told herself that Jordan did this for a living. She'd been doing this for years and years. She was careful and methodical.

Warden Deb Ryder had probably been all those things too, and look where it had gotten her. Hanna stood there staring into the woods until her teeth started chattering.

CHAPTER FIFTEEN

Jordan set her phone to silent and texted her location to her new lieutenant. Given everything Hanna had shared, she knew it was best to stay off the radio, at least for now. She'd shared updates with both the chief and Lieutenant Foley over the past few days. She'd even sent them copies of Deb's notes after her interaction with the sheriff at the discovery of Deb's car. They'd agreed she'd keep working both cases. The missing kayaker and the extorted tourists. The goal being to find definitive evidence to get the Wisconsin Department of Justice involved. Their investigators had the authority to take down a dirty sheriff. Zoey might just be able to provide that evidence firsthand.

Going slow was the key. With the day of steady rain, the footprints were difficult to follow. Zoey's stride wasn't consistent, either. Hopping left, then right around dense underbrush. Luckily, the rain had finally let up enough that it wouldn't erase the trail before she could find its end. Jordan released the tight noose of a top button around her neck and removed the hood of her raincoat. Now, at least she could draw in a full breath of air.

At long last, she spotted a green tarp strung up between two trees and tied off at the lower corners. The ends had been left long enough to fold over and keep the wind out. If this was Zoey's camp, she had some admirable survival skills. Jordan pinned her location on her phone, took a photo, and sent off a text to her lieutenant. *Approaching makeshift camp now. Update to follow.*

Lieutenant Foley: *10-4 Careful*

Jordan pocketed her phone. She drew in a deep breath and let it out slowly. She hoped her approach didn't backfire. "Hello, Zoey, it's Warden Pearce. You can call me Jordan. The warden that was killed, her name was Deb, and she was my friend. Hanna from the diner sent me to check on you. I mean you no harm."

There was a bit of rustling in the shelter. Jordan stayed still, holding her hands out to the sides, hoping to convey a trustworthy presence.

"Hanna sent you? Where is she?" a shaky voice asked from inside the shelter. "I like her. She's kind."

"I wasn't sure what I'd find out here, so I asked her to stay back at the diner. She still wants to cook you a warm meal. Anything you'd like. And like she said, I can keep you safe if you'll let me."

Jordan let the words marinate, worried that if she talked too much, it could do more harm than good. Minutes went by. The saving grace? At least Zoey didn't bolt.

"The warden, the one that was shot, she was your friend?" Her voice still sounded weary.

"Yes. We'd done several trainings together. Some say she was my doppelgänger. Truth be told, I never saw it. Her hair was longer, and she liked to wear ball caps."

The tarp rustled. "You do look a lot like her. She helped me last summer when I first camped on the lake. My kayak flipped, and my gear floated every which way. She pulled me into her boat and helped me get my stuff. This year, I used bungee cords like she suggested. She was pretty cool."

"Indeed she was. It's weird being up here without her." Jordan sat on a nearby tree stump. "Stuff like that is why we do what we do. It makes working in the rain more fun when you can help someone."

"I wish everyone with a badge felt that way."

"Me too." Jordan's response was honest.

The tarp flipped back, and Zoey peeked out. "Can you really keep me safe?"

Jordan remained still, her hands resting on her knees. "Yes, I believe I can."

"How? How will you keep me away from the sheriff?" Zoey asked.

"Well, I've looked into that. There's another agency more powerful than the sheriff's office. The Wisconsin Department of Justice has this special division of criminal investigation, often called the DCI. I can take you to them, and they'll stay with you to make sure you're safe."

Zoey stepped farther out of the opening, staring at her. "Does the sheriff know you're out here talking to me?"

"Nope. I haven't used my radio at all. She has no idea where I am. As far as she knows, I'm still standing next to your car waiting on a tow truck."

The wind swirled a familiar lavender scent around them. Jordan inhaled deeply through her nose. She shook her head. That scent was distinctly Hanna. A twig snapped nearby. Zoey's eyes grew wide. She backed into her enclosure, pulling the tarp across.

"Zoey, it's okay. It's just Hanna." Jordan turned toward the noise. "Apparently, she's too worried about us to stay behind as I'd asked."

Another twig snapped. "Guilty as charged." Hanna stepped out from behind a tree. "It's been a hell of a week. I had to make sure you were both okay."

"And if we weren't, your plan was what?" Jordan held her gaze. "Call the sheriff?"

"Let's not talk about the fact that we both know I had no plan. Can I just say that you're incredible? I had no idea how amazing you were with people. So patient and with such a calming presence. I'd trust you, ya know, if I was on the run. Hi, Zoey." She waved.

"Hey, Hanna. It's weird, but I'm glad you're here. Thanks for the food. It was really good," Zoey said, peeking out of the tarp. "You were right about Jordan."

"She's pretty great, isn't she?"

Jordan pulled her phone out and searched for the sheriff's department website. She pulled up the only photo she could find with Sheriff Reid in it and handed it to Zoey. "Is this the sheriff who harassed you on the water?"

"The picture is super grainy if I zoom in. I don't know. It looks like her, but it's not clear enough for me to be a hundred percent certain."

Jordan accepted her phone back. She looked at the zoomed in picture. Zoey wasn't wrong. It was pixelated a lot. "That helps. I'll see about getting a better photo. It's important to do this right."

Zoey nodded. "Okay, so what do we do now?"

What indeed. Now, it would seem Jordan had two people to keep safe and no truck nearby. She needed help. She pulled her cell phone from her pocket and sent off a quick text. The reply was exactly what she'd expected.

"Zoey, do you have anything personal or important in your tent?" Jordan asked.

She shook her head. "No. None of this is mine."

Jordan knew who most of it belonged to, but she left it alone. She stood and stretched her back. "Okay, if you two will come with me? I encourage you to be quiet. We don't know who else might be in these woods."

Many years ago, Jordan had explored every inch of the woods between the diner, the lodge, and the bar. She knew each swell, boulder outcropping, and valley like the back of her hand. Soon, they were at the edge of the woods near the back of the bar. Beyond lay a clearing that led to the boats on the river's edge where Jordan had met Hanna an hour or so ago.

"Hanna, you go first. Up the stairs to Bobbie Rae's place. She's waiting for us."

"Why Bobbie Rae's and not your cabin?"

"The sheriff knows where I'm staying, but she'd never suspect Bobbie Rae's. She doesn't know about our history."

Hanna nodded. She turned to Zoey. "We've known Bobbie Rae for more than twenty years. She's good people. You can trust her. We do."

With that, Hanna waltzed out of the woods as if it was any other day. She walked up the stairs and rapped on the door. It opened. Bobbie Rae invited Hanna inside, then waved Jordan in.

"Here we go." Jordan said. "Stay between me and the water. If anything happens, run for the river. My boat's down there, and I'll be right behind you. Okay?"

Wide-eyed, Zoey nodded. She stayed glued to Jordan's side in the fifty yards between the woods and the stairs. Jordan guided her to take the lead up the stairs and hoped her larger body would conceal her. Without incident, they arrived at the top landing and were ushered inside. Bobbie Rae closed the door and latched the dead bolt.

"You three okay?" Bobbie Rae asked. "Welcome. It's nothing special, but it's home."

Jordan accepted a handclasp. "I feel much better now. I like what you've done with the place."

"What? Oh, it's probably the first time you've seen it clean without Mom's shit everywhere."

"What I meant was, it looks like I'd expect your house to look like and not your mom's. It looks good. Listen, I've got to get back to Sportsman's Landing and call in about Zoey's car as if I've been there waiting all along. Afterward, I'll pull my boat and park at the lodge. Are you good to keep them stashed until I get back?"

"Hell, yeah. Like anyone with a badge has ever been up here. Well, besides you. Not to mention, every patron in the bar would have my back if needed. I won't let you down. Go, get done so you can get back."

"Thank you," Jordan said and turned to Hanna. "I'll be right back. Do you want me to stop by your aunts' house and pick up some dry clothes? I'll be going by their place once I have my truck."

"Let me worry about getting us dry clothes. You just go finish your shift and get back here safely, okay?" Hanna tugged on her collar.

She leaned down and kissed Hanna tenderly on the lips. "I won't be long."

"I'm going to hold you to that."

Losing daylight, she hurried back to her boat. She released her line and pushed off. Within seconds, she was cruising downriver at full throttle, hoping she'd make it back to the launch in time.

❖

The tow truck arrived fifty minutes after she did. He hooked up but kept his truck in place. "I have to wait for the paperwork. An officer should be along anytime. Apparently, the right hand doesn't know what the left hand is doing today. Like dinner isn't waiting for me at home." He checked his watch for the umpteenth time.

Jordan played along. "Tell me about it. I've been waiting so long that I haven't eaten since breakfast." It was mostly true. Especially the fact that she hadn't eaten, and she was starving.

Sheriff Reid's car pulled into the lot. After hearing the specifics of everything Zoey had experienced and witnessed, the mere sight of Sheriff Reid had Jordan's blood boiling. She was a disgrace to the uniform. Hell, a disgrace to humanity. One thing was certain, she deserved to rot in prison for the rest of her miserable life.

"Warden, I can't make much headway if I have to keep breaking away to collect your next piece of evidence," she said, snapping her gum as she approached. Maybe she'd choke on that gum. An overwhelming cloud of perfume assaulted Jordan's senses as much as the sheriff did. She could go the rest of life without smelling Beautiful by Estée Lauder ever again. "Warden, if you'll sign as the one who discovered the vehicle." Sheriff Reid handed her a file folder.

Jordan read the information on the form. Everything looked accurate, so she signed her name.

"Here's the paperwork, Earl. You can drop the car next to the Camry that you picked up yesterday and drop the file off to Cathy once it's locked in the lot."

"Will do." He grabbed the papers, signed where he was supposed to sign, and hopped into the cab of his truck. Seconds later, he was on his way.

"Any update on the warden's case?" Jordan couldn't resist asking.

"Come on now, you know I can't discuss an ongoing investigation." She hooked her thumb on her duty belt.

"You can, given our interagency cooperation. I think the correct statement is that you choose not to."

"It's early in the investigation. Hell, the autopsy isn't even done yet."

"Did you bring in a medical examiner to do the autopsy, or is good ol' Daniel winging it?" Jordan crossed her arms.

"I can't win with you, can I? I fully intend to do right by Warden Ryder. Mark my words." Sheriff Reid stared at her for a long moment. This was getting nowhere fast.

"Well, I'll let you get back to it then. You know, you could have sent a deputy out here to pick up the car."

"What, and miss out on your sunny disposition? Seriously, I wanted to ask you something. Yesterday, you thought these cases were related, the kayaker and the warden's murder. Do you think this car's owner, Zoey Mitchell, is our missing kayaker?"

"I do."

"Do you think she murdered the warden?"

"No, that's not my working theory."

"You don't think maybe the warden caught her doing something, and it escalated? You don't think a kayaker can pull a trigger? Why do I get the feeling you know something I don't?"

Jordan shrugged. "You've made it pretty clear that you expect me to...oh, how did you put it? Stay in my lane? I'm just a conservation warden, after all. So I'm doing what you asked and focusing my efforts on the missing kayaker, hence the call upon the discovery of her car."

"This whole mess is a clusterfuck, that's what it is. Okay, so tell me, what's your theory?"

Again, Sheriff Reid didn't act like Jordan expected her to. A guilty person wouldn't prod and dig, at least not typically. Was this a fishing expedition? Was Sheriff Reid trying to see how much she knew? Jordan had no intention of tipping her hand. Not if Reid was the one behind all this.

Jordan had another idea: share a bit of truth. If she was right, Reid would deflect at that point and try to steer the theory away from it. If not, she'd keep digging. "I think the kayaker was at the wrong place at the wrong time. I think she might have seen what happened to Warden Ryder. That's my theory, anyway."

"You think the killer is still out there? Do you think the kayaker is dead?"

"It's a possibility, I suppose. I mean, we haven't found her yet. Then again, we haven't found another body, either, and there's been plenty of folks searching the water. Nothing in her camp gave any indication that she was doing anything but camping. There were no drugs. No paraphernalia of such. She was health conscious. She had turkey bacon, for God's sake. Who knows what you'll find in the car, but I saw nothing suspicious through the windows." And, when she hadn't gotten the response she'd expected, she decided a little turnabout was fair play. "Here's a question for you. Why take the plates off the kayaker's car and put them on Deb's car? Why go through the hassle if you're just going to dump it into a ravine?"

"I've been bothered by that myself. Maybe the dump wasn't the plan? The stolen plates were from the same make of car. Color doesn't much matter. Cars get painted all the time. You say the driver drove over the treetops the night of the storm? Maybe it damaged the car? Maybe that changed the plan?" The response sounded genuine and thoughtful, not at all defensive. This conversation was much more like the one they'd shared at the station house instead of the one they'd had yesterday. Had she overreacted yesterday because of the lack of sleep? Could Zoey be mistaken? Could the killer be someone besides Sheriff Reid? Or was Reid a psychopath and a deft liar?

"The treetop did some damage. I still have part of the front bumper in my truck."

"Once all the evidence is collected, I'll see if Banjo and Chipmunk can take a look at the car. See if the treetop broke an oil line or drained the radiator, something that stopped the plan. Or maybe the killer is trying to frame the kayaker?"

"The thought crossed my mind." Jordan watched for any twitch or shiftiness or some kind of tell. Nothing. Sheriff Reid didn't react at all. Wow, she was good.

"Well, if the killer is trying to frame the kayaker, maybe we'll find a gun hidden in the car?"

"That'd be tough to do without breaking a window. Remember, the key fob was submerged in the kayak." Jordan tried to take away an avenue of planting evidence.

"Good point. Ya know, you do have a clever mind for this. Why didn't you become a detective?"

Jordan smiled. "Too much paperwork, and I don't like being stuck at a desk. I mean, this is my office." She held up her arms and turned in a circle.

"Well, you've given me some things to look into. Let me know if you find that kayaker. I'll let you know what I find in the cars. They found that missing child, so the crime scene folks are working on Deb's car as we speak."

That was the last thing Jordan expected her to say. Though, if anyone could plant solid evidence and get away with it, it would be the sheriff. Jordan needed to contact her lieutenant and figure out how to get the division of criminal investigators to take over the case, or Zoey could go away for something she had no part in.

Well, unless she had taken part.

Jordan chewed on that thought all the way to Sturgeon's Bay Landing where her truck and trailer were parked. Eyewitness testimony was sketchy, and she still had no solid evidence to connect Sheriff Reid to the murder or to the tourist extortion. Far too many questions and not enough answers.

CHAPTER SIXTEEN

As had always been the case, Aunt Ruthie had been right there to help. No questions asked. Years ago, no questions didn't necessarily mean no repercussions, but back in Hanna's teen years, that had never been the promise. While times were different now that Hanna was an adult, Aunt Ruthie was still right there whenever her help was needed.

She'd gotten Aunt Dottie settled, given her another half of a gummy, then packed up a bag of clean clothes for Hanna and delivered it to the bar. Hanna couldn't imagine not having her aunts in her corner. Or her life, for that matter. Both were absolute treasures. Fucking cancer. Dottie had to survive. She had to kick cancer's ass because the alternative, the thought of cancer winning, was too much to think about. She shook the darkness from her mind.

Rather than take a shower, Hanna towel-dried her hair and changed into some dry clothes. Zoey, however, lit up when Bobbie Rae offered her a hot shower. Who could blame her? She'd been out in the woods for a week, and the lake wasn't yet warm enough to be a decent substitute. She'd accepted in earnest. After a long while, the bathroom door opened, allowing steam to waft out in billowing plumes.

"There were times I wondered if I'd ever enjoy a blissfully hot shower again. Talk about prayers being answered. That was absolutely magical." Zoey inhaled deeply. "Okay, second only to whatever smells so amazing out here."

Bobbie Rae beamed, standing behind a proverbial feast displayed across the kitchen counter. "Figured you might be hungry. I wasn't sure what you liked, so I made a bit of everything. I might have gone a little overboard. Though, I'm betting Hanna and Jo-Jo haven't eaten, either, given all that's happened. Okay, I have water, milk, all sorts of soda, beer, and about any drink you can imagine. What sounds good?"

"Oh my, everything looks so good, but I can't pay for any of this. The sheriff still has my wallet."

"There's no charge. It's all on the house. What can I get you to drink?"

"Anything at all?" Zoey asked.

Hanna stood back and watched the exchange. Bobbie Rae would do anything to help a friend and might do the same to help a stranger if she was in a good mood, but this was something different entirely.

"Anything."

"After the week I've had, I'm thinking, a bourbon, neat, with an ice water chaser?"

"A woman after my own heart. Bourbon coming right up. How about you, Quinnie?"

"I could do a little bourbon. You pour. I'll get the ice water."

"You two are easy. I don't even have to run downstairs." She pulled a bottle of Henry McKenna out of a cupboard.

"Hey, wait. You don't need to waste the good stuff on me. Hell, Beam is fine."

"Are you kidding? We found the missing kayaker. We're celebrating. My house, my rules."

"You all have been so kind. Thank you." Zoey picked up the bright yellow Fiesta plate. Good, she left Hanna's favorite green one. "Normally, I try not to eat too much red meat, but that burger looks too good to resist." Zoey lifted the bun and spread mayo and ketchup before adding a slice of cheese, lettuce, onion, and tomato. "Oh, onion rings. I love onion rings and steak fries. I think I've died and gone to deep-fried heaven. Wait, deep-fried green beans and cheese curds, too? Pinch me!"

Hanna got a kick out of watching Zoey mound food on her plate. It was obvious Bobbie Rae felt the same way, given her ear to ear smile. Was it her imagination, or was there a little spark there? No doubt Bobbie Rae was kind and protective, but this... the over-the-top grilled and deep-fried spread, the special bourbon that she never pulled out, let alone the expression on her face, was most definitely something more.

"Quinnie, come on, I bet you're hungry too. Go on, make a plate." Bobbie Rae held out the green dish. Hanna loved that she remembered her favorite.

"Ya know, I am hungry." She left out the part about giving her lunch to Zoey earlier. She didn't want her to feel bad. "Everything looks terrific. Thanks for doing this."

By the time Hanna reached the end of the counter, her plate looked every bit as mounded as Zoey's. Bobbie Rae's plate looked sparse by comparison. The three of them sat on the floor around the coffee table in the living room. Bobbie Rae didn't have a dining room, let alone a big table. The six hundred square foot apartment had one bedroom, one bathroom, and the living room and kitchen combo. Her childhood bedroom had been on the old back porch once it'd been enclosed. And she'd shared it with the washer and dryer. Still, like Jordan had said, it was nice and homey and all Bobbie Rae, down to the sexy partial nude of Shakira hanging above the couch. A few tree leaves covered her breasts. It was a striking print.

"So, Zoey, where's home?" Bobbie Rae couldn't seem to tear her eyes away.

Zoey chewed and took a sip of bourbon. "Manitowish. I'm a bartender for the Ding-a-ling Supper Club. No joke."

Hanna laughed. "And all you could come up with was Drunken Loon Saloon?" Okay, maybe the bourbon was already making her feel warm and a bit fuzzy, but really? Ding-a-ling Supper Club? That was rich!

"No way! Seriously, this is the Drunken Loon? I've heard of it. I've always wanted to come up here. I tried to kayak up here last summer, but damn, that was way too far from my campsite." Zoey's eyes sparkled. "This place is a legend!"

"Thanks. I have a lifetime of blood, sweat, and tears invested in this place." Bobbie Rae smiled. "What brought you up to the flowage?"

Hanna was captivated. Beyond the three musketeers, she'd never seen Bobbie Rae so enamored or interested. Asking questions and engaging in conversation wasn't her thing.

"I needed a reset that only nature could offer. Well, that, and I had to get away from my ex. She works at the Ding-a-ling as a server. Seriously, I'm hoping she moves out of town by the time I get back. If not, I just might have to. The thought of watching her mope around all summer is more than I can bear." Zoey ate the last deep-fried green bean on her plate and stood. Was she headed for the sink or seconds?

She returned to the front of the line at the counter, scooping all sorts of food onto her plate. A girl after Hanna's own heart. Hanna devoured the last few cheese curds on her plate and stood, also eager to return to the line. Zoey took a second burger and decorated it as she had the first. Hanna didn't need or want another. Her interests were focused on the deep-fried sides. Zoey snagged a few onion rings from the half-full basket, same with the jo-jo fries. There was still plenty for Jordan. Besides, if anything ran low, Bobbie Rae would call down and have it refilled quickly. Hanna took a few of this and a couple of that, already feeling full, but it all tasted so good, she couldn't resist.

When she returned to the living room, Zoey had switched her seat to the other side of the coffee table next to Bobbie Rae. Each had their legs extended and was leaning back against the couch. They looked too comfortable to ask them to move. Instead, Hanna plopped at the end of the table and sat crossed-legged.

"So when all of this is over, are you going to try for a do-over on your nature reset?" Hanna asked.

"I spent most of my week on the run in the woods with no clean clothes, no shelter or coat, and no food. I think I'm natured out for the moment. What I want now is a warm bed, four walls, and a pile of pillows." Zoey tipped the last of the bourbon from her glass.

Immediately, Bobbie Rae was up and returned with the bottle. She poured Zoey a refill, did the same for Hanna, and set the bottle in the center of the table.

"Your glass is empty too. None for you?" Hanna asked.

"Nope, not right now. Jo-Jo left me in charge. I can't keep you safe if I'm blitzed off my ass, now, can I?" Bobbie Rae held up her water glass. "This is just fine."

"I haven't felt this safe since this crazy ordeal started. There were times I didn't think I'd make it out of the woods. I wasn't sure what would get me. Maybe starvation, hypothermia, or the sheriff, but I seriously thought I was done for. It's been wilder than fiction." Zoey took a bite of her burger.

Who knew what could have happened to her had she not shown up behind the diner? "I'm glad we could help—"

Someone knocked on the door.

Shit. What if it was the sheriff? They hadn't discussed exit plans if they needed to get out of there quick. There was nowhere to hide in here. Frozen in mid-chew, poor Zoey looked absolutely terrified.

With a finger to her lips, Bobbie Rae stood. The way she placed her hand on Zoey's shoulder seemed to calm her a little. She picked up a baseball bat that'd been leaning in the corner and raised it over her shoulder.

"Who is it?" Bobbie Rae asked through the closed door.

"It's me, Jordan."

Oh thank God.

Bobbie Rae stood on her tiptoes and peeked through the peephole. She sighed and released the dead bolt. "Dude, text next time. My heart can't take all this adrenaline." She closed the door behind Jordan and locked it. The bat was placed back in its corner.

"Trust me, I get it." Jordan unzipped her raincoat and hung it on the coat rack.

"Have you eaten? I could warm you up a plate." Bobbie Rae motioned to the counter of half-filled bowls and plates.

"Thanks for doing this. I've got it. You've done so much already." Jordan picked up a plate and made her way down the counter. After the microwave timer dinged, she walked into the living room and sat next to Hanna. "Hey, you," she said, bumping Hanna's knee with her own.

"Hey, yourself." Hanna rested her hand on Jordan's thigh. "Did everything go okay?"

Jordan nodded. "I'm back in one piece, as promised."

That was a nonanswer if she'd ever heard one. Jordan probably didn't want to talk about it in front of Zoey. Still, she couldn't deny being happy to see her.

"Jo-Jo, what can I get you to drink? Bourbon?" Bobbie Rae held up the bottle.

"Not while I'm in uniform. Water would be great."

"I've got it." Hanna jumped up.

"Zoey, you're looking much better than you did when I dropped you off."

"Thanks. I feel much better. I've been wondering, when do you think I could get my stuff back?"

"Honestly, I'm not sure. There's a lot to nail down before anyone can be charged. We'll need a formal statement from you, and you might have to testify to what you saw."

"How can I if people with badges want me dead? She's still after me." Zoey ripped tiny pieces off her napkin.

"Listen, I understand that you're scared. Please know that I'm not going to let anyone hurt you."

"How can you promise that, Jo-Jo?" Bobbie Rae asked. "You can't be with her twenty-four hours a day. What if Mighty Mouse has someone on the inside? It's on the TV, taking out witnesses, so it must happen."

"There's a huge difference between the Wisconsin Department of Justice Investigators and our small-town sheriff. Trust me, they'll want to take down a bad cop. It taints all law enforcement. You'll be protected, I'll make sure of it." Jordan's voice was so calm and assuring.

"You sure?" Zoey asked.

"Yeah, I'm sure. You've got my word," Jordan said.

"Okay. If you'll go with me, I'll do it." Zoey yawned. "Sorry. I'm stuffed and maybe a little buzzed."

"You've earned both." Jordan smiled and picked up her burger. "My lieutenant is trying to locate something we could use as a safe house for the night. It's not something the DNR typically does. As soon as I hear back, we can go. I'll be right there the whole time to keep you safe until—"

"You can't do that," Bobbie Rae said. "You're leading the search. People are going to be showing up in the morning. If you're gone, people are going to get suspicious. Wait a second, you haven't called off the search, have you?"

"No, of course I haven't called off the search. That'd tip our hand and put Zoey in greater danger. Dammit, there are a lot of moving parts right now."

Hanna watched the exchange, fascinated as two people who'd known each other as kids were getting to know each other again as adults. Their mutual respect was on full display.

"Zoey could stay here. She can have my bed. I'll sleep on the couch. My place is about as safe as they come. You need to be out on the water runnin' the show tomorrow."

"Bobbie Rae has a point. We were going to hang out tonight anyway." Hanna perked up at the thought that they'd still have some alone time together.

"You might be right. I need to be visible until we get a positive ID on our suspect and have her in custody."

"Cool. So you two head to cabin seven, and we'll stay here. If you're okay with that, Zoey?"

"Really? You don't mind having me in your space?" Zoey asked.

"I wouldn't offer if I minded. Ask these two."

Hanna laughed. "Just look at her. Does she look like she does anything she doesn't want to?"

"As long as I'm no trouble. Seems no one would think to look for me here. I'm comfortable staying."

Jordan pulled out a phone and sent off a text. Hanna glanced at the screen. Lt. Foley displayed in the upper left. Her lieutenant. Dots bounced in the lower part of the conversation, then a response popped up: *Your call. I trust your judgment.*

"I have my lieutenant's approval."

"See, it's cool, Jo-Jo. You'll be close by if I need you." Bobbie Rae sat up so quickly, it startled Hanna. "Oh, hey, can I have the walkie-talkie thing back?"

"No." Jordan's response was sharp.

Bobbie Rae slumped against the couch.

"I'm sorry, but radio silence is a must. Nothing about Zoey can go across the airwaves," Jordan said in a much softer tone. "It's too dangerous. If you need me, text me a simple 9-1-1, and I'll be here. I sleep light. My phone will wake me, especially under these circumstances."

"Roger that. If there's trouble, I'll text you 9-1-1."

"Thanks for the food. I was starving." Jordan popped the last bite of her burger in her mouth. She stood and carried her plate into the kitchen.

"You cooked. How about we clean up?" Hanna asked.

"Leave it. I'll wash the dishes in the morning."

"I feel like we're being kicked to the curb." Hanna bumped Bobbie Rae's leg under the table.

"Because you are." Bobbie Rae laughed and stood. "Look, Zoey can barely keep her eyes open. Go. Spend some time together. I'll see you two in the morning."

"Thanks for everything. I didn't know who else I could trust. Sorry I pulled you away from the bar. You're still the friend I can count on when shit gets heavy." Jordan held out her hand for a handclasp. It seemed to be their thing.

Bobbie Rae accepted and stepped closer for a half hug. "Hey, man, anytime. I'm always here for you, just like you were always there for me. I'm sure I'll be calling for your help again at some point." She stepped back, turned to Hanna, and pulled her into one of her famous Bobbie Rae hugs. "Quinnie, love you bunches."

Being back made Hanna realize how much she'd been missing her Northwoods family, especially her musketeers. "Love you too." Hanna squeezed and stepped back. She tucked her hand into Jordan's. "Good night, you two."

Jordan was quiet on their short walk to the cabin. She dug through both her front pockets before Hanna realized she was the one with the key. Thankfully, she'd remembered to pull it from her wet clothes that were currently in a bag on top of Bobbie Rae's washing machine. It would have been embarrassing to have to go back and cause another shot of adrenaline with a knock at the door.

But Hanna struggled with the lock. The damned key must have been off or something.

"Here, let me. It's finicky. I've finally figured out the secret." Jordan pulled the key out and slid it back into the lock slowly while turning it at the same time. Voila. It worked.

Bobbie Rae hadn't been entirely wrong when she'd called the Waterdance Lodge a dive. From the looks of the one-room cabin, nothing had been changed since the late seventies. Jordan removed her duty belt and hung it over a post at the foot of the bed. She removed her badge and name tag, setting each on the dresser, then unbuttoned and removed her shirt. The damp white T-shirt beneath stuck to her skin and showed off the outline of her sports bra.

"Do I have time to shower before you have to be back?" Jordan asked. She looked completely exhausted.

As much as Hanna had hoped for a lust-filled evening, it didn't seem like tonight was the best night for it. Besides, Jordan had to be ready to run to Zoey's aid if needed. Hanna stepped in front of Jordan and wrapped her arms around her waist. Her shirt was more than damp; it was soaked through. Jordan had worked all day in the rain, and her raincoat hadn't been all that effective. "I wasn't planning on going anywhere. I'm yours for the night if you'd like a snuggle buddy. I'll take a rain check on the evening I had planned."

"Care to join me? The tub is small, but it could be fun. I may surprise us both and rally." Jordan wiggled her eyebrows. Her eyes told a different story.

Hanna imagined a terrible game of slippery *Twister*, with a torn shower curtain and bodies falling clumsily onto a chilly floor. "As tempting as that sounds, I'll pass. Go. Enjoy your shower. I'll mind the phone for a text from Bobbie Rae."

Jordan leaned down and kissed her tenderly. "You are amazing. Thank you for everything today."

"I think it's you who's amazing. I'm in awe of what you do." Jordan shivered in her embrace. "Shower. Now." Hanna pointed.

Jordan pulled some clothes from her bag and disappeared behind the bathroom door. Hanna snagged one of Jordan's clean T-shirts for a pajama top and opted for nothing beneath it in case Jordan tapped into some energy reserves. She was changed and beneath the covers when Jordan emerged from her steamy cocoon. Dressed in a dry T-shirt and fitted boxers, she tossed her dirty clothes into a laundry sack, checked her phone, and crawled into the bed. Hanna snuggled close. This might not have been what she had in mind, but it felt wonderful. It'd been a good long time since she'd snuggled up in anyone's arms, and she fit perfectly in Jordan's.

"Really? The cologne?" Hanna buried her face in Jordan's neck. "Mmm, you smell so good. Give me strength. I plan on some very sweet dreams."

"Me too. Good night." Jordan shifted onto her side and rested her hand on Hanna's hip. At first, her thumb traced the swell of her hip. Before long, her hand caressed down to her knee with a light, teasing touch, then back up her thigh with a slightly firmer grasp.

How in the hell did she expect Hanna to let her sleep if she was going to touch her like that? The next caress, Jordan didn't stop at her legs. No. She caressed and cupped Hanna's bare ass before moving up along her ribs to the side of her breast. Hanna's breath caught.

That's it. Using her leg for leverage, she pushed Jordan onto her back, rolling on top of her at the same time and straddling her hips. She sat up and in the glow of the parking lot light and watched Jordan's hands explore from her knees to her waist before disappearing beneath her shirt. She closed her eyes and savored in Jordan's tender touches across her stomach, up her back, then she felt her shirt being lifted over her head. And just like that, she was completely naked. For a split second, Hanna felt self-conscious about her pooching belly and thick hips and thighs. No one could accuse her of being a starving model.

"So sexy. Oh, Hanna, you're beautiful."

Hanna looked down into Jordan's eyes, and the flash of insecurity melted away. Instead, she felt savored, sexy, and beautiful. "You make me feel all those things and more."

Jordan traced her collarbone with the tip of her index finger. "There was no way I could go to sleep with your beautiful body pressing against me. At least, not for a few hours yet."

"Good, 'cause I want you way more than I want sleep." Hanna captured her hand and teased her finger with the tip of her tongue.

"Hmm." Jordan surprised her by sitting up.

Hanna reacted quickly enough to pull Jordan's shirt up over her head and flung it to the floor. All that remained were her boxers. Finally, they were inside, on a bed, and all but naked. There was no need to be quiet, not when they were protected by four walls, a locking door, and a roof. Their time in the meadow was sweet heat, but this was going to be hot, unrestricted fun.

Jordan kissed Hanna with fiery passion and dialed the heat index to ten. Desire flooded her senses. Hanna was all about a good, satisfying orgasm, but being with Jordan was already next-level intense, and they'd barely gotten started. Before she knew what was happening, Jordan somehow lifted the two of them up and turned the tables. Hanna found herself on her back in the center of the bed with Jordan kneeling between her legs. Holy hot.

She pulled her knees together, blocking access. "Boxers off. I want you naked."

Jordan stood on the bed, looking at her with a mischievous glint in her eye. "I aim to please."

"No doubt you do," Hanna teased, and yet, her words were a truth she somehow knew deep inside.

Jordan pushed her boxers down and flipped them to the floor with her foot. "Better?"

"Hmm. Much." Talk about sexy. Jordan was a perfect balance of someone who loved both fitness and food. She was the woman of Hanna's dreams. "Dare I say, you're just as sexy in your uniform as you are completely out of it. Mmm, more so." Hanna fanned her face. "Come here, stud. Permission to come aboard has been granted." She rolled her eyes at herself. That sounded way less lame in her head.

The expression and sexy smirk on Jordan's face had her thinking it wasn't so lame after all. Jordan dropped to her knees between Hanna's legs. She leaned forward and looked into her eyes with the sweetest expression.

Hanna needed to feel the pressure of Jordan's body on top of her. She reached up and pulled. They fit perfectly together, and pressure was applied in all the right places. None of her past lovers compared.

Another long, hot, passionate kiss and she was a blazing inferno. Jordan's kisses melted her into quivering magma. The nibbles on her earlobes, the trailing tongue on her neck. Her touches had the power to ignite every single nerve no matter where they landed. Hanna couldn't get enough until she wanted more. Oh, so much more.

Jordan worked her way down Hanna's body. Slowly. Seductively. Nibbling, flicking, and teasing all the right places. It'd been a long, long time since she'd let anyone please her like that.

It always felt too personal, as if it was the next step to something more. Something like a commitment. That wasn't anything she worried about with Jordan. For reasons she couldn't explain, she welcomed both the pleasure and the potential next step. Jordan kissed her left hip, then her right.

"Oh, yeah. Baby. Don't. Stop." She buried her hands in Jordan's short hair, trying not to guide her to where she wanted that talented tongue.

Jordan didn't need any guidance. Not at all. She teased and pleased. Never in her life had Hanna felt such a push-pull pleasure. She had no idea what Jordan was doing to her clit. All she knew was that she didn't want it to stop. While doing miraculous things in just the right place, there was also pressure inside. The perfect amount of pressure. In and out. Wonderfully deep and fulfilling. The pace matched her hips that matched Jordan's tongue. Oh, what a talented tongue. *Don't stop. Don't. Stop.* Hanna began to shudder, quiver, and pulse deep inside. She didn't want to come yet, but there was nothing she could do to keep it from happening. Jordan made her feel so good. *So. Good. Oh. So. Whoa.*

"Jor—Oh…Yes." Hanna couldn't manage a complete sentence. Her brain misfired because her body was firing in double time on all cylinders. Her hips jerked, and she broke out into a sweat. *Don't stop. Not yet.* Fireworks, electrical jolts, and cascading, crashing waves of pleasure. She rode and reveled in every bit of it until she was left breathless and shaking. Still, she savored the aftershocks of pleasure.

Jordan slowed her pace, applying just the right amount of pressure. She kept her fingers deep inside, gently moving with Hanna's heartbeat. She felt all of it. Every blissful twitch enhanced the aftershocks and kept the orgasm rolling. Never before had she known a pleasure like this existed. Never.

At long last, she released the death grip she had on Jordan's scalp. "Come up here. Please." She was still breathless.

Jordan worked her way up Hanna's body, smothering her in gentle kisses and nibbles. Heaven. Absolute heaven. This time, her kiss wasn't fiery fervor. Instead, it was the tender side of passion. All the words, all the looks, all the facial expressions expressed in a sweet, passionate kiss. Jordan kissed her jawline, her earlobe, and her neck before tucking her face into Hanna's neck.

"I feel things with you that I've never felt with anyone before. I hope that doesn't freak you out," Jordan said in a soft and breathless voice.

"I couldn't agree more. Things with you are so different. You seem to know me better than I know myself." Hanna ran her fingers through Jordan's hair. "I only hope I can make you feel as good as you just did for me."

Hanna spent the next couple of hours trying to do for Jordan what she did for Hanna over and over again. Hopefully, the unimaginable pleasure was mutual. If Jordan's moans, quivering, and shaking were any indication, she'd been successful. At some point in the night, she curled up in Jordan's arms and fell fast asleep.

CHAPTER SEVENTEEN

Jordan blinked against the brightness of the parking lot light and rolled over on her side. She must have forgotten to draw the heavy curtains. Hanna shifted ever so gently in her arms. Lovely. She could handle waking up like this every day, though she'd prefer a slightly larger bed. A full-size bed was a tad small for just her, let alone two of them. Even so, it was the best night's sleep she'd had in a long, long time. Lying there, Jordan enjoyed staring at her sleeping beauty.

There was a gentle knock on her cabin door.

"What is it? Everything okay?" Hanna stirred.

"I'll check it out." Jordan leaned over and kissed her. "Good morning."

"Good morning." Hanna's smile lit up the room.

Jordan pulled on her shirt and boxers and peeked out the small window next to the cabin door. "Huh, it's Sheriff Reid." She pulled on a pair of jeans and a sweatshirt and stuffed her feet into her work boots without socks. "I'll be right back."

Jordan had the door cracked open when Hanna popped up out of bed.

"Shit! The diner. I'm supposed to open the diner today. Sorry, I gotta go." Hanna collected her clothes and ran into the bathroom. "It won't always be this crazy. Promise."

The comment had Jordan chuckling. Like her life wasn't just as crazy at the moment. If they enjoyed time with each other while it was all upside down and unpredictable, she imagined how much they'd enjoy savoring some quiet moments.

"Sheriff." Jordan stepped out onto the small porch. A loon called out from somewhere on the water. Was the haunting wail a warning of what was to come? Time would tell.

"Warden, sadly, I don't have much time. I need your help."

The cabin door flew open, then snapped closed as Hanna rushed out. She was dressed in her clean clothes from last night, though the tail of Jordan's T-shirt stuck out below the hem of her long-sleeved shirt. Her hair was sort of combed and back in a ponytail. Even messy and in a hurry, she was absolutely beautiful. "Sheriff."

"Morning, Hanna." Sheriff Reid nodded.

"Come by for some breakfast before you start your day, okay? See ya." Hanna squeezed Jordan's hand.

"See you in a bit." Jordan returned the squeeze.

It was clear Hanna wanted to say more, but the sheriff was standing right there. Keys in hand, she shot into the woods between the lodge and the diner. Jordan glanced at her watch and smiled. Hanna wasn't as late as she thought.

"Sorry, you were saying?" Jordan turned her attention back to the sheriff.

"Did you call the DCI and ask them to take over the case?"

"Me? No." It was an honest answer. She knew her lieutenant had made some calls, but she had not.

"I think it was the CSRU lead. Shit. I need your help. I think I'm being set up." She combed her fingers through her hair.

Jordan couldn't believe her ears. The sheriff wanted her help? "Being set up for what?"

"Ryder's murder. Who knows what else? They found something out at the warden's station house but won't tell me what. Jesus, I could actually go to prison." Sheriff Reid covered her mouth with her hand. She looked totally freaked.

"How about you start from the beginning?" Jordan wished she had a cup of coffee.

"The crime scene response unit arrived yesterday morning. They sent two teams, given all the evidence we had to process. I remembered the code for the lock and walked them through the station house. They found something of interest in the boat but won't tell me what. The other team got to work on Deb's car. Seems they found my prints, my hair, even a drop of my blood in the car. I only know this because Daniel's helping, and he gave me a heads-up.

"Warden, I'm telling you. I've never been in that car. I fully expect to be taken in for questioning. I know I've told you to put away your shiny gold detective badge, but I'm begging you to keep looking into this. Don't assume it's me. You love facts. Find the truth. Follow the facts. It's not me." Sheriff Reid covered her face with trembling hands. Her face was red, and there were tears in her eyes when she pulled them away. "Fuck. What a shit show."

Either she was very, very good at pretending, or she was telling the truth. Jordan didn't know what to believe. Until recently, she'd been ninety-nine percent sure it'd been the sheriff. She had a good idea as to what the CSRU team had found in the boat: Deb's notes. It clearly called out a female sheriff. Sheriff Reid had two deputies. Both were young men in their mid-twenties, newer to the job. So it wasn't like there were several female deputies out trolling the waters. What Jordan needed was a positive ID from Zoey. She was half tempted to grab her cell phone and simply take a picture of her. That would either clear Reid's name or seal her fate. She'd let the facts decide. Much as the sheriff noticed right away, she'd always been all about the facts.

Before she had a chance to step inside for her phone, headlights alerted her to the two cars coming up the road. They pulled into the lodge parking lot, boxing in the sheriff's car. Two officers dressed in professional attire exited each of the vehicles. They approached with their hands on their service weapons.

"Sheriff, we'd like you to raise your arms in the air," one agent said. "I will approach on your right and remove your weapon from the holster."

"Understood." Sheriff Reid held her arms up and stayed still. "Jordan, keep investigating. I'm counting on you."

The unnamed agent removed the sheriff's service weapon with a gloved hand and handed it off to another agent.

"You can count on me to follow the facts of the case," Jordan said.

"Are there any other weapons on your person?" the same agent asked.

"My backup is in an ankle holster on my right leg," Sheriff Reid answered. She looked into Jordan's eyes. "I understand, Warden. Please believe me when I say that someone is setting me up to take the fall."

The second weapon was removed from her ankle, and the sheriff was searched. They removed her duty belt, along with her badge. In all of Jordan's career, she'd never seen anything like it. She almost felt bad for Sheriff Reid. Well, only if she was actually innocent. However, if she was guilty, she deserved everything she got and more.

"Place your hands behind your back." There were metal clicks as a cuff was ratcheted down on one of her wrists.

"Guess it isn't just questioning if I'm getting this kind of treatment. Listen to me, Warden, follow the facts," Sheriff Reid said again while they secured her other hand.

It all seemed to happen in slow motion. As if they could have sat and had tea. A few occupants of the nearby cabins stepped out to watch the scene unfold. There'd be no keeping this under wraps until all the facts were known.

The agents read the sheriff her rights while guiding her toward one of the two cars. They helped her into the back seat. Once the agents were seated in the front, they started the car and left with the sheriff in custody. Jordan had an urge to wave but refrained.

"Can I get your name?" one of the two remaining agents asked.

A tow truck pulled into the lot and parked in front of the sheriff's cruiser.

Jordan stood to her full height, shoulders back. "Conservation Warden Jordan Pearce, badge 1409, Wisconsin Department of Natural Resources. And you are?"

"Agent Catherine Cline, Wisconsin Department of Justice, Division of Criminal Investigation." Agent Cline shook Jordan's hand. "I've been in contact with your lieutenant. I understand you have a witness?" She looked at her phone. "A Ms. Zoey Mitchell? I can take her in for a statement."

There were a thousand ways this could go wrong. Certainly, the DCI was a seasoned, professional organization that she'd been begging to take the lead on Deb's case since the beginning. However, if Sheriff Reid was, in fact, innocent as she'd professed, and the DCI simply took Zoey's statement, then the sheriff could go down for something she might not have done. Jordan knew she'd be overstepping to insert herself in the investigation, but she couldn't help it.

"I promised the witness I'd accompany her. It's the only way she'll give a statement." That wasn't entirely true, but Jordan had promised to keep her safe. "Will you take the statement at the sheriff's office or in Wausau?"

"We'd like to question you too. I understand you found the victim's body?" Agent Cline asked.

"Technically, others in the search party found the location because of activity in the water. It's all in my report. I was the primary to recover the body," Jordan clarified.

"If you and Ms. Mitchell could be at the Wausau location by one this afternoon, that would be great." Agent Cline handed Jordan her card. "Please, ask for me."

"Will do. You haven't mentioned her over the airwaves, have you? I haven't called off the search. Because the suspect"—Jordan motioned up the road—"appears to be in law enforcement, I asked the lieutenant to keep the fact that we found her quiet."

"She conveyed the request. Nothing about Ms. Mitchell has gone across the airwaves. Nothing will until it's confirmed we have the right person in custody."

"Thank you." Jordan nodded and watched the cruiser being pulled up onto the flatbed. When it was secured, the agents returned to their car and followed the tow truck up the road.

There was a lot happening before any coffee. Jordan cleaned up and dressed in a clean uniform, keeping the black band on her badge in honor of her fallen colleague. Before making her way to the diner, she climbed the outside steps to Bobbie Rae's apartment. She knocked and waited. No answer. She texted. No reply. She knocked again. Nothing. What on earth? She called and let it ring until it went to voice mail, then called again and again until at last the call connected.

"Shit," a groggy voice said, then there was crackling and a thud, as if the phone fell to the floor. More static and the call disconnected.

Hoping Bobbie Rae was somewhat awake, Jordan knocked on the door one more time. Time ticked by in slow motion. At last, she heard footsteps. The dead bolt released, and the door cracked open, still chained.

"Jesus, we just fell asleep. It's, like, predawn, Jo-Jo." She released the chain and waved Jordan inside.

Bobbie Rae's spiky eighties Joan Jett hair was wilder than ever with a serious case of bedhead. Her tank top, backward and inside out, only covered one breast. Her right hand covered the other. Her left hand clutched at the lacy panties that were far too big for her delicate frame and threatening to slip right off her.

"Fun night?" Jordan tried to bite back the laughter that yearned to escape.

"I can't find my underwear." Zoey called out from the bedroom.

"I think I have them on." Bobbie Rae looked at her waist. "Yep, these definitely aren't mine."

"How about I give you night owls a minute to wake up? I'll walk over to the diner and pick up breakfast. Any requests?"

"First, you can forget that you've seen any of this," Bobbie Rae said in a hushed tone.

"Haven't seen a thing," Jordan winked.

"Good. I'll have a breakfast burrito and hash browns."

"Oh, that sounds good. Me too. Oh, and I'd love a cup of coffee, with cream and sugar, please." Zoey called out from the bedroom. "Morning, Warden."

"Morning, Zoey." Jordan opened the door. "Lock up behind me. I'll be back."

"Later, gator."

Jordan waited until the door closed and the dead bolt latched. She shook her head and trotted down the stairs. Only Bobbie Rae could turn witness protection into a full-service offering.

The woods between the bar and the diner were alive with vocal spring birds and chattering squirrels. She was certainly wearing a path between the locations. Hanna looked through the pass-through window when the bell jingled above the door. Oh, that smile. Jordan adored her brilliant smile. She came around the counter, wiping her hands off with a towel.

"Sorry I had to rush off like that. Hey, I heard they arrested Sheriff Reid right in front of your cabin. Holy shit."

Jordan reached up and kneaded the back of her neck. "I had a feeling there'd be no way to keep that genie in the bottle."

"Yeah, definitely not. It's been all the chatter this morning. Luckily, it takes the focus off the missing kayaker," she said that last part quietly.

"There is that. I'll call off the search later this morning once I know more." Jordan stretched her neck. She really needed a different bed. "Hopefully, all this can be put to rest soon. I'd really like more uninterrupted time with you."

"Mmm, that sounds lovely. Even if last night wasn't exactly how we'd planned, it was incredible."

"Incredible indeed. It's been a long time since I felt that good and slept that well. Is it too late to run away together and escape the insanity?"

"Don't temp me. Hopefully, we can have some more alone time soon."

"With any luck, we're close to closure. Don't suppose I could talk you out of a cup of coffee? I'll also need three large coffees to go, three breakfast burritos, and three hash browns, if it's not too much trouble."

"Easy peasy." Hanna's smile and sparkling eyes said all the things that shouldn't be said in front of customers.

"Hey, Hanna, can I get a refill?" A man in one of the booths held up his hand.

"I've got it." Jordan stepped behind the counter and grabbed the coffeepot. She poured a cup for herself, then made the rounds. Thankfully, there were only a few customers dining in so far. Before long, Hanna had three to-go boxes stacked in a paper sack and three large coffee cups in a carrying tray.

Jordan put two twenties and a ten beneath her empty coffee cup. "I have an all-day errand to run. I'm not sure what time I'll be back."

Hanna winked and played along. "Well, be safe. Text when you can. I'll see how Aunt Dottie's doing…maybe I could see you later."

"Now that gives me something to look forward to." Jordan returned the wink. "I'd better get going. Thanks for breakfast. I'll be in touch." She found it more and more difficult to tear herself away from Hanna's company.

❖

It felt weird driving the truck without the boat trailing behind. Fed and freshly showered, Zoey fell fast asleep almost instantly.

The two-hour drive left Jordan noodling over a sea of questions. She hoped that her time spent with the fine agents at the Division of Criminal Investigation offered some much needed answers. Often, Sheriff Reid came to mind. So much pointed toward her guilt, yet, despite that, her desperate pleas were sincere and unexpected. A contradiction of epic proportions.

Ten minutes before their arrival, Jordan stirred Zoey back to life. She pulled into a drive-thru coffee shop and refilled the two travel mugs that Bobbie Rae had sent along. "How are you feeling?" Jordan shifted the truck into park and killed the engine.

"Maybe I shouldn't have eaten. I feel a little like I could puke."

"Draw a deep breath in through your nose and exhale through your mouth with pursed lips. Like this." Jordan demonstrated the calming technique. Zoey breathed with her, then again, on her own.

"Does that help?" Jordan asked.

Zoey nodded. "I've never been through anything like this. I'm a nervous wreck."

"If you want me present while you make your statement, just say the word, and I'll be there." Jordan opened the driver's door and slid out of the seat.

"Yes, please. Word, word, word, was that enough words?" Standing next to the open passenger door, Zoey's eyes pleaded her case every bit as much as her request.

"Come on. This is the first step to getting your life back. Let's do this." Jordan walked with Zoey to the entrance and ushered her inside.

Efficient routine had them checked in and waiting in a small conference room. Agent Cline didn't make them wait long, though she struggled with their names. While Jordan admired the efficiencies and resources available in the agencies present in a larger city, she immediately missed the personal element offered in small towns, in little communities like Waterdance, where the plates weren't always overflowing with havoc. A week ago, she wouldn't have even understood that there was a difference. Hanna had been the one who'd opened her eyes to that one.

"Ms. Mitchell, I'll take you back for your statement. Warden—"

Zoey's eyes grew wide. She stepped closer to Jordan. "No, I want the warden to stay with me."

"Agent Cline, at this point, are you prepared for a lineup?"

"Yes, we are. The sheriff's attorney just arrived, so as soon as they're done talking, we can do a lineup."

"Perfect. Let's start there. I haven't had the opportunity to confirm that the person you have in custody is the same woman who Ms. Mitchell dealt with on the water." Jordan almost mentioned other evidence, but she refrained, not wanting to taint Zoey's ID.

"Of course, follow me," Agent Cline said and led them down a long hallway. She opened the first door after a right turn. "You two can wait in here. Her attorney should join soon. I'll make sure we're ready to go. Once the ID is confirmed, I'll get your statement."

Jordan stood next to Zoey at the window. "They won't be able to see us, and unless we shout, they can't hear anything we say. When they come in, see if any of them stand out as the person you saw on the water. Think about the sheriff's voice and mannerisms. If there's something specific you remember her saying, we can have it said by each person for a comparison. Above all else, don't feel pressured. Be honest and take all the time you need."

About ten minutes later, an older woman entered the room, dressed professionally and carrying a briefcase. Likely, she was Sheriff Reid's attorney. Did the sheriff pick someone randomly after she'd been arrested, or did she already have an attorney on retainer? Curious situation to be in, that was for sure. Jordan acknowledged her but didn't speak.

At last, Agent Cline returned to the room. "They should enter at any moment."

Six women entered a room on the other side of the glass. Numbers had been painted on the floor and on the wall above their heads. They were all dressed in a black shirt and dark gray slacks, similar to the sheriff's uniform. None of them had patches on their sleeves or any marking that made them stand out.

Zoey was quiet for a long moment. "The sheriff on the water was super skinny like numbers two, three, and five, but none of them look right. Oh, and the sheriff from the water had a four-leaf clover tattoo on the back of her right hand, between her thumb and her first finger. I don't see the tattoo on any of them."

Zoey seemed to scan the room, focusing on each woman. "Also, she said the word license weird. When she asked for my fishing license, she said it like fish'n lye-sense."

Agent Cline pressed a button. "Starting with number one, please step forward and say fishing license."

One at a time, each woman stepped forward and said the phrase.

Zoey turned to Jordan. "None of them sound right. Maybe if they say, can I see your fishing license?"

Agent Cline pressed the button again. "Starting with number one, please say, 'can I see your fishing license?'"

Zoey sighed. "None of them are saying it like the sheriff on the water. Number two or number five could maybe be her sisters, but I don't think either is her. The lips are wrong, and her hair is a little different."

Number five was Sheriff Reid. Jordan felt a blend of excitement that she hadn't been identified as the killer and sadness because of the same reason. The sentiment surprised her a little.

"Are you sure?" Agent Cline asked. "Because all the evidence—"

"Agent, refrain," the attorney cut her off.

Agent Cline pushed a second button. Shortly after, the side door opened, and the six potential suspects filed out, including Sheriff Reid.

"I think I have the sheriff with the tattoo on video. It should have caught a picture of her or at least recorded her voice."

Reid's attorney perked up. She turned to Zoey. "Where's this video? I'd like to see it."

"Gumball machines have stick-on tattoos. It could still be your client. Lineup is over. You can go." Agent Cline opened the door and pointed down the hall. "Ms. Mitchell, stop talking. Warden, I'd like to speak with you two in the conference room, now."

When the conference room door was closed, Agent Cline spun to face Jordan and Zoey. She had fire in her eyes. "Video? Why am I only now hearing about a video? I had the sheriff arrested in front of her community. I've been interrogating her for hours, and now you're telling me she's not the right sheriff, and you have a fucking video?"

Jordan stepped forward. "Things happened fast yesterday."

"I'm sorry." Zoey's chin quivered. "I forgot all about it until just this moment."

"Everyone's doing their best given the situation. Zoey is scared and has been on the run. I think you'd be happy to get concrete evidence, even if it's after the arrest. Isn't the point to get the guilty party?" Jordan turned to Zoey. This was game-changing news. It would offer definitive proof. "You seriously have a recording?"

"Yeah, the loons were so active that morning. I had the GoPro clipped on the band of my hat. One of those floppy brimmed hats to protect your ears and neck and face from the sun. The way it captured everything I saw and didn't pick up the motion of the paddle was perfect. I tested it out the day before."

"Okay, so where's this camera now?" Agent Cline asked.

"I stashed it. I saw the idea on a TV show, like it would give me leverage if she caught me. Let me think. I stayed hidden until she towed the warden's boat away. I tried to get back to my site, but I was so turned around, I cut across some big open water and paddled forever, then the storm hit. Wow, the lightning was intense. I had to get off the water. I hid under a really dense pine tree that night and still had my stuff. The kayak was onshore but at some point, blew away. The next day, trying to carry loose stuff wasn't working, so that's when I stashed it."

"Do you remember where?" Agent Cline stepped forward. "It's extremely important we get this evidence."

"The morning after the storm, I followed the shoreline forever and walked across the dam. I heard a car coming up the road and swore it had a light bar. At that point, I still had my life jacket and my hat on. I ran along the shore until I found a narrow part. I stripped to my bra and underwear, wrapped my dry clothes in my hoodie, and swam across."

"Wasn't the water freezing?" Jordan asked.

"It wasn't pleasant, but it was better than dead. Once I got to the other side, I ran into the woods. There was this hollowed-out log. I put the camera and my cell phone in my hat. I powered it off so she couldn't use it for tracking, 'cause you know they do that, and put all of it inside my life jacket, rolled them up like a burrito and stuffed them inside that log. I kinda slept there that night and eventually found the Big Island Trail."

"I know the island well. Keep talking, and maybe I can figure out where you hid the camera."

"Well, for a while, it felt like I was walking in circles, but I finally found a spot where the trail teed at the power poles. I remembered seeing that on a map. I went one way, and the power poles kept going when the trail turned to the left, so I turned around and followed them back the other way. Later, I found a campsite with a tent and a cooler, and the people were gone, so I snagged some stuff and some food."

"Campsite F-4. I interviewed that couple after the theft."

"I'm sorry if I ruined their trip. I didn't mean to, but I was cold and starving, and I had to keep going. Eventually, I found the bridge that connects the island to the mainland. I had an idea where I was at that point and made camp in the woods behind the diner. Then, Hanna found me, and the rest is history."

Jordan's mind was reeling with all the information. "Was your phone working when you were kayaking? Maybe it synced your video up to the cloud?"

Zoey shook her head. "I bought the camera on my way up and hadn't set any of that up yet. There wasn't a strong enough signal at my campsite to create an account and sync."

"Do you think you'd recognize where you swam across? We could go out there on my boat." Jordan was antsy to get her hands on that GoPro. She only hoped it had a clear shot of the murderer.

"Yeah, I think I could get us pretty close." Zoey sounded upbeat, almost excited.

"I'd have to insist on tagging along. There's a chain of custody issue," Agent Cline said.

Jordan smiled. She knew that wasn't entirely true. She was a law enforcement officer, and if she found the evidence and turned it over to the DCI, the chain of custody would be intact. Still, she understood Agent Cline's aggravation and why she wanted to see this through.

"If you want to go, we need to head out now. There's a two-hour drive north, and we're burning daylight."

"Are you always this gung ho?" Agent Cline asked.

"Yes, when it comes to facts and data, I'm all in. Can I have two minutes with the sheriff before we head out?" Jordan asked.

"It's entirely up to her."

"I think she'll want to see me. Lead the way." Jordan stepped out of the conference room and followed the agent to a room down another hall. When the door opened, she heard Sheriff Reid sigh. She turned toward the door. Was it Jordan's imagination, or did her eyes light up just a little?

"I wanted you to know. We found the kayaker."

"Really? That's great. Is she okay?"

Not necessarily the response of a guilty person. More and more, Jordan considered the possibility that Sheriff Reid was actually being set up. Still, she'd wait for the proof. "Ms. Mitchell had a GoPro camera with her. She recorded the murder."

Relief flooded her face. "Hallelujah! Thank you. When am I getting out of here?"

"I don't have the camera just yet. I'm headed north now. So you're telling me…it won't be you hassling the kayaker? It won't be your finger on the trigger?"

"Warden, get that camera. It's not me. I'm telling ya, I'm being set up for all of this. I just can't for the life of me figure out who or why." Sheriff Reid scrubbed her face with her hands.

"Stay put. I'll be back as soon as I have solid evidence."

"Like I'm going anywhere." Sheriff Reid gave Jordan a sad look. "Please, get the camera. It will prove my innocence."

Was Jordan hoping for innocence or guilt? Only the evidence could determine that. For now, she needed to get back to the flowage and find that camera.

CHAPTER EIGHTEEN

Sheriff Reid's arrest was the hopping hot topic at the diner. Everyone assumed the charges were murder and seemed to have an opinion as to why she would have killed the warden. It was interesting how no one came to her defense. No one said they had the wrong person. No one urged everyone to hold judgment until the facts could come to light. Total small-town mob mentality at its finest. Had it been a century earlier, would the townsfolk have had her hanging from the nearest tree before the investigation could be final?

It wasn't like Hanna had strong feelings either way, but she'd like to think that the whole "innocent until proven guilty" was a good place to start. She'd known plenty of people throughout her life who were assumed guilty until proven innocent, and that was a tough spot to be in.

Jordan didn't seem like the kind of person who'd jump to conclusions. Hanna could already tell she was a woman of data and facts. Still, when they'd found the car, she was the first to accuse Sheriff Reid of tampering with evidence. Did she know more than she was letting on?

Probably. She was knee-deep in everything that was going on in town. Yet, Jordan had integrity. She'd sworn an oath and didn't talk about open cases.

Yeah, but the day they'd found the car, she'd had fire in her eyes that had blazed so—

"Earth to Hanna." Ruthie snapped her fingers. Somehow, she had snuck out of the kitchen and sat next to her at the counter without her even realizing it.

"Shit. Sorry. I was thinking about all the craziness."

Ruthie smiled. "I could tell."

"What do you think of the sheriff being arrested? Do you think she murdered Warden Ryder? Do you think she's guilty?"

"Ah, honey, I think it's too soon to tell. Nothing's been released. We don't even know why she was arrested. Maybe she has outstanding parking tickets or owes past alimony. Momma always said, don't jump to conclusions."

Hanna patted Ruthie's hand. "See, that's why I love you. Always fair and open-minded."

"Unless you mess with my family, then I'm all protective grizzly, and everyone best stay clear." Ruthie growled and raised her hands like clawing paws.

She wasn't wrong. Hanna had seen her in grizzly mode, and it was some scary stuff. "What'd you need?"

"I wondered what your plans were for the afternoon." She walked around the counter and poured a cup of coffee. She held up the mug. "Want a cup?"

"No, thanks, I've had too much coffee already." Hanna shook her head. "Nothing planned that I'm aware of. Jordan's working. This case has her going twenty-four seven. I'll be so glad when it's over. Why? What's up?"

"Dottie's feeling better and has asked for dinner on the porch. She shouldn't be eating anything from the griddle or the fryer. How about I close up and do prep while you run up to Mercer and grab us a rotisserie chicken and some potato salad? She likes the German kind with bacon. Nothing mayo based. Oh, and a few more cans of peaches. We're about out."

"Wait. Did she ask for chicken? For potato salad? Are you telling me this is Dottie's idea? Oh my God, that's so awesome. Woo-hoo! She'll be able to recover from her treatments so much better with some good food in her system." Hanna reached across the counter and gave Aunt Ruthie a high five.

"I couldn't hardly believe it myself when she called. Honey, you should know whatever Dot wants, I'm gonna get it. Anything to help her be strong enough to kick cancer's ass." Ruthie pumped her fist in the air like Rosie the Riveter. "So if you'll run to the store…"

"Sure thing, Aunt Ruthie. If there's anything else, just text me." Hanna jotted the items down on her order pad as fast as she could. "Okay, I'm off. I'll see you at home with dinner soon."

She was in too good a mood to listen to the scanner and the commotion surrounding Waterdance. Instead, Hanna connected her phone to the stereo system in Aunt Dottie's car and blasted her favorite tunes. The speakers cranked out fun, amping beats that got her in the groove as she rolled down the two-lane highway. Rocking her head back and forth, the fifteen minutes to Mercer melted away too fast and felt too short.

No sooner had the automatic doors at the grocery store whooshed open than she was assaulted with gossip. Men and women alike stood in small huddles, all talking about the sheriff's arrest. While she'd expected the conversations in Waterdance because the arrest occurred right next to the diner, she hadn't considered how fast the news would spread or how much the story would change. Stories ranged from the sheriff being found with a smoking gun in her hand to the sheriff helping pull the body from the water and pretending like she'd never seen the warden before. Typical grade school telephone game stuff where the first kid told the next what kind of sandwich he had for lunch, and the info spread from ear to ear around the circle. Until the last kid was asked what kind of sandwich the first kid ate, and ham became egg salad. It wasn't that Hanna knew the truth, but she knew more than these folks did. At least she'd been there when the body was pulled from the water. And, no, Sheriff Reid's business card hadn't been stapled to her forehead. People were ridiculous.

Hanna wanted to cruise the aisles and get a few new things for Aunt Dottie, but the longer she was in the store, the more she longed to be home. Besides, Dottie wanted dinner on the patio, and she didn't want to delay that. She paid for the chicken, potato salad, and peaches and got the hell out of there.

She blasted her music even louder on the way home. She was looking forward to serving up a good meal for Dottie and spending some time with her. That was precious time that she didn't want to miss out on.

Ruthie's car wasn't in the driveway when Hanna parked. She collected the few bags and made her way up the back porch. The lilac bushes on either side of the porch were in full bloom. Hanna stopped on the top step and drew in a deep breath. Lovely. Only the screen door stood between her and the kitchen, allowing the sweet scent to float on the warm breeze throughout the house. Hanna smiled when the spring on the screen door pulled it closed behind her with the familiar thud. That sound never grew old.

"Is that my favorite niece?" Dottie called from the living room.

"Ha! I'm your only niece." Hanna laughed. Little moments like this reminded her of how good it felt to be home.

"Aye, doesn't mean you're not the favorite." Her aunt's voice sounded strong and cheery.

Hanna smiled. She put the chicken and potato salad in the fridge and walked into the living room. Aunt Dottie was sitting in her easy chair instead of lying on the hospital bed.

"Look at you, all spry and chipper. If this isn't a lovely sight."

"All your remedies, along with a little food in my system, has me feeling stronger. How about we visit on the porch over a glass of iced tea while we wait for Ruthie? She's got you working so much that we haven't had two minutes to sit and chat. It's a beautiful day."

"I'd like that. Front or back porch?" Hanna kissed her aunt's cheek and eyed the portable commode. It was empty, which meant that Aunt Dottie'd had the energy to get to the bathroom on her own. She must have been feeling stronger.

"Front porch. The lilac smells so good out there." Dottie pointed at her walker and pushed up from her chair. "I love having you around again. Such a treat." She patted her cheek.

Hanna helped her get settled in one of the taller Adirondack chairs. It was deep and high-backed like its traditional cousin, yet offered the seat height for someone with a bad back and not so great knees. Bonus, they rocked. Hanna had always loved the style. They were deep and comfy, like sinking into a hug, with a moveable arched footrest, and didn't take a somersault to get out of.

She ran inside and returned with two glasses of iced tea. She set the one with a straw in it next to Dottie. "After dinner, I can cut a bouquet of lilacs for the house if you'd like," Hanna offered.

"You're a good egg." Dottie picked up the glass and took a long sip. "Thanks again for coming home. I know we put a kink in your plans."

The tea was strong, ice-cold, and refreshing. Perfection. "You're kind to say that, but we both know it's been a good couple of years since I've had any plans at all. It's like I've been trying to find my footing again."

"Well, that being said, you certainly didn't plan on running the diner. Years ago, you made it very clear that the diner wasn't your jam." Aunt Dottie used air quotes when she said jam.

Hanna laughed. "Honestly, it's not as bad as I remember it. It's like the hub of our little corner of the world, and the customers are fun, mostly."

"There are a few that will always be grumpy and gruff, but the many make up for the few." She took another sip of tea.

With raised eyebrows, Hanna shot her aunt a look. "Yeah, most of the time."

"Have you heard anything about your Winnebago?"

Where were all these questions coming from? Hanna knew her aunt was getting to a point, but she was taking the long way getting there. "Banjo and Chipmunk think it might have a rod knock. I don't know a whole lot about engines, but I know enough to know that's bad. They said it's already been rebuilt once, something about the cylinders and jugs or whatever." Hanna waved her hand dismissively. "Bottom line, Winnie might need a whole new engine."

"Are you still enjoying life on the road?" Dottie pushed her feet against the footrest, gently rocking her chair.

"I haven't given it much thought. I've been a little preoccupied trying to take care of you and Ruthie, helping at the diner, and all that. Funny, I come home and realize how much I've missed both of you, all my friends, and the area. It's been easy to get back into rhythm. I guess what I'm saying is, I'm not in any hurry to make a decision. Hell, maybe it's time to sell ol' Winnie and figure out what's next." Hanna side-eyed her aunt and waited for the next question. She had a hunch she knew where this was headed.

"A certain conservation warden wouldn't have anything to do with what's next? Would she?" Dottie returned the side-eye.

"Possibly." Hanna couldn't wipe the grin off her face if she tried. "We'll see where it goes. I really can't wait for you to meet her. I know we've just met, but I'm telling you, I can't get enough of her. She's unlike anyone else I've ever been with. She's thoughtful and kind. She's smokin' hot, and she's incredible at her job."

"Ruthie has nothing but good things to say, which makes her all right in my book. It's so good to see you smitten with someone again. I know you've always danced to the beat of your own drum, but ever since that Cuckoo broke your heart, you've insisted on being a solo act. I'm glad to hear you found someone who lights you up inside and makes you feel alive again."

"Kiki." Hanna felt the heat rise in her cheeks. She'd love to erase every moment with her from memory. "Her name was Kiki. My last big heartbreak. But this feels night and day different. Jordan isn't a bad girl. She's a badass cop, and she isn't some emotionally unavailable lost soul. She's completely different. I can't explain it better. It'll be nice to have this crazy case over with so we can actually spend some time together. She's been working nonstop."

"Well, I look forward to getting to meet your warden. I hope she gives you a reason to stick around long term. It's been good having you home. Who knows, maybe you'll rethink the offer to take over the diner someday. It's yours if you want it."

"If you two are done jibber-jabbering, I have the table set and dinner on," Ruthie said from the screen door. Hanna hadn't even heard her car pull in. "Oh, sounds good. I forgot to make myself lunch."

She watched Ruthie help Dottie in the house. Whatever craziness was happening in the world, time seemed to stand still on this property. The slower pace allowed for thoughtful reflection and perspective. Knowing what Jordan was likely dealing with, Hanna almost felt guilty for enjoying a relaxing afternoon with her aunts. Almost. Sitting down to dinner with them was more than she could have hoped for. Dottie gobbled up the chicken and potato salad and seemed to be holding it all down. That was a good sign. Overwhelming emotions came out of nowhere, making Hanna want to cry, but she didn't. She didn't want to spoil the evening. It was too fun, too normal, and everything she treasured about her time up here.

Dottie talked about planting the garden and having fresh vegetables, especially her beloved tomatoes. Hanna closed her eyes and pictured the days of Aunt Dottie eating tomatoes like apples with the juice running down her arm. Good stuff.

Ruthie carried on about some upgrades she wanted to get done at the diner. Maybe expand the dining room for more seating. There were times it was standing room only, and the peak summer months hadn't even hit yet.

It was a lovely dinner. Sharing it with these two, she couldn't ask for more. The robins were busy building a nest in the bushes just off the porch, and the soft calls of the loons out on the water made it all the more enjoyable...until the scanner lit up.

CHAPTER NINETEEN

O h, hey, I think this is where I crossed. I recognize that stump. The way the roots sprawled above ground, I thought it looked like an octopus." Zoey pointed toward the shore of the Big Island.

Jordan aimed for the stump and cut the throttle, gently beaching the boat. With the mooring line in hand, she hopped off the front, just as she'd done countless times throughout her career. Mimicking Jordan's move, Zoey hopped over the side, landing softly by keeping her hold on the side of the boat. Agent Cline tried a different approach, leaping from the top edge of the gunwale. She landed hard, stumbled a few steps, and toppled onto the damp sand.

"Are you all right?" Jordan asked.

"Yeah, that move went better in my head. Luckily, all that's hurt is my pride." She stood and brushed the sand from her slacks. At least she was a good sport about it.

Jordan motioned to Zoey. "We'll let you lead the way."

"I hope I can remember." Zoey looked left and right, then slowly spun. "Okay, yeah, I think I came out of the water over here." She walked past the boat to the far side of the octopus stump. "Yeah, this looks right. When I came out of the water, I ran behind this big pine to get dressed. I couldn't see the shore, so I figured whoever was in the car coming up the road on the other side wouldn't be able to see me. Here, this way."

It all seemed to be coming back to her. She pointed out memorable landmarks like the bush covered in tiny white flowers or the bare limb on a half-dead tree that looked as if it was flipping the bird. Zoey zigged and zagged through the thicket, at times following goat paths created by both people and wildlife, other times cutting through waist-deep ferns. It was in the ferns beneath a dense stand of hardwoods, that Zoey let out a squeal of excitement and dropped to her knees.

"Look, it's still here." She pulled her rolled life jacket out of the hollow log. "My hat, my phone, and the GoPro, just like I said." She held up the tiny camera.

"Let's see what you recorded." Jordan tried to power the device on, but the battery was dead.

"Crap. Maybe I forgot to shut it off," Zoey said.

"No worries." Jordan pulled her portable SD card reader from her pocket. "This thing has come in handy more times than I can count."

She removed the micro SD card from the GoPro and slid it into the portable reader. She dragged the viewing bar back until she saw a clip with Deb's boat. She went back a bit further and hit play. The three of them huddled together like a group of football referees analyzing a replay.

"Oh, here's where I'm showing her that I only had the one fish. See, there she is. Oh, look, I did get a good picture of her face. That's her. Does that help?" Zoey asked.

Her comments in the lineup observation room had been spot-on. This woman had a similar build to Sheriff Reid, but the mouth and lips were wrong. The hair was different too. This woman's hair was slightly darker, with a bit of a wave to it. Jordan paused the video on her face and zoomed in. Her eyes were hazel, whereas the sheriff's eyes were brown like Jordan's. Her mind flashed back to the night of the storm. She tried to picture the woman driving Deb's car. She also had hazel eyes.

Jordan started to pan the frame back to normal but stopped and adjusted it slightly to the right before zooming in a bit more.

Zoey had managed to capture the registration number. With this, she could get a name and an address. *Way to go, Zoey.* She pressed a button to save a screen grab and pressed play again.

The woman wore a black shirt and gray pants, similar to the sheriff's uniform, though lacking the patches typically sewn on the sleeves. She had a black baseball hat on her head, the word sheriff in all caps. Over her shirt, she wore an inflatable life jacket which hid all but a sliver of a badge. The clothing was close enough that an unsuspecting tourist wouldn't question her authority.

In the video, Zoey turned to look at an approaching boat. Warden Ryder. Before Deb could get close enough, the "sheriff" started her boat and took off.

Deb's blue emergency lights flicked on, and the siren wailed as she flew past Zoey in pursuit. The wake from the boat jostled the video, but the camera finally stabilized. The fake sheriff's boat was quickly overcome and corralled into a small cove. Seeing Deb in action, her mastery of her watercraft, and her obvious devotion to her job, invoked both a sense of pride and more profoundly, a sense of loss in Jordan, especially knowing these were her final actions. It was hard to watch.

The video went away from the boats and followed Zoey's path through dense reeds along a shoreline. Intermittently, she'd turn her head and capture shots of the two boats, then turn back to focus on the reeds. A bit of Zoey's kayak came into view. Her hands appeared, picking up the paddle. She extended it, pushed aside the reeds, and opened up a line of sight.

Both boats had stopped. The woman impersonating the sheriff had her gun drawn on Deb. Zoey was too far from the action for Jordan to make out what they were saying. The muzzle flashed, and Deb crumpled to the deck. The shooter stood there as if surprised by what had just happened, then her demeanor changed just as quick. She turned a full three hundred and sixty degrees. She appeared frantic. Was she looking for witnesses? Who knew what she was thinking, really? Holstering her weapon, she opened a compartment and pulled out a large anchor attached to a coil of rope. A moment later, she was in Deb's boat, standing over the body where she dropped the anchor, plucked Deb's badge off her chest, and removed her duty belt. Jordan knew the rest.

Outraged, she vowed to stay the course until this woman was behind bars. She stopped the video, copied it to a blank SD card she kept in the second slot on the camera, and ejected the original.

At last, she had some concrete facts. There were still plenty of questions, but she had definitive proof that Sheriff Reid had been telling the truth all along. For reasons still unknown, she'd been set up to take the fall. Reid hadn't been the one extorting tourists on the water, and she wasn't Deb's killer. Still, several questions hung in the air like the perfume from the night of the storm. She'd have to wait until the killer was apprehended, and even then, there could be questions that might never get answered.

"Seems enough to set Sheriff Reid free and restore her standing. She's clearly no longer a suspect." Jordan secured the micro card back into Zoey's GoPro and handed it to Agent Cline. "Here's your evidence."

"I can't believe it's not Reid. All the evidence pointed to her. That's why we took her down in Waterdance, so we could send a message. Shit, I was not expecting this at all."

"Hell, Reid's been in the area so long, she might help you with motive or ID your shooter."

"If I was her, I'd tell me to take a flying leap. Though, I suppose it couldn't hurt to ask."

"I could talk to her for you."

"I won't say no to that. Also, I'll still need statements from each of you." Agent Cline looked around. "Assuming one of you remembers how to get back to the boat."

"I think it's this way." Zoey shoved her phone in her pocket. Holding her hat and life jacket, she started walking deeper into the island. With that sense of direction, it was no wonder she couldn't find her campsite or where she'd parked her car.

"How about we go this way?" Jordan pointed in the boat's direction.

"Are you sure?" Zoey spun in a circle. "Huh, no wonder I felt like I was walking in circles forever. I probably was."

"It's this way. Trust me." Jordan stepped through the dense ferns and followed the faint path they'd taken in until they were once again on the beach near the boat.

The soft hum of an outboard four-stroke engine grew louder, echoing along the river.

"Do I still have to stay out of sight?" Zoey asked.

"Yes, please. It's almost over. Why don't you and Agent Cline go back behind the big pine where you got dressed? I'll let you know when it's clear."

Nodding, Zoey darted back into the woods with the agent at her side.

Jordan heard the hull splashing against the wind-driven waves before it came into view from the northeast, the same direction as Waterdance. She watched its approach while releasing her mooring line. It was a Lund Pro-V model, somewhat similar to her own boat.

As the boat got closer, the driver came into view. She was a petite woman and wore a black shirt, dark gray pants, and ball cap, just like on the video. Jordan couldn't quite make out the lettering on her hat, but she had a damned good idea what it said.

Then, their eyes met, and there was a flash of recognition. The suspect engaged the throttle and sped off toward the larger part of the lake.

"It's her, the suspect. Cline, stay hidden and call for backup," Jordan yelled. She shoved her boat off the beach with all her might and hopped into the open bow. She lunged for the console. With a twist of the wrist, the motor rumbled to life, and she sped away at full throttle. She flipped on her siren and flashing emergency lights. Her eyes were laser focused on her target. She wasn't going to get away. Not this time. With Zoey protected, Jordan was more than eager to give chase.

She was gaining ground. She reached down and turned on the body cam secured to her uniform just above her mic, then grabbed her mic.

"Badge 1409 to dispatch."

"Go, 1409," a male voice boomed through her speakers.

"In pursuit on the Turtle River heading southeast, approaching the dam. Suspect wanted for murder is considered armed and dangerous. Requesting backup from any and all agencies that can get on the water."

"Ten-four."

Jordan spotted a few fishing boats where the river opened up to the larger waters of the flowage. They appeared to be anchored. She hit her air horn, hoping it'd serve as a warning to pay attention. If nothing else to mind the waves coming from two boats passing by at full throttle. Her suspect cut left and took a shortcut between one of the boats and the shore. The two people in the fishing boat dropped to their hands and knees for balance. At least nobody went overboard. Jordan arched out to the widest opening in her path, losing some of the ground she'd gained in the chase.

"Badge 1409 to dispatch. Now heading northeast at approximately sixty miles per hour toward Fisherman's Landing. Advise any responding agencies with location update."

"Ten-four."

She trimmed up the prop slightly and picked up some speed. This area of the flowage was the most congested, with just shy of a hundred tiny islands and countless little fishing coves. Jordan needed to be attentive to not bust a hole in the hull of her boat or break the prop on an obstacle. Luckily, the suspect faced the same challenges, though it was clear that she knew the waters well.

It always amazed Jordan when people ran, especially on the water. Like, where was she going to go? Jordan heard something whiz by her head, then heard one gunshot and another, followed by two more. She cut slightly and put a few small islands between them.

"1409 to dispatch. Shots fired, I repeat, shots fired at law enforcement."

"Ten-four, backup is en route. ETA fifteen minutes."

The suspect fired a few more times, but at least there were trees and other obstacles to slow or stop the bullets. Shit, she wasn't even wearing her vest. Had Deb been in a similar situation when she wasn't prepared for the bullet she'd taken in the chest? Then again, who was really prepared for a bullet? Still, she'd force herself to wear her vest more often, even if she had to buy one that didn't squish her boobs.

The sound of two more shots interrupted her thoughts. *Stop thinking about this crap and focus.*

The area the suspect was approaching was littered with occupied campsites. Jordan cut between a few islands and took the inside track, hoping to push the suspect out to more open water, away from human targets or shields. It worked. The suspect darted between two larger islands and cut toward old Sweeney Lake, away from the eleven campsites.

Something hit the side of Jordan's boat. Two more gunshots echoed out. She'd take a bullet to the boat over one to her body any day.

She pursued her suspect down around site R-19 near where she'd located the upside-down kayak less than a week earlier and through what was once Baraboo Lake. The frequent rock outcroppings made the area difficult to navigate at this speed. The suspect cut her boat hard to the right to avoid something in the water. *Zing*, another bullet whizzed by, followed by the sound of the shot, then two, three, or was that…four more?

"1409 to dispatch. Location now over old Baraboo Lake. Shots continuing. Not returning fire. Going to try to force her down to old Horseshoe Lake to keep her away from campers."

"Ten-four. Will relay location once backup is on the water."

She took her eyes off the water for a second to secure her mic and looked up just in time to dodge a large boulder just below the surface. She cut wide, trying to keep the suspect away from three more campsites. It worked, but her maneuver put them both into extremely shallow water. Jordan remembered her close calls the night she had been checking on campers. There were four sites down in this area, but that was better than the twenty sites along the Flambeau River just to the north.

The suspect cut between two islands when her boat stopped so fast, the stern flipped up out of the water while the engine continued to scream. Arms and legs flailing, the suspect was launched in slow motion as if she was running through the air.

"1409 to dispatch. Suspect's boat down, suspect ejected. Location is due west of old Horseshoe Lake. Searching water now."

"Ten-four, backup launching now."

Jordan lowered her speed and had her weapon at the ready as she carefully navigated around the damaged vessel. The stalled boat creaked and popped. There was a large hole in the port side of the hull. She drew in a deep breath and tried to steady her heart rate, scanning the water for any movement.

Suddenly, the suspect popped up out of the water on the starboard side of the boat, pistol pointing directly at Jordan.

In a fluid motion, Jordan shifted the boat into neutral, turned slightly to her right, and took aim. Adrenaline coursed through her veins. She was pumped and pissed and trying to figure out if she'd heard fourteen or fifteen shots. Not that there was anything she could do about it now. She released the safety on her gun, knowing there was a round already in the chamber. "Drop your weapon and put your hands in the air. You're under arrest."

"I'm not going anywhere. I'll shoot you dead just like the other warden before I let you arrest me." Her hand was shaking like crazy. Jordan wasn't sure if it was the situation or the cold water or maybe both. One thing was certain, she wasn't wearing a vest.

Regardless, Jordan watched for even the slightest twitch of her trigger finger. Where was the backup? "I have a full clip, and if I'm not mistaken, you're out of ammo."

Was it as unnerving for the suspect to look down the barrel of Jordan's gun as it was for Jordan to do the same? Her focus remained on even the slightest twitch.

She heard a boat or boats approaching. *Please let it be backup.* She saw a familiar flash of sparkling ruby red out of the corner of her eye. She risked a glance, hoping it was friend and not foe. Banjo and Chipmunk's flashy red boat, she'd recognize it anywhere. Chipmunk had a short, double-barrel shotgun aimed at the suspect.

Chipmunk? Seriously?

"I'd do as the warden asks. So much as flinch, and I'll turn you into chum before you get a round off." Chipmunk had a hell of an icy stare. Who knew she was such a badass?

"Drop your weapon, and put your arms up." Jordan commanded. Still, she stared into the barrel of the suspect's gun. This wasn't anything she'd ever get used to.

Another boat approached. "You're surrounded. I'd do what the warden says."

It was Bobbie Rae in her old Lund. She had two regulars from the bar with her, though Jordan didn't know either of their names. They were huge dudes, each armed, one with a handgun and the other with a shotgun. This was her backup. These were her people. She'd never felt more grateful to have true friends in her corner. Nothing like this would have happened in the southern counties.

The suspect's shoulders dropped, then her pistol fell from her hand into the lake. Jordan pressed the button to engage the shallow water anchors off the back of her boat, then cut the engine. She secured her weapon and carefully jumped over the side. The water was barely thigh deep. Beautiful by Estée Lauder assaulted her senses as she approached the suspect.

"Do you like the perfume, or was it just another link to Sheriff Reid?" Jordan asked, cuffing the suspect's hands behind her back. While holding the suspect's right hand, Jordan noticed the green four-leaf clover tattoo in the fleshy part between her thumb and first finger. *Gotcha. Way to recall details, Zoey.*

"Lawyer."

"It was you, wasn't it? Driving Deb's car the night of the thunderstorm, it was you. You thought I was Deb, and you freaked. Now your reaction makes sense. You couldn't figure out how you could shoot someone in the chest, weigh her body down with an anchor, only to come face-to-face with her in the middle of a wicked thunderstorm. Is that why you ditched the car?" Puzzle pieces were starting to fit together.

"Lawyer."

"Do me a solid, and ask me for my fishing license," Jordan said while turning the suspect's pockets inside out.

"Fishing lye-sense?" She shook her head. "Lawyer." Two more points for Zoey. She was proving to be a wonderful witness.

"And…you're under arrest. You have the right to remain silent." Jordan rattled off her Miranda Rights.

"Mick, Terry, stay ready. Banjo and I'll help the warden get her in the boat." Chipmunk flipped the safety on and set her shotgun down.

Banjo maneuvered his boat next to Jordan's and engaged his shallow water anchors as well. Once they were in Jordan's boat, they reached over the side and pulled the suspect up. She probably weighed less than half of Deb's waterlogged body.

"1409 to dispatch. Suspect in custody. Location is due west of old Horseshoe Lake. Be advised, armed civilians present assisting in apprehension. Scene is secure. I repeat, the scene is secure."

"Ten-four, backup approaching any minute. I'll convey."

Jordan secured her mic. "Chipmunk, next to my seat is a pair of gloves. Would you hand them to me?"

"They're brand-new. You're going to ruin them in the water." Chipmunk pulled the gloves apart and handed them down to Jordan.

"Won't be the first time or the last." She pulled the gloves over her wet hands and crouched. She felt around the rocks and sand until, aha, there it was. Keeping the muzzle down, she pulled the pistol out of the water, removed the clip, and pulled the slide partially back. Her heart stopped beating for a split second. She'd miscounted. While the clip was empty, one round remained in the chamber. With the slightest squeeze of the trigger, her life could have ended, just when it was getting good. The thought shook her to the core. Thankfully, her friends had arrived in time to keep her from the same fate as Deb. There wasn't a doubt in her mind that the suspect would have fired had they not arrived when they did. Jordan released the hammer and applied the safety.

Two sheriff's boats approached, lights flashing and sirens blaring. *Better late than never.* They cut the sirens as they coasted closer.

"Sorry it took so long. Things have been out of whack with the sheriff out of pocket."

"Understood." Jordan couldn't say more. It wasn't her place to proclaim the sheriff's innocence. "Do you have an evidence bag? There's still a round in the chamber." Jordan asked. "I didn't want to eject it into the lake. Please hold the suspect until the DCI can take custody. It shouldn't be long."

"Will do, Warden." The deputy gloved up and accepted the pistol and the clip.

Jordan waded to the back of her boat and climbed the ladder. Her body ached. Boy, she really needed a vacation.

More than anything, she wanted to roundhouse the smug-ass Reid impersonator. The suspect was transferred to the deputy that had taken possession of the pistol, and once she was secured, they left the scene. The other deputy called for a barge to help with the disabled boat.

Finally, Jordan felt like she could breathe. "I can't thank you all enough. You really saved my bacon." She shook Banjo's hand. She turned to shake Chipmunk's and was surprised when she pulled her into a hug. Wow, she was a good hugger.

"We heard your calls on the scanner. No way they'd launch in time. We were fishing down by Mud Lake. Saw some of the chase. You're one hell of a navigator. Kept between her and the campers wherever you could." She clapped Jordan on the shoulder.

"You two carry a twelve gauge in your boat when you're out fishing? When did that start?"

"Ev...ever s...since we helped w...with the warden's b... body and heard about the other t...troubles on the wa...water."

"We texted Bobbie Rae. Figured she could rustle up some help. Her boat fits through the shortcut at the tip of the big island at ol' Merkle Lake." Chipmunk motioned to the trio in the old Lund.

"Mick and Terry had to crouch so we could get under the footbridge. Don't ticket me for being over max capacity for my little boat. So it wasn't Mighty Mouse after all. Instead, it was a lowly, half-drowned rat." Bobbie Rae stepped out of her boat and into Jordan's, quickly pulling her into a hug. "I'm glad you're okay. Don't want to think about what could have happened." She leaned closer to Jordan's ear. "Give me a nod if you-know-who is safe."

She nodded. "All good. Thanks for being here." Jordan released Bobbie Rae and stepped back. "Thank you, everyone. I owe all of you a round or five and an unbelievable amount of gratitude for making sure my heart kept beating. Listen, I sincerely appreciate everything you all did, but I've gotta go. I was on a call when all this came down. I'm sure they'll let me know if they need statements, but my body cam should be enough. I'll see you all later, okay?"

"Happy to help anytime. We'll catch up later." Chipmunk accepted Banjo's help into their boat.

Bobbie Rae gave Jordan an extra squeeze and stepped over the gunwale down into her boat. "Later, Jo-Jo. Go take care of that call, would ya?" She shot Jordan a wink. Not much got past her. She knew Zoey had been with Jordan all day. No doubt she was wondering why they were out on the water.

Jordan pulled out her phone to text Agent Cline: *Suspect in custody. Sheriff dept holding. I'm on my way back to you.*

Agent Cline: *Wonderful news. We'll stay hidden until you're back.*

Jordan sent a thumbs-up and stowed her phone. She waved at Banjo and Chipmunk, then at Bobbie Rae, Terry, and Mick as the two boats took off in separate directions. Bobbie Rae no doubt headed back toward the bar, while the other two were likely headed home. It'd been a hell of an event for all of them, Jordan included. She brought up her ladder and the shallow water anchors, then started her boat and made her way back to the octopus stump to pick up Zoey and Agent Cline. With the real suspect in custody, it was almost over.

When she'd submitted her transfer request, she'd done so because of a desire for a slower pace. With any luck, now that they had the real suspect in custody, she'd get a chance to experience it.

CHAPTER TWENTY

Thanks for taking Zoey's statement on your cell while I chased the suspect around the lake. She's been through enough and doesn't need to spend another moment in hurry up and wait mode," Jordan said on the short walk back to the lodge parking lot.

Agent Cline nodded. "She sure seemed happy to see whoever was waiting for her above the bar."

"Yeah, I think they're kindred spirits." Jordan chuckled. "She'll be even happier when her stuff is released, and she can move on with her life. She's kind of stuck without her car, not to mention her wallet. With any luck, they'll recover it in the search. It'll be interesting to hear what all is found in the suspect's house."

"Hopefully, we can get Zoey squared away in a day or two. Not the vacation she expected, I'm sure. I'm sorry for what she went through. The entire ordeal is heartbreaking." Agent Cline stopped walking in the parking lot. "Is there a hotel nearby where I could get a room? We could make the trip to Wausau in the morning. If one of these cabins is available, I could stay here."

"I really hoped we could make the trip tonight. I'm sure the sheriff is chewing her nails to the quick. If it were me, I'd want every effort made to get me released once the truth was known."

"You're a thoughtful person, Warden. If I'd been wrongfully arrested, I'd want you as a friend."

"Trust me, Reid and I aren't friends. Until today, I thought she was guilty and wasn't all that upset to watch her get cuffed. But the facts prove she was telling the truth, and now that I know she's innocent, I can't let her just sit there. Call it a professional courtesy."

"Like I said, I'd want you around. Friends or not, you've kept an open mind. Okay, we'll make the trip tonight."

Jordan unplugged the trailer lights and disconnected her boat trailer from the truck. "Listen, I need to make one more stop before we head out. There's someone special who needs to see that I'm okay. I know she heard everything on the scanner, but based on the texts I've been getting, she's pacing the floor. Is that all right? If not, I can drop you at the sheriff's office and catch up with you later."

"Ah, the transport team is still twenty minutes out. If you don't mind a tagalong, I don't mind a detour. The deputies aren't too keen on my presence, having arrested the sheriff and all. Talk about a cold shoulder."

Jordan chuckled. "Hadn't thought of that. Hop in."

"You're lucky to have someone care so much about you." Agent Cline offered a sad smile and climbed into the passenger seat.

"Come on, no one's pacing the floor for you?" Jordan asked and started her truck.

"Nope. Not for a few years now. I'm divorced because apparently, my work was more important than my marriage. At least, that's what she told me. Hell, maybe she had a point. Look at us, more than twelve hours into our day, and we're still at it." Her honesty was refreshing.

"I'm sorry to hear that, but I do understand. Hazardous part of our jobs, I'm afraid." Three miles later, Jordan flipped on her blinker and turned into Hanna's aunts' driveway.

The front door flew open before she even had the truck completely in park. Jordan couldn't recall a time when anyone had been so excited to see her. Others in her orbit had always been the center of attention, the ones everyone was excited to see, like her mom and her sisters, even the women she'd dated before her time with Dr. Knoedel. Because of this, Jordan always faded into the background. She was the solid, stable one. Not the one a beautiful woman leaped off porches to see. It warmed her deep inside to see Hanna jump from the top step without a care in the world. This was a new feeling, and it felt good. They met in front of the truck, and Hanna launched into Jordan's arms with much enthusiasm, wrapping her arms around her and kissing her.

"Am I ever happy to see you." Hanna held her tightly, then just as quickly pulled back. "Let me look at you. Are you okay? No nicks or bullet grazing?" She stepped back and slapped Jordan's arm. "What were you thinking chasing an armed lunatic? You forget I was there when you pulled the other warden out of the lake? You could have ended up puffy turtle food just like her. Christ, you could have been killed. I just met you. I'm not ready to lose you."

Jordan cupped Hanna's face. "Whoa, hey, I'm okay. I'm good." She didn't dare tell Hanna about the round in the suspect's chamber or how close she'd actually come to pulling the trigger herself. Throughout her career, she'd never taken a life, but if she'd had to fire her weapon, she hoped her aim to be true and to be the last one standing. Hell, a shootout had been a real possibility had it not been for Banjo, Chipmunk, and Bobbie Rae's crew. Just thinking about the close call had Jordan's heart hammering in her chest. She tried to brush it off. "I'm better now that I get to see you. No bullet wounds, I promise. Maybe some sore muscles from the boat chase, but all's good." Jordan held her arms out, and Hanna stepped back into her embrace. Holding her felt like home.

"I've been worried sick," Hanna's voice was muffled against Jordan's shirt.

"I had a feeling. The gazillion texts you sent were a pretty solid clue. It felt wrong just to text you back with an 'I'm okay.' I figured you'd want to see for yourself." Jordan rested her chin on the top of Hanna's head.

"You figured right." Hanna nuzzled closer.

"That's why I wanted to stop before heading back to Wausau."

"Wait, you have to go back? Isn't it over? On the radio, you said the woman was wanted for murder. Has there been another murder? Are there two cases?"

"No, just the one case, one murder, and one killer. It's over, but my part of the job isn't done. I need to see this through. We have to meet some agents and head back to the DCI's office."

"We?" Hanna stepped back and looked around.

"Hanna, this is Agent Cline with the Division of Criminal Investigations." Jordan motioned to the side of the truck where the agent was standing.

"Nice to meet you." Hanna offered a wave before turning back to Jordan. "Are you coming back tonight?"

"Yeah, I'll be back, but it might be late. Do you want the key to my cabin?"

Hanna nodded. "Yeah, if you don't mind. I don't mean to sound needy. God, I feel like I'm being needy. What is going on with me? Who am I right now?"

Jordan laughed. "Hey, definitely not needy. I was hoping you'd want to stay with me. I want to be with you too." She pulled the key from her pocket and dropped it into Hanna's waiting hand. "I'll be back as soon as I can."

"I look forward to spending some non-murder investigation time with you." Hanna had the cutest expression on her face. "Thanks for getting me. I'll pack a bag and wait for you at the cabin. Maybe I'll walk over and hang out with Bobbie Rae for a bit so I'm not pacing in a new room." She tugged on Jordan's collar. "Promise me you'll be careful. No falling asleep at the wheel."

"I promise. I'll see you tonight." Jordan kissed her good-bye. While they hadn't known each other long, they fit so perfectly together.

It was almost too much watching Hanna standing in the driveway, waving, while Jordan backed onto the road and drove away. There wasn't a doubt in her mind that Waterdance was home, and even after a crazy week, she already knew that she wanted Hanna to be part of her life, a big part.

❖

Jordan peeked through the small window in the interview room door. Sheriff Reid looked lost and forlorn sitting alone at the small table, as if she'd already lost hope. She didn't even look up when Jordan opened the door.

"I've said all I have to say." The sharp edge in her voice had her sounding even more like Holly Hunter, if that was possible. She scrubbed her face with her hands.

The door latched behind Jordan. She took two strides and set the sheriff's badge on the table. Its black band, just like hers, honored a fallen colleague: Deb. This and other little gestures she'd discovered throughout the day had Jordan respecting the sheriff more and more. "I believe this belongs to you."

Reid covered her mouth. Her face reddened briefly before she drew in a deep breath. Tentatively, she reached for her badge as if waiting for Jordan to take it back. With a delicate touch, she traced the star. "Warden Pearce, I wondered if you'd come back tonight. Hell, if you'd come back at all. I also wondered if you weren't a little bit happy to see me hauled away." She looked up. "I wasn't real welcoming when you came to town." Her eyes were puffy. Her nose was red. It was clear she'd been crying.

"Had you been guilty, I wouldn't have shed a tear." Jordan sat in the chair across from her. "I followed the facts, and the facts proved your innocence."

"Oh, thank God." For the first time, Sheriff Reid looked directly into her eyes. "Better yet, thank you."

Jordan nodded.

"Who was it?" she asked.

"Darcy Barrows."

"Darcy Barrows?" Sheriff Reid tapped her finger on the table. "Why do I know that name? Wait, I interviewed her for a deputy position this past winter. I decided not to hire. If I recall, there was some hinky stuff in her psych eval. Huge red flags." She sat a little taller in her chair. Perhaps it was sinking in that she was cleared of all charges.

"I'd say. She holds you personally responsible for crushing her dreams and ruining her life. She had this notion that if she harassed and extorted the tourists on the water, word would get out, and you wouldn't be reelected. She was sure she was a shoo-in to replace you."

"How's the warden's murder figure into all this?" Reid asked.

"Warden Ryder had been getting complaints from the tourists about a sheriff on the water threatening them with a ticket if they didn't give her cash. Time and again, the tourists refused to file complaints because the sheriff had copies of their driver's licenses, including their addresses, and promised to make life a living hell for them if they said anything. Little did any of them know, she wasn't really you."

"Holy shit. Come to think of it, she was about my height and body style."

Jordan nodded and leaned back in her chair. "She was hassling the kayaker when Deb caught her in the act. The audio is garbled on the video, so I'm not sure why Deb didn't draw her weapon. Hell, maybe it was too late by the time she realized it wasn't you. Either way, the murder and the dumping of the body are on video. That and I had my body cam on today when I caught her. She confessed to everything. We have her dead to rights. Get this, she even wore your perfume, like took on your entire persona. That's why I thought you'd been in Deb's car."

"So it was her in Ryder's car the night of the storm?" Reid asked, attaching her badge to her uniform.

"Yep."

"So what was with dumping the car and switching the plates?"

"I wondered the same thing. It was like you thought. A brake line ruptured when she drove over the tree. That's why she dumped the car. As far as the plates, Agent Cline got it out of her. Zoey was the loose end. Somehow, she thought swapping the plates would tie Zoey's murder to you, assuming she could find Zoey. After she towed Deb's boat back to the station house and bleached it, she went back out to kill Zoey, but the storm hit and messed with her plans, so she decided to make it look like Deb had bolted by sending the resignation email and stashing her car. All hoping to buy some time, but she must have forgotten to switch the plates back. The tree fell across the road and threw her another curve. When she saw me through the rain with a ball cap on, she thought I was Deb and had come back from the dead. It really freaked her out."

Sheriff Reid leaned back and squinted. "I guess you do look a lot like her, if your hair was longer, and you wore a ball cap. I'll be damned."

Jordan rolled her eyes and shook her head. "Barrows searched for Zoey most of the next day but came up empty. That's why, on my first tour, campers were telling me that the sheriff was by but had ignored them when they'd called for help. Lending to my suspicion of you. Then, I found Zoey's kayak and abandoned campsite, and we started the search, which kept Barrows off the lake for a day or two. Bottom line, she was hoping to set you up for both murders."

"Well, shit."

"What she didn't count on was Hanna finding Zoey in the dumpster behind the diner and convincing her to come forward. Zoey Mitchell and her last-minute decision to buy a GoPro are the main reasons you're not going down for Deb's murder. As twisted as Darcy was, she did a hell of a job setting you up. She even followed you until she saw you toss some gloves into the trash at a scene. That's how she planted your prints. Your blood was from a Band-Aid in your trash."

"Fuck me. I guess I need to be more careful."

"They're processing her now. The DA will expunge your arrest tomorrow. You're once again the sheriff of Iron County, back in good standing. How about I give you a ride home?"

"I won't say no to that. Get me out of this room, hell, out of this building. I don't know about you, but I'm ready for a drink!" She stood and held out her hand. "Hey, Jordan, thank you."

It was the first time the sheriff had used her first name. Did this mean they were friends? Maybe just friendly. "You're welcome." Jordan accepted her hand but couldn't bring herself to call her Ang or Angela, especially when she looked like a Holly.

When they exited the building, the sun was dropping below the horizon, offering an incredible sunset brimming with deep reds, brilliant oranges, and splendid rich shades of fuchsia against a mottled, cloudy sky. A beautiful conclusion to a crazy day, hell, a crazy week. At least it was something beautiful in the review mirror as she and Sheriff Reid headed northeast, away from the insanity.

CHAPTER TWENTY-ONE

Aunt Dottie was doing so much better that Ruthie encouraged Hanna to take the next couple of days off and have some fun. Hanna had a sneaking suspicion that Ruthie had overheard Jordan saying that she was taking the next couple of days off as well. Who was she to spoil her aunt's matchmaking fun?

Since she didn't have to work first thing the next morning, nothing was stopping her from having a couple of drinks with her friends while she waited for Jordan to return from Wausau. She sent out a group text and walked the fifty feet from cabin seven.

The bar was quite subdued for a Friday night, as if the insanity of the week had everyone longing for the safety of home. Regardless of the reason, it suited Hanna just fine. She plopped down on the same stool Jordan had sat on before they'd gone for their walk and fooled around in the hidden clearing. Well, more than fooled around. Hanna shivered and held on to the memory.

"Hiya, Hanna. What can I get for you? Bourbon neat?"

"Bourbon sour, please." Hanna turned toward the familiar voice. "Zoey? Hey, weren't you with Jordan?"

"I was. She dropped me here before heading back to Wausau."

"Are you working here now?"

"Ah, I wish." Zoey set a coaster on the bar. "Naw, I'm just helping out. Someone called in sick and left Bobbie Rae scrambling." She grabbed a glass and filled it with ice, added bourbon, lemon juice, simple syrup, and topped it off with an orange slice and cherry garnish. "She's done so much to help. You all have, really. Covering the bar seemed like the least I could do to offset all my mooching. Here ya go. I hope you like it."

She set the drink in front of Hanna. It was perfect and just like Bobbie Rae made them. "Mmm. Wonderful."

Zoey smiled. She looked around like she should be doing something, but the bar was neater than Hanna had ever seen it. Everything was stocked. Not a dish in the sink.

"Where's Bobbie Rae?"

"She ran upstairs to take a shower. Said she needed to calm her nerves. She should be down soon."

"How are you holding up?"

Zoey leaned in a little closer. "I'm so relieved it's over. Ya know, now that I've officially been found and all. I mean, I know it's not over, over. I still don't have my stuff, and I'll probably have to testify. But I'm not cold and hungry and alone in the woods, running for my life and sleeping under a tarp. I'm glad that part's over. The debt I owe you all, especially you, is more than I could ever repay. Honestly, I don't think I'd be here if it wasn't for you tossing that bag in the dumpster when you did. I didn't know who I could trust."

Hanna reached across the bar and wrapped her hand around Zoey's. "I can't believe how well you're handling this. I totally would've lost my shit. I'd be huddled in a corner, terrified and rocking uncontrollably. I admire you so much."

"Trust me, I was close to cracking when you found me. Like I'd turned feral or something. Seriously, I had to be on the edge to dumpster dive and chow down on people's half-eaten food."

"Well, I, for one, am glad you didn't snap. The circumstances are pretty fucked-up, but I'm really glad we met. You fit in with us well." Hanna gave her hand an extra squeeze.

"Thanks. I feel the same way. At least something good came out of the craziness." Zoey picked at the corner of a cardboard coaster. "Can I ask you something?"

"Sure, anything."

"Is Bobbie Rae a player?"

Hanna choked on both her drink and the question. Lemon juice and bourbon were not kind to the sinuses. She grabbed a few napkins in the nick of time. Sneezing lemon juice and bourbon was as unpleasant as breathing it in. She blew her nose, then wiped her eyes with a clean napkin. Wow, that was the last question she'd expected. "What? Why would you ask me that?"

"We slept together last night. Okay, not so much slept."

"You and Bobbie Rae?"

"Yeah, I thought for sure Jordan would have told you, even if Bobbie Rae asked her not to say a word. She woke us up this morning, and Bobbie Rae answered the door wearing my, well, your underwear."

Hanna laughed at the mental image of Bobbie Rae trying to hold up her underwear. "Jordan didn't say a word. She wouldn't if Bobbie Rae asked her to keep it a secret. I'm learning that Jordan has a strict moral compass, and she and Bobbie Rae share some kind of blood oath or something. I have no doubt they'd fight to the death for each other. Would you believe that until a week ago, they hadn't spoken in, like, twenty-seven years, and it's like they picked up right where they left off."

"That's cool. Having friends who have your back like that. Just makes me want her that much more. The things she did to me, well, let's just say I've never come so hard and so many times. So is she a player? Or do I believe her when she says she wants to see more of me?"

Hanna shivered at the memory of a similar experience with Jordan from the night before. The power of her multiple orgasms could not be overstated. With any luck, she'd get a replay tonight.

"Crap, your face got all screwy. She is a player, isn't she? I should have known." Zoey scrubbed her face in her hand.

"No. No, she's not. She's totally not a player. The opposite, really. Like I said last night, Bobbie Rae doesn't say or do anything she doesn't mean."

"But your expression?"

Hanna waved at the heat in her cheeks. "Trust me, I wasn't thinking about Bobbie Rae. Jordan…well, seems we both had an awesome night last night. Holy wow, a totally awesome night."

"Yeah, she knows how to curl your toes? How long have you two been together?"

"She definitely knows how to curl my toes." Hanna kept fanning her face. "I'm not sure I can even say we're together. I've only known her for six days. Granted, it's been the most intense and crazy but also incredible six days ever."

"Shut up!" Zoey slapped the bar. "You two totally meld."

Hanna pulled the cherry off the spear and slowly chewed it. "We do, don't we? For someone who's sworn off love, I'm falling fast. I can't picture a future that doesn't include her."

"I know what you mean. I just met Bobbie Rae, and while the sex was incredible, it's not just that. It's her. Everything about her. I want to climb on the back of that Harley and ride off into the sunset with her. She totally lights my fire."

A warm fuzziness emanated from deep within Hanna. She got it. She understood everything Zoey was saying on a deep level. Swap out Bobbie Rae with Jordan and swap the Harley for the boat, and she was all in. Was it the intensity of the week or was Jordan "the one?"

"What?" Zoey pulled Hanna out of her thoughts.

"Well, I was just wondering if we would feel this way if the week had been different. Say you met Bobbie Rae while camping, and I met Jordan at the diner, without the murder and the chaos."

"Are you wondering if you'd feel the same or if the orgasms would be as good?" Zoey's question came with an all-knowing smirk.

"You're right, even the question is ridiculous. I was smitten with Jordan the second I laid eyes on her and that first kiss…wow, talk about curling your toes."

"That's what I'm saying. The crazy circumstances might be what brought her into my life, but it's not why I'm interested. Trust me, I've been pondering it all day."

"What have you been pondering? If it's how to stay another night with me, all you have to do is ask. I'm in," Bobbie Rae said, walking in from the back of the bar. She strolled up next to Zoey and draped her arm over her shoulders. "Hey, beautiful." They were adorable together.

"Hey, sexy." Zoey beamed with happiness.

Hanna looked at her phone. There was a text from Carol that she wouldn't make it over to the bar. She was tired and crashing early. Not entirely unexpected. She started her days early to have freshly baked goods for delivery. Oh, and look, one from Jordan. *Just dropped Sheriff Reid at her house. Should be home in a few minutes. Are you at the cabin or the bar?*

It'd come in almost fifteen minutes ago. How had she missed the text? Jordan was probably already at the cabin, and Hanna wasn't there. Smiling, she stared at the text. Jordan had actually typed the word home. The thought warmed Hanna's heart. Home.

Hanna: *I'm at the bar, missed your text*

Jordan: *I just got out of the shower. I'll be over.*

Hanna: *Stay. I'll come to you. Do you need food?*

Jordan: *No, but I'd take a drink.*

"Well, lovebirds, it's time for me to bid you a good evening. Can I get a couple of these to go?" Hanna rattled the ice in her empty drink.

"After the day Jo-Jo's had, she deserves the bottle."

Hanna wanted to ask specifics, then decided it was probably best she didn't know.

Bobbie Rae pulled out a large plastic beer pitcher and poured in some lemon juice and simple syrup. She grabbed a second pitcher and filled it with ice, resting a few skewered orange slices and cherries on top, then she picked up a bottle of Jim Beam. It was close to empty. She reached to the right and spun the bottle of Maker's Mark. It was more than half-full. "This'll do. Can you manage all of it?"

Hanna pulled some cash out of her back pocket. Normally, she didn't carry cash, but Ruthie had shoved it in her back pocket on her way out earlier.

"Nope. Your money's no good here tonight. No arguing."

"Consider this a tip, then." She tucked a couple of twenties beneath her coaster and slid her phone into her pocket. Hanna grabbed both handles of the pitchers with one hand and the bottle of bourbon with the other. It was manageable. "I've got it."

"Oh wait, cups." Zoey ran around the counter and put a few red solo cups upside down over the neck of the bourbon bottle. "May your toes curl many times tonight," she said, grinning from ear to ear.

"I wish you the same." Hanna winked. Zoey gave her a thumbs-up and an exaggerated nod.

Bobbie Rae looked between them and shrugged. "You two have a secret code?"

Hanna and Zoey laughed.

"See you two tomorrow, Quinnie."

"Maybe at some point." Hanna had hoped to spend the next few days in bed. "We'll see you when we come up for air."

❖

Movement outside the window caught Jordan's eye, and she rushed to open the door. "That's some drink."

"Bobbie Rae didn't want you limited. Said you deserved more than one." Hanna laughed and set the two pitchers on the counter next to the microwave.

"Since I'm officially off the clock for a few days, I won't say no to that. Plus, I have good news to celebrate. I've been offered the post permanently. I'm officially the new warden for the Turtle Flambeau Flowage." Jordan held out her arms.

"Really? That's fantastic news!" Hanna jumped into Jordan's waiting arms. Holding her felt like home. "Best news ever. I'm so glad it's over. You're home safe, and things can get back to normal. How are you holding up?"

"Better now that I'm holding you. When you're with me, everything is better." Jordan rested her chin on Hanna's head. There was so much she wanted to say. All of which could be summed up with three little words, but it seemed too soon to profess her love, didn't it? Too soon or not, her feelings for Hanna just kept getting stronger. "How is it we've only known each other a week, and you're the one I want to celebrate with? You're the one I want to lean on when I need held up? You're the one I want to share my good news with and hold after a tough day? No one else will do. I only want to be with you, for all of it, for everything. I'm totally falling for you. Who am I kidding? Hanna, being with you is night and day different from anything I've ever experienced. I've fallen...I'm all in."

Hanna snuggled a little closer. That was a good sign. At least Hanna hadn't made a beeline for the door. "I feel the same way. First, you captured my attention, then you captured my heart. When the bell jingles on the door at the diner, I can't resist looking to see if you're coming to see me. When it is you, and you give me that look and that smile, it's all I can do not to rush into your arms. Jordan, I'm all in too. You know how we were talking on the boat about looking for a home, for a place where we belonged? I totally feel like my place is here with you."

"I couldn't agree more." Jordan pulled back and cupped Hanna's face. "Really? You'd stay to be with me? What about your work?"

"Let's just say, my interests have shifted. Waterdance is home. I want to be with you and my aunts and our friends. Ruthie and Dottie aren't getting any younger. For years, they've begged me to take over the diner. Seventeen-year-old me used to hate working there. Funny how much I'm enjoying it now. Let's just say, I'm open to the idea when Ruthie's ready to pull the plug. Jordan, I mean it when I say I'm in." Hanna's smile lit up the room. "The feelings I have for you are unlike anything I've ever experienced."

Drinks forgotten, Jordan guided Hanna to the bed. Making love felt like the perfect way to express everything that words couldn't.

EPILOGUE

Five months later

Jordan sat in the big wooden swing on the deck facing the river. It was now her favorite place to sit and enjoy a cup of coffee, especially with Hanna sitting right next to her, her legs draped across Jordan's lap. Heaven. The loons, along with the sandhill cranes and the great blue herons, were beginning their fall migration. She loved listening to the different calls and songs reverberate off the water.

"This is magical." Jordan squeezed Hanna's hand. "I love you."

"Mmm...I love you too, babe." Hanna leaned forward and kissed her.

Preparations were finally finished. Covered card tables and an eclectic variety of chairs were set up on the deck and around the yard. The firepit popped and crackled with a roaring blaze, ready for both hotdogs and marshmallows. With a push of a button, the Weber would be primed for grilling burgers, brats, and chicken. It was a day of celebration indeed.

The distinctive rumble of a Harley Davidson pulled into the driveway. Bobbie Rae parked the bike on the concrete apron in front of the pole shed. Zoey sat on the back holding a Crock-Pot in her arms. Before Jordan could get up to help, Zoey handed the pot to Bobbie Rae, dismounted from the back seat, and took the pot back. Bobbie Rae lowered the kickstand and swung her leg off the bike.

"It's like you two practiced that," Hanna called from her comfy spot on the swing.

"Well, Quinnie, we wouldn't want you to have to get up or anything." Bobbie Rae opened one of the saddlebags and pulled out a bottle of Grey Goose vodka and a small paper sack. "Dottie still likes her martinis, right?"

"You know the way to her heart." Hanna swung her legs off Jordan's lap and stood to hug their friends.

"Where's the food going?" Zoey asked while accepting a sideways hug.

"I have a couple of banquet tables set up in the dining room. There should be plenty of power strips." Hanna pointed into the house. "Bobbie Rae, the booze can go in the kitchen."

While Hanna had spent most every night there since Jordan had moved in, she'd only recently officially moved out of her old bedroom at her aunts' house. Each day just kept getting better and better. Jordan couldn't imagine not having Hanna as a constant in her life.

It didn't take long for the driveway to be packed with cars and the chairs filled with those near and dear to the guest of honor. Most weren't much more than familiar faces, but others Jordan considered dear friends. Banjo and Chipmunk, Carol, even Sheriff Reid, out of uniform for once, came out with a dish to pass. She'd even asked for help on a case recently. Their relationship had definitely improved.

Hanna stood at the edge of the deck with Auntie Ruthie and Aunt Dottie at her side and let out a loud whistle. "Can I have everyone's attention, please?"

The crowd quieted down to a soft murmur.

"I'd like to thank you all for coming out today. We couldn't be more grateful to have each of you in our lives, especially given this past year. I'd like to ask you to stand and celebrate with us." Hanna motioned to Dottie, who picked up a piñata stick and struck the large bell hanging from a tall post on the deck several times.

"I'm cancer free," Dottie screamed at the top of her lungs and pumped the fist of her free hand.

The crowd erupted in applause and whoops of celebration. Dottie handed the stick to Ruthie, who rang the bell a few more times. Indeed, a day of celebration. Jordan couldn't help but brush a tear off her cheek.

Hanna whistled again, settling down the crowd. "Jordan's running the grill. There's a buffet line in the dining room and drinks in the kitchen. Everyone, it's time to eat!"

Most of the group migrated out once bellies were full, food was wrapped and put away, and congratulations had been shared. Jordan swallowed the nervous lump in her throat and touched the small box in her pocket. It was almost time. Maybe she should wait. What if Hanna said no?

Those who remained at the party were in comfy camp chairs surrounding the firepit. The sun sat low in the sky, bathing the yard in a golden glow. Now. Now was the perfect time. She bit her lip and stood.

"Can I have everyone's attention for just a minute?" Jordan clasped her hands behind her back to keep from fidgeting. "I want to thank each of you for agreeing to hang out a little bit longer. Each of you has been asked to be here this evening because you're special to me, to us. I can't imagine not sharing this moment with all of you." She cleared her throat. It was next-level dry. *Just nerves. You know what you want to say, so say it.* She drew in a deep breath and wiped her sweaty palms on her jeans.

"Banjo and Chipmunk, you have no idea the impact you've had on my life. You gave up your quiet afternoons to spend time with me. You talked to me like I was a person and treated each other with affection and kind words. Back then, it might have only been about the fishing, but you two helped me see that there can be healthy, loving relationships when all I knew of relationships was fighting, arguing, and ignoring the hard stuff. I thank you for that. I hold those lessons dear."

Jordan drew in another deep breath and turned to her left. "Bobbie Rae." She placed her hand over her heart. "There are no words. You came into my life when I most needed a friend. You taught me about trust and unconditional love and friendship. You taught me how to talk about the stuff we're told not to talk about. With you, I learned how to depend on someone, how to laugh until I cried, and that even when things sucked, life was to be savored and enjoyed. I know we lost touch for a good long time, but you never stopped being my best friend. I'm glad you and Zoey found each other. She's a wonderful addition to our little family.

"Carol, the other musketeer. I look forward to getting to know you better. I know Hanna treasures your friendship." Jordan pivoted to the other side of the group. "Dottie and Ruthie, it has been such a pleasure and an honor getting to know you two. You are incredible people and amazing role models. Thank you for taking Hanna in when you did. I'm so grateful that you beat the cancer that called her home and brought her into my life. I can't imagine not having met her, and I can't imagine not having the two of you in my life for many years to come."

She dug into her pocket and pulled out the small box. Hanna gasped and covered her mouth. Good, she was surprised. Another long, deep breath and Jordan dropped to one knee in front of her. "Hanna, you captured my attention the moment we met, and every day, I find you more and more irresistible. I love you with every fiber of my being. I can't imagine a future without you. Will you marry me?"

Tears streamed down Hanna's face. Jordan felt tears of her own. Tears of happiness. With her hand still coving her mouth, Hanna nodded. Jordan slid the diamond ring onto her finger. It fit perfectly.

Hanna slid out of her chair and into Jordan's arms. "I love you. Yes. Yes, I would love to marry you."

"I love you too. You just made me the luckiest woman in the world."

Whoops and catcalls erupted. Jordan felt people slapping her on the back and shoulder. She'd acknowledge them in a minute, after her first kiss as an engaged woman. Tears continued to fall while she kissed her bride-to-be. When she stood with Hanna at her side, she realized there wasn't a dry eye to be seen.

This was her chosen family. These were her people. And with Hanna, she'd found her home.

About the Author

Nance Sparks is a Goldie Award winning author of lesbian romance. She lives in south central Wisconsin with her spouse. Her passion for photography, homesteading, hiking, gardening, and most anything outdoors comes through in her stories. When the sun is out and the sky is blue, especially during the golden hour, Nance can be found on the Wisconsin River with a camera in hand, capturing shots of large birds in flight.

Books Available from Bold Strokes Books

Close to Home by Allisa Bahney. Eli Thomas has to decide if avoiding her hometown forever is worth losing the people who used to mean the most to her, especially Aracely Hernandez, the girl who got away. (978-1-63679-661-1)

Golden Girl by Julie Tizard. In 1993, "Don't ask, don't tell" forces everyone to lie, but Air Force nurse Lt. Sofia Sanchez and injured instructor pilot Lt. Gillian Guthman have to risk telling each other the truth in order to fly and survive. (978-1-63679-751-9)

Innis Harbor by Patricia Evans. When Amir Farzaneh meets and falls in love with Loch, a dark secret lurking in her past reappears, threatening the happiness she'd just started to believe could be hers. (978-1-63679-781-6)

The Blessed by Anne Shade. Layla and Suri are brought together by fate to defeat the darkness threatening to tear their world apart. What they don't expect to discover is a love that might set them free. (978-1-63679-715-1)

The Guardians by Sheri Lewis Wohl. Dogs, devotion, and determination are all that stand between darkness and light. (978-1-63679-681-9)

The Mogul Meets Her Match by Julia Underwood. When CEO Claire Beauchamp goes undercover as a customer of Abby Pita's café to help seal a deal that will solidify her career, she doesn't expect to be so drawn to her. When the truth is revealed, will she break Abby's heart? (978-1-63679-784-7)

Trial Run by Carsen Taite. When Reggie Knoll and Brooke Dawson wind up serving on a jury together, their one task—reaching a unanimous verdict—is derailed by the fiery clash of their personalities, the intensity of their attraction, and a secret that could threaten Brooke's life. (978-1-63555-865-4)

Waterlogged by Nance Sparks. When conservation warden Jordan Pearce discovers a body floating in the flowage, the serenity of the Northwoods is rocked. (978-1-63679-699-4)

Accidentally in Love by Kimberly Cooper Griffin. Nic and Lee have good reasons for keeping their distance. So why does their growing attraction seem more like a love-hate relationship? (978-1-63679-759-5)

Fatal Foul Play by David S. Pederson. After eight friends are stranded in an old lodge by a blinding snowstorm, a brutal murder leaves Mark Maddox to solve the crime as he discovers deadly secrets about people he thought he knew. (978-1-63679-794-6)

Frosted by the Girl Next Door by Aurora Rey and Jaime Clevenger. When heartbroken Casey Stevens opens a sex shop next door to uptight cupcake baker Tara McCoy, things get a little frosty. (978-1-63679-723-6)

Ghost of the Heart by Catherine Friend. Being possessed by a ghost was not on Gwen's bucket list, but she must admit that ghosts might be real, and one is obviously trying to send her a message. (978-1-63555-112-9)

Hot Honey Love by Nan Campbell. When chef Stef Lombardozzi puts her cooking career into the hands of filmmaker Mallory Radowski—the pickiest eater alive—she doesn't anticipate how hard she falls for her. (978-1-63679-743-4)

London by Patricia Evans. Jaq's and Bronwyn's lives become entwined as dangerous secrets emerge and Bronwyn's seemingly perfect life starts to unravel. (978-1-63679-778-6)

This Christmas by Georgia Beers. When Sam's grandmother rigs the Christmas parade to make Sam and Keegan queen and queen, sparks fly, but they can't forget the Big Embarrassing Thing that makes romance a total nope. (978-1-63679-729-8)

Unwrapped by D. Jackson Leigh. Asia du Muir is not going to let some party girl actress ruin her best chance to get noticed by a Broadway critic. Everyone knows you should never mix business and pleasure. (978-1-63679-667-3)

Language Lessons by Sage Donnell. Grace and Lenka never expected to fall in love. Is home really where the heart is if it means giving up your dreams? (978-1-63679-725-0)

New Horizons by Shia Woods. When Quinn Collins meets Alex Anders, Horizon Theater's enigmatic managing director, a passionate connection ignites, but amidst the complex backdrop of theater politics, their budding romance faces a formidable challenge. (978-1-63679-683-3)

Scrambled: A Tuesday Night Book Club Mystery by Jaime Maddox. Avery Hutchins makes a discovery about her father's death that will force her to face an impossible choice between doing what is right and finally finding a way to regain a part of herself she had lost. (978-1-63679-703-8)

Stolen Hearts by Michele Castleman. Finding the thief who stole a precious heirloom will become Ella's first move in a dangerous game of wits that exposes family secrets and could lead to her family's financial ruin. (978-1-63679-733-5)

Synchronicity by J.J. Hale. Dance, destiny, and undeniable passion collide at a summer camp as Haley and Cal navigate a love story that intertwines past scars with present desires. (978-1-63679-677-2)

The First Kiss by Patricia Evans. As the intrigue surrounding her latest case spins dangerously out of control, military police detective Parker Haven must choose between her career and the woman she's falling in love with. (978-1-63679-775-5)

Wild Fire by Radclyffe & Julie Cannon. When Olivia returns to the Red Sky Ranch, Riley's carefully crafted safe world goes up in flames. Can they take a risk and cross the fire line to find love? (978-1-63679-727-4)

Writ of Love by Cassidy Crane. Kelly and Jillian struggle to navigate the ruthless battleground of Big Law, grappling with desire, ambition, and the thin line between success and surrender. (978-1-63679-738-0)

Back to Belfast by Emma L. McGeown. Two colleagues are asked to trade jobs. Claire moves to Vancouver and Stacie moves to Belfast, and though they've never met in person, they can't seem to escape a growing attraction from afar. (978-1-63679-731-1)

Exposure by Nicole Disney and Kimberly Cooper Griffin. For photographer Jax Bailey and delivery driver Trace Logan, keeping it casual is a matter of perspective. (978-1-63679-697-0)

Hunt of Her Own by Elena Abbott. Finding forever won't be easy, but together Danaan's and Ashly's paths lead back to the supernatural sanctuary of Terabend. (978-1-63679-685-7)

Perfect by Kris Bryant. They say opposites attract, but Alix and Marianna have totally different dreams. No Hollywood love story is perfect, right? (978-1-63679-601-7)

Royal Expectations by Jenny Frame. When childhood sweethearts Princess Teddy Buckingham and Summer Fisher reunite, their feelings resurface and so does the public scrutiny that tore them apart. (978-1-63679-591-1)

Shadow Rider by Gina L. Dartt. In the Shadows, one can easily find death, but can Shay and Keagan find love as they fight to save the Five Nations? (978-1-63679-691-8)

The Breakdown by Ronica Black. Vaughn and Natalie have chemistry, but the outside world keeps knocking at the door, threatening more trouble, making the love and the life they want together impossible. (978-1-63679-675-8)

Tribute by L.M. Rose. To save her people, Fiona will be the tribute in a treaty marriage to the Tipruii princess, Simaala, and spend the rest of her days on the other side of the wall between their races. (978-1-63679-693-2)

Wild Wales by Patricia Evans. When Finn and Aisling fall in love, they must decide whether to return to the safety of the lives they had, or take a chance on wild love in windswept Wales. (978-1-63679-771-7)